Dear Readers,

The Red Hat Society embraces women from all walks of life. Most have been home-makers, wives, and mothers. Many have also pursued busy careers outside the home. Some are married; some are divorced or widowed. But even though each of us has been dealt a different hand, we have all played in the same game of life.

As the Red Hat Society has grown, its members have come to realize that, as different as we are, we do share one special personal quality. Each of us has come through the years with our optimism and sense of humor intact. Rather than gritting our teeth and fearing whatever comes next, we march out to meet life with smiles on our faces and hope in our hearts.

Yet even the strongest woman occasionally falters. That's when the value of having "sisters" becomes most important. This new official Red Hat Society romance takes us into the mind and heart of a divorcée whose own resources have run dry. As her story progresses, she is the beneficiary of a great deal of love and support from her new neighbors—the red-hatted Queens of

Woodlawn Avenue. As they plop a hat on her head and teach her to play the game of bridge, they also deepen her understanding of how to play the hand now dealt to her. From these generous women, she learns how to accept the things that she must, and how to change the things that she can. And she finds that she is *far* from being "done."

Is there magic in a red hat? You betcha!

In friendship,

Sue Ellen Cooper

The Red Hat Society®'s

QUEENS OF
WOODLAWN
AVENUE

Regina Hale Sutherland

DOUBLEDAY LARGE PRINT HOME LIBRARY EDITION

WARNER BOOKS

NEW YORK   BOSTON

Warner Books
1271 Avenue of the Americas
New York, NY 10020

ISBN-13: 978-0-7394-7180-7

Printed in the United States of America

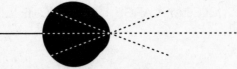

This Large Print Book carries the
Seal of Approval of N.A.V.H.

 **CHAPTER ONE**

Fifty-Two Card Pick-Up

I could smell the pound cake through my closed front door. Vanilla, sugar, butter—luscious scents mingling in a heavenly aroma that promised rapture. Of all things, why did it have to be pound cake—my sugar-addicted Achilles' heel?

"Mrs. Johnston? Ellie? Are you in there?"

The nasal voice reminded me of Gladys Kravitz, the nosy neighbor on *Bewitched.* Unfortunately, I didn't possess Samantha's supernatural powers to rid myself of this unwanted visitor. Which meant that the only way I was going to get the cake and/or make my neighbor go away was to open the door.

Honestly, I'd have had no dilemma at all if it weren't for the pound cake. For the past two weeks, I'd been closeted in the house, safely hidden from the outside world. All I wanted was to lick my wounds, marinate in endless bubble baths of grief and regret, and eat whatever was handy. I had consumed the entire contents of my kitchen. Campbell's chicken noodle soup. Krispy Kreme donuts. Butter pecan Häagen Daz. Betty Crocker brownie mix. No saturated fat or carbohydrate had escaped me, because for the first time in my adult life, I was eating whatever I wanted. Two weeks, though, of consuming my way through the kitchen had yielded a predictable result. Like Old Mother Hubbard, my cupboard was now as bare as my bottom was wide.

I wanted to be left alone to grow old and die in solitude, cut off from the outside world in this tumbledown 1920s Tudor, the symbol of my wretched post-divorce existence. I could keep drifting from room to room, looking glassy-eyed out the windows at my overgrown backyard with a cup of cold coffee in my hand. The drone of late-night infomercials would keep me company during the long, sleepless nights I spent flipping through photo albums of the life I had lost. I could depend on the stray tabby cat that pawed through my garbage can for my social interaction. But if I didn't replenish my food supply soon, I was going to grow old and die much more quickly than I'd planned.

"I made pound cake. To welcome you to the neighborhood." Her temptress's voice, along with the scent of vanilla, slid through the cracks around the edge of the door. My new neighbor was scarily persistent. I had simply ignored her earlier visits, but now I didn't have the luxury. Who would ever have believed it would come to this?

Once, I'd been Mrs. Eleanor Johnston, wife of a successful surgeon and pillar of the Junior League. Now I was nothing but another high-end Nashville divorcée who'd been banished from her 37205 life by her husband's wandering eye. I had become nothing but a cliché, and not a very interesting one at that.

"I think you'll feel better if you eat some of this," the voice said through the door. God, but this woman was not going to give up, was she?

And she did have pound cake.

My hand shook as I reached for the doorknob. The warped wood stuck tight, and I had to give it a strong yank before it gave way, revealing the perky middle-aged woman standing on my front porch.

"There you are." The woman's bright blond hair competed with her paper-white teeth for brilliance. With a start, I recognized her from her advertisements on bus stops all over town. She owned one of the big real estate firms and I had probably even met her at one fund-raiser or another, but I couldn't remember her name.

"I was beginning to worry about you." Uninvited, she stepped across the threshold and into my inner sanctum with the same determination that must have gotten her to the top of the Nashville real estate market. I had the grace to blush at the state of the living room. Twinkie wrappers and empty Coke cans littered the scarred coffee table. The sagging couch that once had done duty in our bonus room—I'd considered it fit only for small children and teenagers—was now the centerpiece of my living room suite.

Sadly, it classed up the joint, a strong indication of the general condition of the house.

"I knew you'd open the door eventually," the woman trilled as she brushed past me and headed toward the kitchen as unerringly as if she'd traipsed through the house a million times before. "My pound cake never fails."

I stood rooted to the spot, mouth gaping for several long moments, before I realized I was supposed to follow her size-2 frame. By the time I caught up with her in the kitchen, she had placed the cake on my cutting board, unwrapped the cloth like a priest preparing the host for the congregation, and was using a lethal-looking knife to slice off a wedge of the promised ambrosia.

"Got milk?" she chirped.

My mouth watered so heavily I had to swallow twice before I could form a reply.

"Um, no. I'm out."

"That's okay. We can have coffee instead."

I paused and cleared my throat. "Well, I don't actually have any coffee either."

Her eyebrow arched. "You've gone through it all, then?"

My stomach twisted. I feigned ignorance.

And hauteur. "What do you mean, I've gone through it all?"

Her laugh was like silverware clanking in a drawer. "Honey, I know how it goes when you're newly on your own. Eating your way through the refrigerator is practically a rite of passage."

"I haven't—" A flush crept up my neck.

"It's nothing to be ashamed of, honey." She placed a hunk of cake on a paper napkin from the stack on the counter and thrust it toward me. "And you look like you need this."

My hand froze, fingertips an eyelash away from the cake. For a moment, I saw myself through my nosy neighbor's eyes. Greasy hair that hadn't seen shampoo in a week. Dressed in my son's cast-off sweat pants and a paint-stained Vanderbilt sweatshirt. Had I even brushed my teeth that morning?

With a laugh that was two parts humor and ten parts shame, I ran a hand over my hair to smooth down the inevitable bed head. "I don't really . . . That is, I'm sure . . ."

The other woman smiled, this time with no condescension at all. "It's okay, honey. We've all been there."

That got my back up. Because, *pardon*

me, not everyone had been where I was now. Not everyone was eating off Chinet while a DD-cup tramp ate off her Haviland china and drank from her Waterford crystal.

"I don't know what you mean." Indignation kept me from reaching for the cake.

"It's no secret, sugar. News travels fast on the Woodlawn Avenue grapevine. We're practically psychic."

Years of good Southern upbringing kept me from making a sharp retort. I didn't need the final humiliation of a public airing of my dirty laundry in my new neighborhood. Wasn't it enough that I could never hold my head up again in Belle Meade? I'd lost everything. My husband. My beautiful home. My place in society. And now I was nothing more than fodder for gossip over the backyard fences of Woodlawn Avenue?

My neighbor remained undaunted by my silence. "I'm Jane, by the way. Jane Mansfield." She laughed, showing off her blinding teeth again. "I know, I know. But you can't pick the last name of the man you fall in love with. Or out of love with, for that matter."

Jane Mansfield. Now I remembered. Her publicity photo on the bus stop ads showed her dressed in fifties attire with a matching bouffant hairdo. She was ten years or so older than me, but at the moment, she looked a decade younger. She probably felt that way, too. Because right then, I must have looked at least a hundred and five.

"It's my birthday," I said, the words falling from my lips of their own volition.

The woman nodded. "Good thing I showed up. Every woman deserves a cake on her birthday."

I nodded, my throat too tight for speech. When was the last time I'd had a birthday cake I hadn't made with my own two hands? Jim had been good with presents but bad with remembering to order something from Becker's Bakery, and none of my children had inherited my homemaking gene. As I'd learned over the years, there was something inherently sad about providing one's own cake.

"I'm Ellie," I finally rallied enough to blurt out. "Ellie Johnston. I mean, Hall. Ellie Hall." Another change that was going to take some adjustment.

One of Jane's perfectly waxed eyebrows arched. "It's final, then, your divorce?"

A lump formed in my throat. "I signed the papers yesterday."

"Hell of a birthday present."

I didn't know whether to laugh or cry at the irony of it all. "Yes. Yes, it was a hell of a present."

Jane stood up straight, all ninety-eight or so pounds of her. "So today's the day you start over. New house, new life, new you."

That point of view had never occurred to me. I'd been so focused on what was coming to an end, I hadn't given much thought to what might be beginning. The very idea made me queasy, so I took a bite of pound cake.

A profusion of flavor exploded on my tongue. "Oh my God," I moaned through the ecstasy melting in my mouth. "I can't believe this cake."

Jane smiled. "Well, there's more where that came from." She reached down and sliced off another piece. "So, Ellie Hall, do you have plans for your birthday?"

I sighed and leaned against the counter. "No. Not really. Since it's Saturday, Oprah and Dr. Phil won't be expecting me."

"Good." Jane took another paper napkin from the pile and brushed the crumbs from the counter into her hand. As casually as if it were her house instead of mine, she opened the cabinet door under the sink and tossed them into the waiting trash can. "We've been waiting for a fourth."

"A fourth? A fourth of what?"

"A fourth for our bridge club."

"Oh. I'm sorry, but I don't play bridge."

Jane smiled. "That's okay, honey. I didn't play either when I moved into my house. But I learned."

The woman might bake heavenly pound cake, but she was clearly a bit loopy. "I'm sorry, but what does your house have to do with a bridge club?"

"Follow me."

Jane stepped around me and led me back through my dining room to the archway that separated it from the living room. The heart-shaped arch had mocked me from the moment my realtor had first shown me the house. But it had been one of the few in this rapidly gentrifying neighborhood south of Vanderbilt University that I could afford. It was as close to Belle Meade as my budget would allow. In time, I could channel my inner Martha Stewart to drywall the offending arch into another shape. A dagger, perhaps, for sticking through Jim's faithless heart.

Jane ran her hand over the curve in the

plaster, caressing it. "Didn't you wonder about this when you bought the house?"

I shrugged, not wanting to reveal the depths of my pain or my sensitivity about the arch. "It's important for some reason?"

"All four houses have them. One for each suit."

"All four houses?"

"Built by the original members of the club."

"Someone built houses based on a club?"

"Not just any club. Their bridge club. The Queens of Woodlawn Avenue."

That drew a rare chuckle from me. "Queens of Woodlawn Avenue? You've got to be kidding."

Jane shook her head. "Nope. I'm the Queen of Diamonds. Grace on the other side of you is the Queen of Spades. And Linda, in the Cape Cod on the other side of me, she's the Queen of Clubs. We each have the dining room arch for our suit."

Okay, her pound cake was sinfully good, but this woman was starting to frighten me a little. "Look, I appreciate the invitation, but really, I don't think I'd make very good company right now." Not to mention my complete ineptitude with card games of any variety. While some of my sorority sisters in college had been bitten by the bridge bug, I'd declined to be infected.

Jane waved away my words with a flick of her expensive manicure. "You'll learn. We all did." She stepped back into the living room and I followed like an obedient puppy. "In fact, I think we should meet tonight. You need backup on your birthday."

"Look—" Okay, I was starting to get perturbed. Couldn't this woman see that I just wanted to be left alone?

"Seven o'clock at my house," she said over her shoulder as she tugged open the obstinate front door. "And wear a red hat."

"Wear a what?"

"A red hat."

I sagged against the arm of the sofa. "I'm not sure I own a hat, much less a red one."

Jane smiled, again blinding me. "Then you can borrow one of mine. We never play bridge without our hats. Chapter rules."

Chapter rules? Great. Not only had my husband thrown me over for a Hooters waitress, but I had spent all the money from my divorce settlement on a house in a neighborhood of crazies.

"Bring a dish, too. That's another rule."

"A dish of what?"

"Hors d'oeuvres. Casserole. Dessert. Whatever you feel like."

"But I don't have anything in the house."

Jane smiled again. "Then I guess you'd better run to the grocery store." Her eyes traveled over my sweatshirt and sweatpants. "You might want to change first. In this town, you're going to see someone who will report back to him."

"Report back?"

"To your ex. He'll hear about your every move. So you can decide what kind of report he's going to get. Would you rather be the spurned woman in scruffy sweats or the fabulous divorcée who embraced life and moved on?"

Truthfully, I'd rather be able to dial the clock back nine months so that none of this had ever happened. But she did have a point. Jim was bound to hear about it if I schlepped to the grocery store in our son's castoffs. When it came to demographics, Nashville might be a major metropolitan area, but in all the ways that mattered, it was still a small town. I'd learned never to say anything bad about anyone, because you could count on the fact that the person you were speaking to was somehow related to the person you were disparaging.

"Seven o'clock?" I said weakly, and Jane beamed.

"Good girl. You're going to be okay."

I wanted to believe her, but reason and hard truth were not on her side. I was a fifty-year-old broke divorcée, living in a run-down, eighty-year-old house and wondering how I was going to pay next month's electric bill. But even at my lowest, I still had my pride. It was about all I had, but for the time being, it was going to have to be enough.

Jane waved good-bye and disappeared through the front door, leaving me alone with the pound cake. I straightened my spine, walked to the coffee table, and scooped up the Twinkie wrappers and Coke cans. Whether I wanted it or not, two things were apparently going to happen.

With or without Jim, life was going to go on.

And much to my consternation, I was going to learn to play bridge.

 **CHAPTER TWO**

The Declarer and the Dummy

I had heard about those Red Hat Society ladies, had seen them at tea rooms around Nashville and traveling in flocks through the lobby of the Opryland Hotel. I just never envisioned a scenario where I would actually contemplate becoming one. But desperate times called for desperate measures, and, after all, the women I'd seen looked pretty normal, despite the purple outfits and feather boas that went with the hats.

Surely it was just a harmless pastime. But

as I discovered promptly at seven o'clock that evening, the petite Jane Mansfield's red hat collection made the number of shoes in Imelda Marcos's closet look paltry.

"Veil? No veil?" Jane asked over her shoulder as she opened one large hat box after another. "Or flowers, maybe?"

They had their own room, her hats. She had not been kidding when she said the Wood-lawn Avenue Bridge Club only took two things seriously: their food and their head-gear.

"A veil," I murmured. "The better to hide behind." That afternoon, I had girded my loins with crisp capri pants and gone on an expedition to Harris-Teeter, the nearby gro-cery store. At first I'd been tempted to stock up on Hershey's miniatures and potato chips, but self-preservation had reared its head and forced me to spend some quality time in the produce aisle. I now had enough fruits and vegetables to open my own stand. Way too much for one person, and I'd spent more than I should have, but it had felt good to do something positive for a change.

"Voilà!" With a rustle of tissue paper, Jane pulled a red monstrosity from its nesting place. "Now *this* is a birthday hat." She swooped over and plopped it atop my head before spinning me around to look in the mirror. "You can't help but celebrate when you're wearing this."

From beneath the numerous plumes, I nodded my agreement. Weird as it might be, I did feel marginally better with the thing on my head. I felt a bit regal and, well, a little more powerful. But did I really have the panache to carry off meeting two total strangers while wearing it?

"Don't worry," Jane said, as if reading my thoughts. "If anything, you'll be the tame one in the crowd."

And as it turned out, I was.

The other two women arrived in a flurry of red hats and hot dishes. Jane introduced me as she tended to the arrangement of the food on the sideboard in her dining room.

"This is Grace, our Queen of Spades," Jane said, deftly sliding hot pads under the dishes that required them. Grace had to be eighty if she was a day and her towering confection of a hat would have been right at home in Marie Antoinette's court.

"I buried three husbands," she said as we hovered around the dining room table. "And every one of them died with a smile on his face."

"And this, of course, is Linda, our Queen of Clubs."

Even with her hat's full portrait brim dipped low over one green eye, I recognized Linda St. James. As always, her hair shone like polished mahogany and her smile appeared gracious. We'd worked on several fund-raisers together through the years, and were slated to be on the planning committee for the Cannon Ball, Nashville's most prestigious charity event. Or should I say *had* been slated. The first meeting of the planning committee was in a few days, and my invitation must have been lost in the mail, because I hadn't heard a word about it.

"Yes, we've met." I tried to smile graciously, too, but fear churned through my stomach. I hadn't counted on one of the Queens of Woodlawn Avenue being someone I knew. Nashville society could be as cutthroat as it could be caring, and I didn't know Linda well enough to determine which of the two she might be. I'd been deserted by enough of my so-called friends over the last nine months that I'd grown wary.

"Welcome, Ellie," she said, her eyes soft with compassion, and I breathed a sigh of relief.

"We're glad you're here," Grace said, patting my hand.

"Now our Red Hat chapter is complete. Come on, girls. Time to get started." She shooed us into our chairs.

How long had it been since I'd been surrounded by three people so determined to be kind to me? Jane sat across from me and shuffled the cards while Linda, on my right, wrote something on the score sheet. I started to get nervous. Should I confess my complete ineptitude with cards up front, or let them discover for themselves what they'd done by inviting me to join them?

"I'm afraid I've never played before," I said.

Jane set the cards in front of Linda, who simply tapped the top of the deck. "Cut the cards and you cut your luck," she advised me.

"I'm going to deal this first time," Jane said to me, "but we're going to let you be the declarer and play the hand." With practiced movements, she picked up the cards and began distributing them with the efficiency of a Vegas pit boss. If her real estate business ever went sour, she definitely had a skill to fall back on.

"We each get thirteen cards," Linda advised me. "Sort them by suit, and then arrange them from highest to lowest. Ace is high."

Okay, well that I could probably manage. I reached for the growing pile in front of me, but Grace stopped me with a wrinkled hand. "Good bridge etiquette means waiting until all the cards have been dealt, honey."

I flushed as red as my hat. And then I got a little mad. Because it's not fair when people expect you to know the rules before they've told you what they are. Sort of like how my husband told me he was leaving before he ever mentioned anything about being unhappy.

"We won't worry about bidding tonight," Jane said as she flicked the last card onto my pile. She sat across from me. "That can come later. Right now, we'll just concentrate on the play of the cards."

The other two nodded their hats in agreement.

"Grace will lead," Jane continued. "All we have to do is follow suit. If she plays a spade, we play a spade and so forth. The one who plays the highest card takes the trick."

Well, that seemed pretty straightforward. Surely I could do at least that much.

Grace laid a jack of spades in the middle of the table. "Shouldn't we start with a dummy?" she asked. "Let her learn to play the dummy from the start."

I snorted. Too late. I had recently acquired a great deal of experience in that area.

Jane must have seen my thoughts in my expression, or at least heard them in my snort, because she laughed and shot me a reassuring smile. "In bridge, whoever wins the bidding is called the declarer. That's you for now. Their partner, the person across from them, becomes the dummy. The dummy—me—lays her cards down, and the declarer ends up playing both hands."

I sighed and put my cards down. After two weeks alone in my house, I still wasn't ready to face the world. People meant well, but even the kindest of them wanted me to buck up and do better. "Look, ladies, I'm just not up to this. You should find another fourth."

Grace tut-tutted. "We can't do that, Ellie. You live in the house. You have to be the Queen of Hearts."

Tears welled in my eyes. This was just too bizarre and I didn't have the emotional energy left to deal with it. I was also tired of being told what I had to do. I'd listened to enough admonitions and lectures over the last nine months from my children, from my lawyer, from the judge. When was it going to be my turn to decide what I wanted to do?

"I just can't," I managed to gasp as the tears overflowed, and everyone at the table knew I wasn't referring to the card game. "I'm not the woman I used to be." There, I'd said it. Named the fear that had taken up residence in my head and heart. Again, I was a walking cliché, because somewhere along the journey of marriage and motherhood, I'd lost myself.

Grace reached over to pat me again. "There, there, honey. It's going to be okay."

Linda was more straightforward. "Crying will get you nowhere, Ellie. Relationships are like bridge. You can be the one who plays the cards, or you can be the one that gets played. In a good relationship, it goes back and forth. But in a bad relationship . . ."

"Never the declarer, always the dummy," I said through my sniffles.

Jane passed me a handkerchief across the table. "Here. This will help."

I smiled a watery thanks and lifted it to my nose for a good blow.

"Stop!" Linda cried. "That's not what it's for."

"Take off your hat," Jane instructed, "and put the handkerchief on your head."

My disbelief was obviously reflected on my face.

"Really," Linda said. "It's a bridge tradition. To change your luck."

She had to be kidding.

Feeling foolish, a state with which I had become depressingly familiar, I pulled off the hat and draped the handkerchief over my head. If nothing else, it was cooler than the hat, which had started to itch.

"That very handkerchief brought me Charles, my second husband," Grace said with a smile and a wink.

The last thing I needed was another husband. The first one had proven to be more trouble than he was worth. The fact that I still loved him made it even more irritating.

"Okay," I said, picking my cards back up. Jane was right. I could spend weeks on end moping around my house, feeling sorry for myself, or I could try to move forward with my life. "Teach me how to be the declarer."

Linda clapped her hands together. "Bravo, Ellie. All right, now you have to play for me since I'm the dummy. I'll lay my cards down like this, so you can see what you've got to work with."

"You mean everyone gets to see them?" I didn't see much advantage in being the de-clarer if the other team got to look at the dummy's cards, too.

"Yes, everyone sees them," Linda said, "but only you know how these cards do or don't complement the ones you're holding. Only you know what they're worth to you."

To my novice eye, the dummy hand didn't look like much to work with at all, but it was better than nothing. So was my ramshackle house, and this odd assortment of new friends. After all, I had no place to go but up, and I couldn't afford to turn down help wherever it was offered.

Or maybe I was just so unused to it being offered that it was hard to accept it when it finally showed up.

We played three more hands of bridge that night before stopping to eat, and for an hour I had the pleasure of thinking about something besides the upheaval in my life. I had grasped the basic concept of following suit and taking tricks. I'd even mastered learning to count the high card points in my hand. Aces were worth four. Kings, three. Queens two, and jacks one. Jane said I'd need to know how to count my hand when it came time to learn about bidding. The enormous task of retaining all this new information overwhelmed me, so I consoled myself with generous helpings from Jane's sideboard.

I also quickly learned why Jane had seemed so at home in my house. Her floor plan was identical to mine, although her immaculately decorated home looked like something out of *Veranda* while my décor was more *Goodwill Weekly.* I asked her about the similarities in the layout as we worked our way through Linda's poppy seed chicken and Grace's mouthwatering squash casserole.

"Flossie Etherington, the original Queen of Hearts, built your house," Jane said, eager to talk about her first love, real estate. "Joyce, her best friend, was the Queen of Diamonds. She built mine."

"They played bridge back then? In the

twenties?" The ladies would have been from my grandmother's generation.

"At the time, bridge was the most popular game in America," Grace said. "My mother taught me to play when I was barely old enough to hold the cards. She was the first Queen of Spades."

"And the club has been around that long? Since the houses were built?"

"In one form or another. Flossie was the last of the founding members." Jane's smile spoke of fond remembrance. "She suggested the red hats when we needed something to revitalize us, so we formed our own chapter—the Queens of Woodlawn Avenue. Flossie played bridge right until the end. We had our last foursome in the hospital. Whoever was the dummy played her cards for her."

"I'm surprised I've never heard of the group." I'd have thought the *Tennessean* or *Southern Living* would have done a feature on the houses and their connection.

"We don't want publicity," Jane replied, and Grace and Linda nodded in agreement. "Not beyond Red Hat circles. If everyone knew about us, it wouldn't be the same."

I could see her point. Sometimes women

needed a little something for themselves that wasn't subject to the scrutiny of the outside world.

"All right, you two. Time to get back to work." Grace tapped the table top. "Ellie's got a lot more to learn."

Truer words had never been spoken, and when Grace winked at me, I knew she was talking about a lot more than bridge.

To my surprise, and not a little delight, I began to get the hang of simply playing out a hand. I made mistakes, true, but the other ladies were patient. Sometimes, they'd take back their cards and let me try again. Little by little, my confidence grew. By the time Jane went to turn on the coffee pot, the hour was growing late and my head was spinning as I tried to remember what they'd taught me. After Jane handed around the delicate china cups steaming with decaf, she put the cards away.

"Ladies, as another duty of our chapter, I think it's time for us to help Ellie develop some goals for her new life."

My head popped up, at least as much as it could in its exhausted state. A mixture of embarrassment and apprehension settled in my very full stomach. "Really, you don't need to . . ." I never got to finish the sentence.

"But, dear," Grace interrupted, "it's what we're here for. That's why we're the Queens of Woodlawn Avenue."

I refrained from uttering an undignified "Huh?"

"I'm assuming you need to earn a living." Jane didn't mince words. "Alimony's not what it used to be. So we need a financial goal."

The truth was that even though Jim made a very good living as a surgeon, we had always seemed to spend as much as he brought home. A well-appointed house in Belle Meade, private school tuition, Jim's love of all forms of transportation—cars, a boat, a Harley. And now, with two kids in college, we were really strapped for cash. He could hardly have paid me much alimony in any event, but I'd been too proud to ask for it.

"I was going to start looking for a job. I just haven't. . . ." My voice trailed off, because I didn't want to lie nor did I want to be honest. Since I'd never dreamed I would need it again, I let my nursing license lapse long ago. Jim and the kids had been my full-time job for more than twenty-five years.

Jane's look sized me up. "Do you really want to work for someone else, after all the years of setting your own schedule?"

"Well, no," I answered honestly, having never thought of it quite that way before. "But I don't have much choice."

Jane smiled. "The one thing you do have, Ellie, is a choice. Maybe not an easy one, but a choice nonetheless."

I had no idea what she was talking about.

Jane pulled the score pad from our bridge game toward her, ripped off the top sheet, and wrote *Ellie's Goals* on the fresh page. All the hairs on my neck stood on end.

"Okay, first item: develop a business plan for Ellie. As Queen of Diamonds, that's my job. I deal with money—how to make it and how to keep it." She wrote down *Business Plan* on the pad and drew a diamond next to it.

"A plan? What do I need a plan for?" I hated the feeling of not being in control. I'd experienced it far too often in the last nine months, and to have this enjoyable evening suddenly turn from a friendly game of cards to an "analyze Ellie" session was disquieting, to say the least.

Jane's brow remained calmly smooth beneath her blonde hair and red hat. "A plan for establishing your own business. We'll get together, talk about your interests, your passions, and figure out how to turn them into a positive cash flow. Trust me, that's the way to go."

The only way I wanted to go was across the lawn to my house, but I refrained from saying so. After all, Jane was only trying to help.

"I'm next," Linda said, reaching for the pad. "We need to resurrect your social standing." She made a face. "Why is it that when the man bails out of the marriage, he doesn't have to give up the club or his friends? But the wife, well, she might as well have been swallowed by a black hole." Linda scribbled something on the pad, and then drew a club beside it. I leaned over to read what she'd written.

It said *Ellie to chair next year's Cannon Ball.*

I burst out laughing. I couldn't help it.

Because she was from an old Nashville family, Linda might be the Queen of Clubs in the literal sense of the word, a bastion of Nashville society events despite her Woodlawn Avenue address, but she might as well have written *Ellie to land on the moon.* The unfortunately named Cannon Ball, a fundraiser for the local children's hospital, was the most prestigious occasion on Nashville society's competitive calendar. It was named for General Conrad Cannon, a Confederate leader who had spent his dotage in Nashville. With Jim's full support—because it was a heavy time commitment—I'd worked my way onto the planning committee over the last few years. I had thought that this year, finally, might be the year I was named chair-elect. The moment Jim announced he was walking out, though, all my hard work began to circle the drain.

"I'm on the committee, too, this year." Linda drew a club on the pad next to what she'd written. "I can pull some strings, but you have to do your part."

As much as I appreciated her willingness to champion me, the very thought of tackling the last leg of my social climb under my current conditions made my stomach hurt. At the higher levels of involvement, volunteers were expected to give more than time and energy—they had to offer up copious amounts of money as well. Without Jim's checkbook at hand, I had no way to meet that expectation. My invitation to the first planning luncheon hadn't been lost just because I was single.

"I don't really think I'm the one to reverse years of social practice." The muffled laughter, the whispers, the promised invitations that never arrived. I'd seen enough divorcées take a tumble to know what I would be up against, even with Linda's support. Sure, if I could snag a bigger catch than Jim in the next two weeks, all might be forgiven. But a single woman chairing the Cannon Ball? It was never going to happen.

Linda, though, didn't look like she was going to take no for an answer. "It's late. Don't decide anything tonight. In fact, why don't I come over Monday morning? I'll take you shopping."

"Why would I need to go shopping?" Plus, it wasn't like I had any actual money to go shopping with.

"You're going to buy a smart new suit to wear to the first planning meeting for the ball."

"But—"

"It's not an extravagance. It's an investment. In your social standing. For your business, even."

"But I don't have a—"

"Not yet," Linda soothed, "but with Jane behind you, that won't take long. Besides, I know where I can get you a really good deal on the most amazing clothes in town." She winked one of those green eyes at me. Then she passed the pad over to Grace. "There's only one thing left, then."

I couldn't imagine what that might be. The elderly Grace was the Queen of Spades. What that had to do with planning for my future, I couldn't say.

"We can get to work on your garden right away. It's gone to pot since Flossie's children put her in that nursing home." Grace pursed her lips in disapproval. "They never had the proper appreciation for that garden." She jotted down her contribution on the pad and drew a warbling spade beside it.

Gardening? Now I was really sorry I'd had that second helping of squash casserole. "Not a great idea." I couldn't return Grace's smile. "I've got the world's brownest thumb."

Grace was undeterred. "There's no such

thing, dear. All you need is a little help. I can teach you what you need to know."

"But—" How had this happened? How had they wrenched what little control I had left over my life out of my hands so quickly and efficiently? Was there something in the casserole besides squash?

"It would certainly add to the value of your house." Jane, as a realtor, would be the one to know. "Landscaping always does."

"Digging in the dirt will do you a world of good," Grace added. "Best way I know to bury your grief."

Her frank acknowledgment of my bereavement both stung and soothed. "Okay, okay. I surrender." I threw my hands up in the air. "But don't say I didn't warn you the first time I kill a cactus."

"We have your goals, then." Jane ripped the list off the score pad and pushed it across the table toward me.

"But—" I looked at all the notes written there. I hadn't agreed to all of that, had I? Evidently my assent wasn't necessary, though. From the determined looks on the faces of the other Queens of Woodlawn Avenue, I wasn't going to get away with hiding in my house anymore. These ladies clearly weren't the type to let me continue my Krispy Kreme Pity Parties in solitude.

I knew I wasn't ready for all they were proposing, but it felt good to have their support. That feeling had been missing from my life since before Jim walked out the door and drove away in his BMW Roadster. How had it happened, over the years, that the one person I most enjoyed spending time with became the person I saw the least? But Jim had his practice, his patients, his hospital responsibilities and the occasional teaching stint at Vanderbilt Medical School. I'd lost myself in the children, the church, PTA, Scouts, and sports. Like continental drift, our estrangement had been immeasurable to the eye, but slowly, over time, the gaps between us had grown steadily wider.

"I'm not sure what to say."

"You don't have to say anything," Linda squeezed my shoulder. "You're one of us now."

And that's the moment, with Linda's simple words of acceptance and the concurring nods of Grace and Jane, when I truly felt I'd become an official member of the Queens of Woodlawn Avenue.

CHAPTER THREE

Taking Tricks

I awoke the next morning with yet another carbohydrate-induced hangover, but also with the knowledge that my life had very nearly been hijacked by three would-be fairy godmothers in red hats. Sure, last night, all four of us had some fantasy that I could somehow be gotten back on track. But in the light of that April Sunday morning, as I nursed a cup of Sanka on the cracked concrete patio and tried to pretend it was a nonfat latte from Starbucks, I knew otherwise. Building my own business, chairing a prestigious charity event, even reclaiming the tattered garden where I sat—all were far beyond my limited resources.

The phone rang inside the house, and I reluctantly stood up and went inside to answer it. The old princess phone I'd dug out of Courtney's things didn't have a Caller ID screen. I had to answer, though, because it might be one of the kids.

"Hello?"

"Ellie? It's Jim."

My stomach sank. "Good morning." I forced myself to sound cordial, if not particularly warm. I hadn't seen him since the last mediation session several weeks before. How unfair that the rich timbre of his voice still resonated in my heart as it had done from the first time I met him.

There was a long moment of silence as I walked back outside and waited for him to say something. Finally, around the tightness in my throat, I said, "Did you need something?"

"Um, well . . ."

It had been a long time since I'd heard Jim utter such tentative syllables. In fact, the last time he sounded so awkward was right before he proposed. The memory of that moonlit night, his hands holding mine as he looked into my eyes, was too painful to be revived, so I wrapped the phone cord tightly around my finger, hoping the pain would keep me from drowning in the past.

"What is it? Is it one of the kids?" His terseness scared me.

"No, no. Nothing like that."

I could hear Our Lady of the Hooters singing Britney Spears in the background. The fact that she had the same musical tastes as my twenty-year-old daughter might have made me feel culturally superior, but it also made me feel old.

"What's the matter, Jim?" As my fear receded, impatience took its place.

"Nothing's wrong. I just thought I should be the first to . . . That you should hear it from . . ."

When had my socially adept, well-educated husband lost the ability to formulate a complete sentence? Clearly the Hooters hottie had taken a toll on his IQ.

"Hear what?"

"I just thought you should know that, well, Tiffany and I are getting married."

Well, of course they were. I couldn't suppress the bark of laughter that erupted from my throat. But the dark humor was a cover for a deeper, lethal pain. I looked down at the cracked linoleum beneath my feet, wondering how I managed to remain upright. Could the black hole that had just opened up in my midsection spread to the floor below me? And here I thought I'd already found the bottom of my emotional pit.

"Congratulations, Jim. I always knew you had it in you. You've finally made a total ass of yourself."

"C'mon, Ellie," he said in that tone of hurt/annoyance that had crept into our marriage over time. "You don't have to be that way. You're going to have to accept what's happened."

When pigs fly, I thought, but it was a sentiment I kept to myself. "Pardon me if it takes me a bit longer to forget about the last twenty-five years, but one of us had a significant head start."

"If you're going to be that way, I'm hanging up."

"Since I didn't ask you to call in the first place, that will really be no hardship for me." I reached over and opened a cabinet to pull out a glass.

"Was there anything else?" I really made an effort to sound detached. In an attempt to make things seem normal, I reached into the refrigerator for a pitcher of iced tea.

"Just a small thing."

Right. I poured the tea into the glass. The last "small thing" Jim had dumped on me was the news that he was taking me off his health insurance plan. At the moment, if I were to be hit by a car, I'd have to be left on the side of the road like a stray dog.

"How small?"

"It's about my alimony check. With all the wedding expenses, it's going to be a few weeks late."

"A few weeks?" I hated it when I shrieked. After the last time we went to divorce mediation, I'd sworn not to anymore. But I couldn't help it. It was gut instinct, born of terror.

"Jeez, Ellie, why don't you do that a little louder so the whole neighborhood can hear you?"

I swallowed, took a sip of tea, and tried to remember that somewhere underneath this walking midlife crisis was the man I'd loved, and who had loved me, for most of my adult life.

"When can you send it?" The only bright spot about tying up most of my available cash in this new house was that I had a month's grace period before I had to make the first payment. Jim, though, didn't need to know that.

"We're getting married in June. I'll get it to you after that. I promise."

"June?" It was April. "And what am I supposed to live on for the next three months?"

I could hear him bristle through the phone line. You would have thought by that point he'd have learned to avoid the word "promise" within my hearing.

"If it's more than two weeks late, I'll take legal action." If only my heart could be iced down like the glass of tea in my hand.

"Ellie, don't say that. We both know you haven't got the money."

"Then I'll pawn something. Or I'll borrow it. I don't think you want your partners to know you're a deadbeat."

If I had to end up garnishing his paycheck, everyone in his medical practice would know, because the bookkeeper was the biggest gossip since Rona Barrett and she was on my side—her husband had dumped her for a pole dancer. Amazing how shared suffering created those bonds.

"Okay, okay. It'll be there on time." He paused for a moment. "I was hoping you'd be at least a little happy for me."

"Then you're a bigger idiot than I thought."

The weird thing about everything that had happened since the day of Jim's big announcement was that he still wanted my approval. At first it had infuriated me. Then it galled me. Now I was starting to see it for the pathetic need to shirk responsibility that it was, the emotional equivalent of his beloved Harley-Davidson. I wondered, not for the first time, how other couples managed to navigate their midlife crises and still be married. Clearly there was some secret formula to which Jim and I hadn't been privy.

"Good-bye, Jim." There was no point in prolonging the agony. Or the anger. He mumbled a good-bye of his own, and I hung up the phone. The agony receded, but the anger remained. Suddenly, I craved a Twinkie with every last fiber of my being.

No. I pounded my hand on the kitchen counter, hoping the physical pain would replace the emotional scourging. I had to stop. I wanted to stop. With a sob, I sank down, my back scraping the cabinet handles on the way down, until I rested on the scarred linoleum.

I couldn't stop the thoughts swirling through my head. I couldn't stop wondering what I'd done wrong. What I should have done differently. How I could possibly have prevented myself from growing older.

That thought hurt the most.

Because no matter what, turning fifty was the one thing I couldn't have changed.

Linda St. John was a woman of her word. She showed up at ten o'clock on Monday morning, looking chic and polished in a linen sheath dress and strappy sandals. I couldn't remember when I'd last had the energy to iron linen or the well-maintained feet to carry off such dressy sandals. Linda's pedicure glowed brightly enough to signal the space station. I wiggled my own pathetic toes in my plastic Target thongs. How could I even think of doing what Linda wanted me to do? But after Jim's phone call the day before, after I'd dried my tears and scraped myself off the floor, I had acknowledged to myself that I was tempted by her offer of help. My inner Amazon, the long-buried warrior woman who was raging mad, well, she had apparently begun to stir down there in the tomb where I'd incarcerated her.

"Come on." Linda stood just inside the front door. "We're going shopping."

"I still don't understand how one outfit's going to save my social standing."

Linda smiled. "You'll see."

"I may need a minute to get ready." Since Jim's phone call, I'd come to at least one conclusion. I didn't want to continue to sit home consuming vats of Rotel-and-Velveeta cheese dip and speculating just how gaudy Tiffany's wedding invitations were likely to be. If Linda could help me keep my spot on the planning committee for the Cannon Ball, maybe I should give it a try. I couldn't humiliate myself any more than Jim had already done. Well, okay, I could, but at least it would be at my own hands and I would be the instrument of my own downfall, not simply an unwilling victim of another woman's DD-cup bra.

"Give me a few minutes to change, and I'll be ready," I said to Linda. She nodded, and

I headed back to my tiny bedroom and my even more minuscule closet.

I'd always heard that Linda St. John knew two things: how to manipulate people and how to dress them. I wanted to take advantage of her talents, but I also didn't want to be evicted from my squalid little house when it came time to pay the mortgage, assuming the arrival date of Jim's alimony check wouldn't do that for me. I would rather have a roof over my head than silk shantung from the new spring line on my back.

So, of course, half an hour later, Linda led me into Elliott's, the most glamorous store in town, like she owned the place. I slunk in behind her like I planned to shoplift a few items while no one was looking. Furtive is as furtive does. Well, at least I could look around, and then maybe we could go find a comparable designer knockoff at TJ Maxx.

An elegant saleswoman named Carol introduced herself, and she and Linda hugged like long-lost college roommates. During my marriage, I'd tended to be more Chico's than chic for a number of reasons. One, I liked to hide my lack of a bustline behind draping tops and jackets. And, two, because I'd spent most of my clothing allowance on our home, making it beautiful and comfortable so Jim and the kids couldn't wait to come home at the end of the day.

"A suit, I think." Linda gave me the once-over with a practiced eye. "But not too busi-ness-y. Very 'ladies-who-lunch.'"

Carol nodded and looked me up and down. Then she took my hand and led me to the front of the store so she could study my complexion in the harsh daylight streaming through the plate glass windows. She turned me this way, then that. I wished I'd kept that last appointment at Illusions to touch up the blonde highlights in my other-wise ordinary brown hair. Salon visits, too, were now a thing of the past.

"Blue," she finally pronounced. "This way."

She spun on her stiletto heel and headed toward the back of the store. "Follow me," she ordered over her shoulder, and I did just that, too intimidated not to.

At Elliott's, the price tag amount increased with each square foot you progressed into the store. At my best guess, we were al-ready twelve feet beyond my budget. Oh, who was I kidding. We'd passed my budget out in the parking lot.

Carol went all the way to the back, and I saw where she was headed long before we got there. The suit—a stunning confection of robin's egg blue—hung like a crucifix above the holy altar of fashion. Any woman who wasn't legally blind would have fallen to her knees and worshipped that suit. And there was no way the price tag had less than four numbers to the left of the decimal point.

"Perfect." Linda nodded with approval. Carol pulled a carbon copy of the suit in my size from the rack on the wall.

"If you'll follow me." She walked away, and I understood that it was a command, not an invitation.

The changing room was bigger than my new bedroom and far more elegant. I slipped out of my clothes and into the suit, knowing all the while that it was certain to fit perfectly, the way that clothes you can't afford always do. There was no point looking at the price tag. Slowly, I turned toward the full-length mirror.

The suit echoed the classic lines of Chanel, with three-quarter-length sleeves and a tightly fitted waist. Despite my recent junk food binge, the skirt clung to my curves in all the right places. The tiny ruffle around the lapels and the slightly fluted skirt made me look thoroughly feminine. If I died on the spot, I would want to be buried in that suit. It looked so good I would easily have agreed to spend eternity wearing it. Figured.

"Come out and let me see," Linda called.

I drew a deep breath and headed out of the changing area. Not only was I going to have to do battle with my own common sense, I was also going to have to convince Linda that there was no way I could possibly afford the suit.

"I knew it," Linda said the moment I stepped into view. "Absolute perfection."

I hated that she was right. "Yes. It is. But, Linda, I can't—"

Linda ignored my protest and turned toward Carol, who was looking thoroughly pleased with herself. "She'll take it. And she'd like to set up a house account in her husband's name."

"But—"

"Certainly. Let me just get my notebook." Carol practically sprinted to the cashier's stand.

"Linda," I said in a stage whisper. "I can't buy this suit."

Linda waved away my protests with an airy hand. "You aren't paying for it. Your husband is."

"He's not my husband anymore." I couldn't bring myself to tell her that he was, in fact, about to become someone else's legally wedded spouse.

Linda's smile hinted at her more predatory instincts. "Yes, well, we're not done shopping yet. We're going to pick out a little something for his hootchie mama as well. When she gets it, he'll be so busy taking credit while she demonstrates her gratitude that he won't look at the bill twice."

"Won't he wonder who charged it to him?"

"I think he'll be far more concerned with keeping his floozy happy. What's he going to do? Tell her she has to return it?"

My mouth dropped open. It was too underhanded. Too devious. Too perfect.

"That will really work?"

"That's the beauty of Elliott's," Linda whispered as Carol crossed the store toward us. "They still have those old-fashioned house accounts where you say, 'Charge it, please, and thank you very much.'"

I was aware those kind of social conveniences had been part of the Nashville I'd grown up in, though not in my modest neighborhood. My mother's budget, solely funded by her salary as an office nurse for a local pediatrician, had run more toward layaway at JCPenney's than impulse purchases at exclusive Green Hills boutiques.

Carol materialized next to me and handed me a form to fill out, and Linda went to browse for something for Jim's girlfriend. Thirty minutes later, we emerged from Eliott's with the robin's egg blue suit in a garment bag and the receipt for a special delivery order to my old house in Belle Meade for one Tiffany Trask. The Fendi bag ought to ensure that she kept Jim happy for some time to come. And I got at least a little compensation for my husband's impending nuptials. Excuse me, my *ex*-husband.

"So you're set," Linda said as we drove back to Woodlawn Avenue in her big, black Lexus. "The planning luncheon is day after tomorrow at Roz Crowley's house on Belle Meade Boulevard. I'll pick you up at eleven."

My stomach lurched at the mention of that name. *Roz Crowley.*

Linda was so pleased with herself, I didn't want to spoil her fun. But if I'd known the first meeting was at Roz's house, I'd have never left home this morning. I knew just what would happen the day after tomorrow. A lunch catered by the most sought-after firm in town. Exclusive society. The most prestigious address. And the exact public humiliation I'd most feared.

"Linda . . ."

"No weakness, Ellie. It's just like junior high. Never let them see you sweat. Never doubt yourself. Head high. Shoulders back. And I'll be right beside you."

Just like junior high. Linda had no idea just how right she was about that.

"Why? Why are you doing this for me?" I couldn't believe a simple bridge club could inspire this kind of loyalty, red hats or not.

She smiled in a sort of half-regretful, half-amused way. "Let's just say it's a form of payback."

She didn't seem inclined to say any more, and I decided not to push. Whatever Linda's reasons—whether it was simply loyalty to the legacy of the Queens of Woodlawn Avenue or a generous spirit—I was grateful for her help. Terrified. Squeamish at the thought of leaping into a huge societal breach. Especially in the home of a woman who had despised me since we were twelve. But I was grateful to Linda nonetheless.

"Get a manicure the day before," Linda admonished me when she'd pulled into my driveway and I was slipping out of the car. "Pedicure, too."

I would have liked to, but I couldn't see any way to charge a mani-pedi to Jim as we'd done with the suit. I'd have to do my nails myself and hope the results would pass muster.

"Thanks, Linda," I said as I shut the car door. "I do appreciate it."

"My pleasure." She smiled bracingly. "You promise, don't you, Ellie, to go to the luncheon with me?"

I hesitated, wondering which would prove greater—my fear of Roz's wrath or my need for the new friendships I'd found.

And at that moment, my inner Amazon struggled a few more layers upward. Maybe it was the suit. Maybe it was exacting a little payback on Jim. But suddenly I felt stronger than I had in months. "I promise."

I watched Linda back out of the driveway, give me a little wave, and turn her car toward her house two doors down. In a lot of ways, I felt like a peri-menopausal Alice in Wonderland who had fallen down her own personal rabbit hole. I had no idea what might happen next, and that both excited and terrified me. Disaster and triumph loomed in equal proportion. But at least I was feeling something besides grief.

 **CHAPTER FOUR**

Discards

The Queens of Woodlawn Avenue were clearly not women to let any grass grow under their feet. I hadn't been home from my shopping expedition with Linda more than thirty minutes when Jane knocked on my front door. Thankfully, she arrived without any additional pound cake. Given my weakness for it, I was glad not to be tempted. After all, I didn't want to jeopardize the fit of my new ill-gotten designer suit any more than I already had.

"Linda's had you out shopping?" Jane asked, but I knew by the way she breezed by me without waiting for an answer that it was a rhetorical question. Linda had no doubt already called Jane and filled her in on all of the details of our Elliott's expedition. I wasn't ungrateful, but I bristled at the idea of my two new friends talking about me. After months of feeling I had to fight every battle on my own, of dealing with jaded lawyers, budget movers, and fearful friends who treated me like a pariah, I suppose I should have relished the well-meant interference of my three fairy godmothers. But I wasn't quite ready to sign away all rights to my self-determination just yet.

Jane made her way unescorted to my dining room, so once again I found myself following in her wake. She laid her red alligator briefcase on the table, snapped open the clasps, and lifted the lid. With crisp efficiency, she took out a sheaf of papers, a legal pad covered with writing, and a couple of pens. With her professionally manicured hand, she motioned me to join her at the table.

"We don't have a lot of time to draft your business plan, so I took the liberty of making some notes."

Jane flipped through several pages of writing, picked up a pen to make several more notations, and then set the pen down on top of the pad, all without noticing my silence in response to her comment. "So, let's see what we can do about generating some revenue streams."

"I can't think of anything I'd rather generate." I sounded more than a little annoyed, but she just laughed.

"Good. It's going to take a lot of hard work, but I've found there's nothing as satisfying as running your own business. So, let's get started. What's your background, workwise?"

I wonder if Cinderella had felt like she was being similarly steamrolled while her fairy godmother flew around singing "Bibbity-bobbity-boo." As a matter of fact, now that I thought about it, I don't think Cindy was ever consulted on the pertinent details of her transformation. I now knew how she felt.

Jane wanted to know about my qualifications. Well, I'd always thought that my efforts as Jim's wife and my children's mother had constituted the best work of my life. However, I doubted knowing how to simultaneously make a three-egg omelet, tutor a high school freshman in algebra, and extract a headless Barbie from the dog's jaws would count for much in the cutthroat world of commerce.

"Well, my degree is in nursing."

"Okay." Linda flipped to a clean page of her legal pad and wrote *Nursing* at the top. "And you'd like to get back into it?"

"Actually, no. And my license lapsed a long time ago, so it would take some doing to get back up to speed."

"Have you considered going back to school?"

I had, actually, in the long nights I'd laid awake right after Jim announced his change of heart about our marriage. But it hadn't taken me long to realize I didn't want to go back to school, and I definitely didn't want to go into debt just so I could work twelve-hour shifts as a floor nurse. The thought of working in a doctor's office, as my mom had done all those years, depressed me even more. She'd made enormous sacrifices so I wouldn't have to follow in her literal foot-steps. Despite the long hours I'd labored and the often thankless tasks I'd performed for my family over the years, I'd relished the freedom of setting my own schedule. I'd also enjoyed not having to pinch every penny. My unpaid labor had freed Jim up to bring home a whole lot of bacon.

"I don't think more schooling is the answer," I told Jane, and she nodded.

"What other experience do you have?"

"The only thing I'm qualified for is to be somebody's wife or mother," I said to Jane morosely, hating the self-pitying tone in my voice. Jane nodded, commiserating, and she looked pensive—at first. But a moment later, her eyes lit up.

"That's it!" she cried, her smile spreading across her face. "It's perfect."

"What's perfect?"

"I can't believe I didn't think of it immediately."

Considering I had no idea what she was talking about, I wasn't surprised about anything. "What do you mean?" Maybe all that red hat–wearing was starting to scramble her otherwise astute head for business.

"You said the only thing you're qualified to be is someone's wife or mother. Well, I can think of plenty of men who need the services of a wife."

"Prostitution wasn't exactly what I had in mind," I said, trying to laugh because I was sure that wasn't what Jane meant. At least, I was pretty sure.

She laughed too, which was reassuring. "No, I mean that I know lots of single businessmen who need help with the tasks a wife would normally perform. Picking up dry cleaning. Playing hostess for a business dinner. All the little details someone needs to coordinate so they can concentrate on making money. You'd be perfect for that."

"Well, I'm certainly experienced." Jim had often said he'd never have advanced as far in his field as he had if it weren't for me. Of course, the down side had been that he spent so much time at work, and I spent so much time making sure he could, that our marriage had been the ultimate casualty of both our efforts.

"I think you could find women clients, too," Jane said. "Working mothers, or even some high-end, stay-at-home moms who volunteer so much they might as well be working."

"And something like that would generate the income I'd need?" It sounded like a lot of work, which I wasn't necessarily adverse to, but it also sounded very inconsistent. I'd been hoping for a steady paycheck if nothing else.

"Well, let's see." Once again, Jane started writing on her legal pad. This time, she was jotting down columns of numbers. "You wouldn't have much overhead, which is great. And your mileage would be tax deductible. The biggest start-up cost would be advertising and the usual office stuff— business cards, stationery, that sort of thing. Oh, and you'd need a Web site. That's mandatory."

A Web site? I could barely figure out how to check my e-mail on a semi-regular basis on the cranky, aging computer I'd gotten in the divorce.

"I don't know, Jane," I said more irritably than I'd intended. I had a sudden, intense craving for more of her pound cake. Or at least that last two-pack of Twinkies I had stashed in the hard-to-reach cabinets above the ancient refrigerator.

Jane smiled, and the compassion in her expression made me want to weep. Which only made me crankier. I was tired of being the belle of the dumped housewives' ball.

I want to be the belle of the Cannon Ball. That ridiculous, hopeless thought came out of nowhere, but it took hold and I couldn't push it out of my head.

"Ellie, I'm going to be honest with you." Jane reached across the table and took my hand in hers. "I know it's rough right now. But no white knight is going to come along and rescue you. If you want to change your life—no, if you just want to take your life back, then you're going to have to be the one to do it. No one else is going to do it for you."

There it was. The plain, unvarnished truth. Laid out on my dining room table without fanfare.

I looked around the room, at the cracks in the plaster and the scuffed hardwood floors badly in need of refinishing. My new surroundings couldn't be more different than what I'd known for the last two decades. But Jane was right. No one—man, woman, or child—was going to come along and pluck me out of my hovel as if I were a princess in a fairy tale. If my life was going to get better, I had to make it that way.

My throat was thick with tears, but I pushed the words past them. "A Web site? How much does that cost?" My watery smile threatened to slide off my face, but I kept it pasted on by sheer dint of will.

Jane nodded approvingly. "Depends. Are any of your kids computer addicts?"

"My son, Connor. But he's away at college."

"That's the beauty of the Internet," Jane said. "Your Webmaster can be in New Guinea, for all it matters."

"I can ask him." I leaned over to look at the other items on her list. "And my friend, Karen, her family owns a printing business. She might be able to get me a discount."

"Excellent." Jane started making more notes. "As soon as you're up and running, I'll start spreading the word. You could have clients as soon as next week."

"Next week?" The thought seemed overwhelming.

"Is that a problem?"

"I guess not." Since I had no idea if Jim's alimony check would arrive at all, I couldn't afford to dilly-dally.

Dilly-dally. Another of my mom's favorite words. Well, she'd managed somehow all those years. Worked hard and kept me fed and clothed. There was no reason I couldn't do the same.

"What should I do first?" I asked Jane, and she was happy to spend the next few hours crafting a plan. We made up a price list, identified local publications where I might want to place ads, and set up an office in my second bedroom. By the time she left, I'd lost my resentment at being the latest project of the Queens of Woodlawn Avenue, and I'd gained a new appreciation for how compassionate other people could be.

Okay, I'd let Linda talk me into taking my fight for a place on the planning committee of the Cannon Ball right to my old nemesis. And I'd been a willing participant in Jane's incipient efforts to turn me into a business-woman. But when Grace showed up on my doorstep the next morning, a garden spade in one hand and a bag of potting soil under her liver-spotted arm, I knew I had to draw the line.

"Really, Grace, it's not fair to inflict me on those poor plants."

Grace pointed the trowel at me and said, "There's no such thing as a brown thumb.

Besides, every clod of dirt you turn over only raises the value of your house."

Well, she certainly knew the one argument that might persuade me to start digging. The financial one.

"I don't know. . . ."

And I didn't. I mean, how many projects could any semi-sane divorcée undertake at one time? I was going to have more than enough on my plate battling Roz Crowley and trying to launch my own business. I didn't need to court certain disaster by trying to putter in the garden.

On the other hand, I didn't want to hurt Grace's feelings. She was nice enough to try and help me, and how would she feel if I let Linda and Jane work their mojo on me but ignored her offer? I had always been a sucker for making other people feel better, and so I took the spade she offered me and pasted a smile on my face. "Okay. You can try and turn me into a gardener, but don't say I didn't warn you."

Grace chuckled. "By the time I'm done with you, Ellie, *Better Homes and Gardens* will be calling for your advice."

Twenty minutes later, Grace had lost some of her amusement and she'd quit predicting my launch as a horticulturalist of some renown. We were on our knees in the back-yard, ready to attack the jungle that had once been beautiful landscaping. We wore matching pink paisley gardening gloves, and the sun beat down on our uncovered heads.

"No, Ellie, dear. That's not the weed. That's the plant."

I think she was gritting her dentures, be-cause her jaw beneath her wrinkled skin was pretty tight.

"Are you sure? It looks pretty weedy to me."

"You can't always tell by how it looks," Grace said, stooping down to pull my hands away from their intended victim.

"Then how do you know?"

"I suppose because somebody teaches you which is which. Like I'm doing for you. My mother taught me, just like she taught me to play bridge."

I could picture Grace and her mother in old-fashioned clothes, working together in the yard or sitting across a card table from one another. Grace's hair would have been in braids down her back, and her feet would have dangled a few inches off the floor in one of the straight-backed dining chairs. The image tugged at my heartstrings. My mother had been far too tired in the evenings to do anything but soak her aching feet while I heated more water and dispensed Epsom salts into the tub. Our weekends had been filled with shopping for groceries, trips to the Laundromat, and cleaning house. I couldn't recall any times when we'd planted flowers or played a game together. The closest we'd come to a recreational activity had been sitting side by side in church.

Grace motioned for me to come closer, so I half-crawled, half-scooted toward her until the five feet between us was reduced to inches.

"Try it like this," she advised me, grabbing a weed—I still wasn't clear how to identify one—at the point where it sprang from the soil and pulling it slowly but firmly toward her. "You have to get all of the roots, or it will just grow back."

"Okay," I said, my eyes searching the tangle of greenery as I tried to identify a weed of my own to pull. I located what I thought was one of the offenders, reached down the stem as far as possible, and gave it my best yank. It broke off in my hand well above the roots. I looked at Grace, clutched the plant, and waited for the inevitable scold.

Instead, she laughed, her frustration withering as quickly as the poor dead plant in my hand.

"You tried to warn me, didn't you?" She smiled.

"Let's just say that my potential as a bridge player far exceeds my possibility as a gardener, and you know that's not saying much."

Grace slipped off her gardening gloves and used the back of her hand to wipe perspiration from her forehead. Her skin resembled the crepe paper I'd always used to festoon the dining room for one of my children's birthday parties.

"Ellie, who convinced you that your only value lies in how well you do something? Don't you get any credit just for being you?"

Perspiration slid off my forehead, too, stinging my eyes as sharply as Grace's question stung my psyche.

"I don't know what you mean." Of course I knew exactly what she meant, but I wasn't ready to go there.

"I mean who convinced you that you have

no intrinsic value?" She tugged her gloves back on. "Sometimes it's the mother." She yanked at another weed and it came up easily, roots and all. She tossed it over her shoulder onto the crabgrass-infested lawn. "Sometimes it's the husband. Even the children." As she ticked off each offender, another weed flew through the air to join the pile.

"You're way off base," I snapped, but we both knew my flash of temper came from Grace's words hitting too close to home.

"Am I?" She pulled two more weeds and began to hum under her breath. I couldn't quite make out the tune.

"I'm not one of those sad women who give up their sense of self because they stay at home all day."

"I didn't say you were."

"You implied it." I couldn't believe we were having this conversation, and I found it even harder to believe that I was letting her get to me. She was obviously a well-meaning old busybody, but the last thing I needed was a red-hat–wearing, gray-haired Oprah trying to analyze me down the path to empowerment.

"I know my own worth." I reached out,

fingers desperate to find the right green thing to pluck out of the dirt. Frustration blurred my vision.

"Do you?"

Great. I really was being psychoanalyzed.

"Look, Grace, if you have something to say, please just say it." I started plucking at plants indiscriminately. Since I couldn't tell the good ones from the bad ones, why not just uproot everything and start from scratch?

"Wait, wait. Don't pull up the daisies."

My hand stopped in mid-pluck. "I might as well just clear the whole thing out and start over," I said, and suddenly I knew I wasn't just talking about my flower beds. I'd been pushing Jim's phone call to the edges of my consciousness.

"But you don't need to start over." Grace looked me straight in the eye. "There's plenty here worth saving. It just needs a bit of discernment."

Discernment?

She nodded her head like she'd heard the question in my thoughts. "You just need some time to sort out the good from the bad."

I sank back on my bottom, arching my

back to ease the ache there. "How much time will it take for me to learn how to garden?" We both knew my question had to do with a lot more than rescuing my yard from encroaching chaos.

"That depends," Grace said.

"On what?"

"On how patient you're willing to be."

"I don't have time to be patient." I needed a new life, and I needed it now. I had mortgage payments to make, a charity ball to commandeer, and an ex-husband who couldn't wait to race down the aisle with a woman who made Pamela Anderson look like a Rhodes Scholar. I needed to be fabulous, and I needed it now.

"I don't think you have any choice."

"I don't know why not. It would be much simpler that way."

"I suppose. But it wouldn't be nearly as satisfying."

At that point, though, I didn't have much interest in feeling satisfied. I just didn't want to feel so desperate anymore. But when I thought about it, I realized that the rest of the day stretched before me like a yawning, empty cavern. I had no plans. Nowhere to be. The only thing on my "To Do" list was to e-mail my son about setting up a Web site and to call Karen about a discount at the print shop. Together, those tasks might take fifteen minutes. I looked at the length of the flower bed as it stretched along the side of the yard, across the back fence, and back the other way toward the house. What Grace proposed was a formidable task, but, again, it was better than sitting in the living room and eating Twinkies.

"All right. I'll try. But I may pull up more plants than weeds."

"You might at first," Grace said. "But I bet you'll learn to tell the difference."

I didn't answer. I hoped she was right. If you looked at the last few years of my life, it was hard to make a case for the brevity of my learning curve.

"Okay, so what do I look for in a weed?"

Grace nodded her approval. "The thing to realize is that calling something a weed is an arbitrary designation. It's only a weed because we say it is." She looked me straight in the eye again to emphasize her point. "You know, we call something a weed because it's hardy, tenacious, and outgrows other kinds of plants." She paused for a moment. "Not much of a reward for thriving where others can't, huh?"

Were my conversations with Grace always going to have this many levels? Between that and the hot sun, my head swam.

"So that's why the only way to tell them apart is to have someone show you the difference?"

"Yes. But you also have to remember that what makes a weed is only a matter of opinion."

"Point taken, Grace."

Because of course that's how I'd been feeling since the separation. Like a hothouse flower that had suddenly been declared a nuisance. I bent over next to Grace again and wrapped my gloved fingers around several long, green stalks. "Weed or plant?"

Grace looked over. "Weed. Definitely."

"All right, then." I yanked it up with a newfound ruthlessness. "Just keep an eye on me so I don't kill the real thing."

"I plan to." Grace smiled again, and we spent the next hour pulling up the unwanted plants in companionable silence.

 **CHAPTER FIVE**

The Power of the Trump Suit

By that evening, every muscle in my body ached from bending over flower beds all day. My joints screamed in protest when I pulled off my grimy T-shirt and faded khakis and stepped into the shower. The ancient plumbing ran as hot and cold as my life at the moment. Relief and hope morphed with breathless rapidity into stretches of panic and fear. Maybe this house was the right one for me after all.

I had just stepped out of the shower when

the phone rang. Wrapping a threadbare towel that had seen better days around me as far as it would go, I padded down the hall to the kitchen where the phone was. Thankfully, all the curtains were closed. Jane and Grace, as helpful as they'd been, probably didn't want to see their new neighbor in the buff. *I* didn't even want to see me in the altogether; gravity had more than taken its toll in the years since my virginal wedding night with Jim.

I caught the phone between slippery fingers and fumbled with the receiver until I wrestled it to my ear. "Hello?"

"Ellie? It's Linda. Sorry for the short notice, but it's an emergency chapter meeting. The Queens are going to play bridge tonight."

"Tonight?" My gaze flew to the clock on the counter. It was already after six.

"We're celebrating your terrific start on your new life."

Terrific start?

I hadn't accomplished much except to swindle my husband out of a suit, make phone calls to my son about the Web site and to my friend who owned the print shop, and give myself the beginnings of carpal tunnel syndrome with all the weed pulling.

Hardly a day's worth of revolutionary activities.

"You don't have to bring anything," Linda said, not waiting for a response from me. "Be at my house at seven."

"I still don't have a red hat." I don't know why I said that, but Linda just laughed.

"Well, I may not have as many of them as Jane, but I bet we can find one here that will suit you. Oh, and wear something purple. That's one of our requirements, too."

Purple? Oy. I'd planned to spend the evening doing my nails in preparation for the big luncheon tomorrow, but I decided I could wait and do that the next morning. Truthfully, I was tired of spending evenings alone on my decrepit couch clutching a pint container of Häagen Daaz and a spoon. Even wearing purple clothes and a red hat seemed a preferable alternative if it got me away from overdosing on butter pecan.

"Okay, I guess. I can be there."

"Great. We'll see you at seven."

We said good-bye, and I returned the receiver to its cradle. Then I made a beeline for my room and began to pull clothes out of my closet, searching for something purple. The towel slipped and I let it go, but I was careful to avoid my reflection in the full length mirror on the back of the bedroom door.

"Tonight, we're going to teach you about trump," Linda said as she shuffled the cards. A red pillbox hat perched atop her brunette French twist. Evidently whoever hosted the bridge-game-cum-chapter-meeting would take the lead in my education. Linda sat across from me, so she was my partner for the evening.

"Aren't those like wild cards or jokers?" I asked.

Linda passed the cards to Jane on my right and she began to deal, but she did so with the cards facing up instead of down. "Exactly. Whoever wins the bidding determines which of the four suits will be trump."

"And trump cards win against anything in another suit—even aces," Grace chimed in. She had been pouring iced tea for everyone and set my glass in front of me before sliding into her chair on my left.

Jane finished dealing out the cards, and I sorted mine out by suit and then from highest to lowest as they'd taught me the last added, pointing to the four hearts in her hand and the four in mine. "You can almost always catch an extra trick when they're distributed like that."

"Why?"

"Because one of you can usually trump in on one of the other team's high cards. Then, between you, you can still take four more tricks with your trump."

"Huh?"

"Let me show you."

And she did. Linda removed all the clubs from my hand and traded them for other cards. "Suppose Grace leads her ace of clubs," she said, pulling it to the middle of the table. "If you're void in clubs, then you can play a trump card." She pulled the three of hearts to the center of the table and put it on top of Grace's ace. "Voila! The enemy is neutralized. You have the lead, and you can pull trump."

"Pull trump?"

"You can keep leading your high trump cards and winning all the tricks until your opponents are out of them. Then the rest of your high cards are all winners, no matter what suit, and your opponents can't trump any of yours."

time. Then we all laid out our cards, face up, so that everyone's hand showed.

"Trumps allow you to neutralize your opponents' strength," Linda said. "Whenever the first person leads a card, you have to follow suit if you can. But if you're void in that suit—if you don't have any diamonds or spades or whatever it is—then you can play a trump card."

Sort of like my husband had when he'd given me my walking papers.

"So whoever wins the bidding decides which suit will be trump?" It was like the whole weed versus plant thing all over again, all in the eye of the beholder, so to speak.

Linda nodded. "You want to have at least eight cards from one suit between you and your partner before deciding to make it trump. That's called an eight-card fit."

"How do you know if you have eight cards without looking at your partner's hand?"

"You communicate that when you bid. We'll get to that later. For now, let's just practice playing the hand with one suit as trump."

"It's ideal if you and your partner each have four of your eight trump cards," Linda

I liked the sound of that. My sure winners had been trumped enough by other people's cards lately.

"Let's play the hand so you can do it yourself."

And we did. Once again, when I made mistakes, the other ladies took back their cards and let me try again. I couldn't remember a time in my life when I'd been allowed to learn, and fail, in such a supportive environment. By the time we'd demolished Grace's mint brownies and a gallon of iced tea, I could pull trump with the best of them.

"We still haven't played a real hand of bridge, though," I said later as we were tidying up the kitchen. The camaraderie had taken my mind off my aches and pains, both physical and mental, for long enough that I felt more relaxed than I had in a long time.

Linda made a final swipe at the kitchen countertop with the dish cloth. "Patience, Ellie. You don't want to go into battle without all the weapons you're going to need."

A sudden vision of Linda and I walking into Roz's house the next day flashed in front of me. "It may be too late for that already," I said morosely.

"That's why you have a partner." She

wrung out the cloth one last time and draped it over the faucet. "In case you need backup. If you're the declarer playing the hand, the dummy can provide some extra winners, even if you have a few cards that are losers in your hand. Don't forget that."

She looked at me so meaningfully that I knew she wasn't just talking about bridge.

"A trump suit gives you special powers," she added as we walked toward the front door. Grace and Jane were juggling their purses as well as the empty dishes of bridge treats, so I opened the door to let them out. "I'll pick you up at eleven-thirty tomorrow," Linda called as I followed the other two out the door.

"I'll be ready," I answered over my shoulder. The evening had definitely taken the edge off of my anxiety, but I didn't feel nearly as confident as I sounded. Pulling trump at Linda's card table was one thing. Neutralizing an enemy like the one I was going to face the next day—well, that was another thing entirely.

Roz Crowley (née Smith) gave doctors' daughters everywhere a bad name. She had been raised with just enough money and social status to make her feel important but not enough to make her an automatic player in Nashville society. Her ruthless climb to the top of the Belle Meade set had been aided by, in succession, her marriage to an older wealthy financier, her single-minded devotion to cultivating all the right friends, and her relentless insistence that her children attend the best schools and make friends only with the offspring of VIPs.

The only reason I knew all these things was because my mother had worked for Roz's father as a nurse in his pediatric practice. During my growing up years, my mother was constantly admonishing me to be either more or less like Roz, depending upon her latest achievement or escapade. That alone would have given me significant cause to dislike her, but the fact that I was privy to the intimate details of her life gave Roz cause to dislike me.

So as I headed up Roz's front walk with Linda by my side, I was filled with deep gratitude for the robin's egg blue suit. Fortunately, I already owned a pair of beige Stuart Weitzman pumps and matching purse as well as some killer pearls Jim had given me on our twenty-fifth anniversary, so I was armed for battle. This particular showdown between Roz and me had been brewing for several years. We'd both put in our hours on the Cannon Ball's lesser committees—pre-parties, mailings, seating arrangements. Last year, Roz had surprised everyone by managing to get herself named chair-elect, leapfrogging over half a dozen other women who were in line for the job. This year would be her crowning glory as she reigned supreme as Chair of the Ball. It was as close to getting yourself crowned queen as one was likely to come in Nashville.

But as socially successful as she was, Roz was not well-liked, whereas I had always enjoyed a full circle of friends. *Had,* of course, being the operative word, because my divorce had sent those so-called friends fleeing like I'd contracted bubonic plague.

Roz's formal living room held a larger than usual number of attendees for the Cannon Ball Planning Committee Kick-Off Luncheon. A photographer from the *Tennessean* was already making the rounds as the ladies preened and posed, artfully concealing their early-bird martinis behind their skirts when the flash went off.

My goal for the luncheon was to prevent my total ostracism from society. Linda, I knew, had much higher hopes. She was one of the folks Roz had shunted aside to claim the chairmanship of the ball. Perhaps that, more than her position as the Queen of Clubs, was the reason she had appointed herself my champion in the social arena.

"You can't let her push you out," Linda had advised me in the car on the way over. "She knows you have as much claim as anyone to be the new chair-elect. Keep a foot in the door, no matter what."

I wondered if she meant that figuratively or literally. While I didn't think Roz would actually deny me admittance to her home, I knew she wouldn't pass up an opportunity to deal me my social comeuppance. No way was she going to name me her heir apparent for the Cannon Ball.

"Linda! There you are." Roz came swanning into the living room reeking of Opium. Her sharp, dark eyes darted to me and then away again. "We need your advice on the theme. Angela says it's too over the top, but I don't think it's so *outré*." She snagged Linda's elbow and proceeded to tow her across the room with all the determination of a tugboat pushing a barge. Her intention, to leave me standing alone in the middle of the room, could not have been more clear. Or more perfectly executed.

"Ma'am?" The young photographer materialized at my elbow. "Can we get you in this picture?"

I looked over to see three women I'd known for years congregated by the fireplace, ready to have their photo taken. I hadn't moved in my normal social circles for the past nine months, and other than smiling and nodding in the grocery store, it was the first time I'd seen most of them since Jim walked out. Pasting a smile on my face, I nodded. "Certainly," I said and moved toward the group. Only the strangest thing happened. Actually, the most humiliating thing happened. Before I could reach them, the trio dissolved. By the time the photographer and I reached the fireplace, the antique rug in front of it was empty.

The photographer shot me a quizzical glance. "That was weird," he said.

What could I say? A divorcée in their midst might be contagious. In my present state, I was the embodiment of all their worst fears—no husband, no money, no

Belle Meade address. The only person they'd be less likely to accept in their midst than me was Jim's Tiffany. I looked around for someone, anyone, to rope into having their photograph taken with me, but the rest of the women in the living room were either turning to make their way through the archway to the dining room or studiously avoiding my pleading look. Linda's advice from yesterday morning—never let them see you sweat—rang in my ears. I refused to crumble at the first instance of adversity.

"You'll want to get a shot of that group there," I said to the photographer, motioning toward some women who were huddled together, talking animatedly, on Roz's sofa.

"Sure. Thanks." The photographer cast me one last pitying glance before he, too, fled from my presence.

Roz appeared in the archway between the vast living room and the cavernous dining room, ringing a little silver bell.

"Luncheon is served," she called, and the women all picked up their cocktails and followed her like obedient sheep. Well, okay, most of them weren't sheep. They were just hungry. And, in fact, not more than a handful probably realized the bad feelings between Roz and me. But those few who did were enough to make me stiffen my spine, and my resolve along with it. Thankfully, Linda reappeared in the archway beside Roz and motioned for me to join her.

We moved *en masse* through the dining room to Roz's enormous solarium, which I knew she'd built for occasions such as this. Of course she'd been named chair of the ball. After all, how many women in Nashville could host a seated luncheon for forty? It was a far cry from any of the dining rooms of my new Red Hat friends.

"Here we are," Linda said, motioning to the table where Roz was taking her seat.

I must have balked like a mule, because Linda put a hand on my shoulder and practically pushed me into the chair. The table seated six, and Linda had shoved me into the seat next to Roz. She took the one on the other side of me and smiled graciously at the other women at the table as she took her intricately folded linen napkin and placed it in her lap.

Roz turned toward me with a smile that looked like a hyena sizing up a lamb chop. "So, Ellie, how is your new house working out? I drove by the other day, and I was so surprised to see *rental property* across the street." She said the two words in a whisper, as if she'd been forced to utter an obscenity in polite company.

"The house is coming along," I said blithely, imitating Linda by reaching for my napkin and draping it across my lap.

"The location doesn't bother you, then?" Roz was never one to dig in the knife without giving it a good, hard twist. "I'd be devastated to leave Belle Meade."

She'd led a high card, and I cast about desperately in my mind for a trump, but I couldn't think of anything to say. The other ladies at the table might be sipping water from crystal goblets or tucking their own napkins in their laps, but I could see from the corner of my eye that they were hanging on every word of our exchange.

"I live next door to Ellie," Linda said, jumping to my defense. "I love my neighborhood. It has the most darling houses. Give me character and charm over some of these McMansions any day of the week."

Roz couldn't prevent the corner of her lip from curling up for the briefest of moments, a snarl that revealed her for the bitch she was. I beamed at Linda, who had trumped Roz for me.

"My new neighbors are the best part of moving," I said. "Linda's been lovely, welcoming me to the neighborhood."

I might have taken the trick, but I knew better than to think Roz would throw in her cards easily.

"I got the cutest little invitation yesterday," she said, looking around at the other ladies at the table. The catering staff were beginning to circle the room, and one slipped a spinach salad under Roz's carefully sculpted nose. I remembered vividly the day when I was fourteen and my mother came home from work and confided in me that Roz had undergone plastic surgery. At the time, we'd been struggling to find the money to buy my school supplies.

"Invitation to what?" Linda asked politely before taking a bite of her salad, and a sudden, icy fear struck me.

"A wedding," Roz said with a laugh. "At first, I thought it was for a baby shower, it was so pink. I've never seen anything quite so . . . well, childish, I guess is the word."

At the far end of the table, a dark-haired woman's eyes lit up. She set down her fork,

prepared to feed on something more substantial than the spinach salad. "Who's the
lucky couple?"

The dark-haired woman was probably the
only person at the table who hadn't received one of the pink monstrosities. Roz
smiled at me in triumph. "I'm sure you can
guess, Ellie."

Everyone at the table froze, as if waiting
for the *Tennessean* photographer to take a
picture. Five pairs of eyes fixed on me.
Once again Roz had led a high card, but this
time I couldn't look to Linda for help. I had
to trump her on my own.

Should I laugh it off? Feign indifference?
For a moment I froze, until Linda nudged me
with her foot beneath the table.

"I'm surprised," I said, trying to look non-
plussed. Roz looked so pleased with herself, and I dearly wanted to take that self-
satisfied look off of her face.

"What surprises you, Ellie dear?" Roz
asked.

I took a sip of iced tea from the Waterford
crystal in front of me. "I'm surprised you
didn't get your invitation earlier. Mine came
a week ago."

I was not going to give her the satisfaction, no matter what it cost me. Around the table, the other women whispered and tittered. Linda smiled her approval.

"Really?" Roz pretended to look aghast. "Oh, Ellie, surely you're not going to attend the wedding? I mean, well, that would be just too humiliating, wouldn't it?"

I gripped the edges of my chair, safe in the knowledge that the drape of the immaculate table cloth would hide my agitation. I was determined, as Linda had advised, not to let Roz see me sweat. "Jim and I parted mutually, and we'll always share the children." I forced out the words, but they tasted as bitter as they were false. "I wish him the best."

Roz looked around at the others and snickered. "Well, then you're a better woman than I am. I could never be in the same room again with a man who'd betrayed me like that. And with a Hooters waitress, too."

"So then you're not planning to attend the wedding?" I sent her back the same icy smile masquerading as a pleasant expression she'd been giving me since I'd arrived. "I'll be sure to give Jim and Tiffany your regrets."

Roz's brow furrowed despite the quantity of Botox lodged there, and then she rallied for one last try at uprooting me.

"Yes, well, perhaps we should leave the small talk for now and discuss the plans for the ball. I've made the committee assignments."

At this, even the ladies at the adjoining tables fell silent, as if they'd all been listening, one ear cocked, for just such an announcement. My heart thrummed in my chest. I knew better than to hope for any mercy from Roz, and there was no way she was going to name me chair-elect. I held out a faint hope that Linda might get the nod. At least then I could expect something better from the next year's committee assignment. Assuming I wasn't working as a waitress at Waffle House by then.

Roz stood up and tapped her crystal with her sterling silver flatware. "Ladies, if I could have your attention please."

I'd pulled trump with Roz as best I could, but she still held the highest card. I gritted my teeth and tried to look like I was enjoying myself.

"I know you're all eager to get your assignments, and so I won't wait any longer."

We held our collective breaths as Roz proceeded to announce who had been selected to chair which committee and what women were assigned to help her. As Roz went down the list, I gripped the arm of my chair more and more tightly, but my name was not mentioned. I had hoped at least for decorations. Or perhaps even the thankless task of rounding up donations for the silent auction. But one by one, my hopes were whittled down until nothing remained but a nub.

"And our last committee. Transportation."

It was the junk assignment, the one given as a clear indication of the chair's lowly status. In this case, a woman would prefer to simply be named to the committee rather than to chair it. Then she could fade into oblivion or perhaps move to another city to make a fresh start.

"Our transportation captain this year will be Ellie Johnston." Roz stopped, pressed her fingers to her lips, and giggled. "Excuse me, I mean Ellie *Hall*."

I couldn't count the number of pitying looks sent my way. I nodded graciously to Roz and then to the other ladies as if I'd just been crowned Queen of the May. Linda might teach me all about pulling trump, but the truth was, if you weren't holding the ace, you could never take the last trick.

 **CHAPTER SIX**

Opening Bids

"I've found your first client." Later that afternoon, Jane's bright voice penetrated the thick gloom that had settled over me after the luncheon at Roz's house. I hadn't made the gloom any lighter when I came home and proceeded to drag out the photo album from my wedding. The pictures of Jim and me, arm in arm, smiling and laughing, had pulled me even further into the Slough of Despond. Sitting on your Goodwill-ready couch in scruffy sweats imagining the face of a Hooters waitress on your wedding portrait was not conducive to a positive mental state.

So when Jane knocked I'd debated once again whether I should open the door, but the manners my mother had drilled into me at an early age prevailed. Now Jane was perched on my pathetic couch drinking a glass of iced tea, and I sat to her right in a cheap wooden rocking chair Jim and I had picked up at a garage sale. I smiled at her, doing my best to cover my turbulent emotions, and nudged the wedding album a little farther under the coffee table with my toe.

"First client?" Jane's enthusiasm only made my despair deeper. "But I haven't done any of the other stuff yet. Web site. Business cards. I don't even have a name for my business." I twisted the glass of iced tea in my hands, wishing the rest of me could be as numb as my fingers.

Jane set her iced tea down on the coffee table, careful to use one of the coasters even though another ring or two on that table would hardly have attracted notice. "All you need to know right now is how much you're going to charge Henri." She said the name in a lilting French accent, hardly pronouncing the "h" at all.

"Henri?" I echoed. The rocking chair was as uncomfortable as it had been cheap. We'd planned to put it on the porch of the lake home we dreamed of buying some day.

"Henri Paradis. He's in Nashville for the next six months on business. I helped him lease a condo on West End today. Very exclusive. And very expensive." Jane's eyes twinkled as brightly as her teeth shone. "He mentioned how overwhelmed he felt, what with working sixty hours a week and no time to acquaint himself with the city. He told me what he really needed was a wife, and *voilà*!" She reached into her pocket and retrieved a small white business card. "Your first client, Ellie. Isn't it exciting?"

Sure, except for the fact that I had no idea what my duties would be, how much I'd charge for them, or whether Henri Paradis thought Jane was a madam taking care of more than just his housing needs.

"It's too soon." Setting goals was one thing, but coming up with the courage to try and obtain them was another matter entirely. And after the smackdown at Roz's luncheon today, I wasn't feeling particularly lionhearted.

Jane, per usual, waved away my objection with her well-manicured hand. "You have to start sometime. Why not now?"

I could think of a million reasons why not now—I had more moping to do, more refined carbs to eat, more pity to indulge in—but none of them would hold any water with Jane. She laid the business card on my scuffed coffee table and then nudged it toward me with one poppy red fingernail.

"You can name your price, the man's so desperate."

"I don't want to practice extortion. I just want to earn a living." I began to rock, despite the discomfort of the bare wood against my backside.

"So we'll see what he needs, estimate how long it will take you, and multiply that by an hourly rate."

"Today?"

"When were you planning to start?"

"I don't know. Maybe next week?" *As long as I can afford to be in denial.* And then I thought again about Jim's phone call and the likelihood that I might never see his alimony check at all. Nothing like the prospect of a little poverty to provide an antidote to fear and trembling.

"It won't be any easier next week." Jane pushed the card even closer. "Why don't you give Henri a call right now?"

With tentative fingers, I picked up the card from the coffee table.

M. Henri Paradis
Chief Financial Officer
The Triumph Group

The address was in one of Nashville's largest downtown office buildings. I'd never heard of the Triumph Group, but if the man was working with Jane, who handled real estate matters for a healthy slice of the city's wealthiest elite, then he must be a solid citizen. Or at least as much of one as a Frenchman could be. I remembered my mother, who had done a semester as an exchange student in Paris, telling me as a child never to trust a Frenchman. The thought of my mother, though, was the one thing that could get me to summon my courage. She'd faced just what I was facing and had never shirked from the challenge.

And I was my mother's daughter. At least, I hoped I was.

"All right. I'll call him. Although I don't have the foggiest idea what I'm doing."

Jane stood up and I did the same. "That's okay, Ellie. Neither does he. In fact, he'll probably need you for a lot more than picking up dry cleaning."

"Like what?" Suddenly I was suspicious again, because Jane *was* sounding like a madam now.

"Nothing like that." She laughed. "Although, if you're given an opportunity to socialize with the man, don't turn it down on principle. He's—how do they say it?—*magnifique.*"

"Don't you make it a policy not to date clients?" I didn't know why I was even asking, since I had no interest in dating anyone. Ever. Again.

Jane's brow creased. "Well, I guess that depends."

"On what?"

"On what you need more—the date or the client."

Since I couldn't imagine ever opening myself up to a repeat of the pain Jim had inflicted on me, that shouldn't be a problem.

"Call him," Jane said again as she let herself out the front door. She didn't wait for me to answer, yanking the warped wood closed behind her as best she could.

I took a deep breath, and fearing that if I procrastinated I'd never find the courage, I walked to the phone. Then I picked up the receiver, punched in the number on Monsieur Paradis's business card, and flung myself farther into the abyss of my brand new life.

Of course he was out of the office. Isn't that always how it goes? His assistant put me through to his voice mail while I leaned against the kitchen counter and watched through my curtainless window as three squirrels raced around my backyard.

"Monsieur Paradis," I said after the beep, hoping my four years of high school French had not been in vain and that my inflection was at least passable. "This is Eleanor Hall. Jane Mansfield gave me your card and said you might be in need of my services." Ouch. Did that sound suggestive? I hadn't meant it to. "I'd be happy to discuss your needs at your convenience." Oh, shoot. That was even worse. I left my phone number and ended with, "and welcome to Nashville." I tacked on that last bit as an afterthought, but at least it sounded hospitable.

With an exasperated sigh, I shoved away from the counter. If nothing else, waiting for Henri Paradis to return my call would take my mind off of Jim's upcoming wedding as well as my demotion to Transportation Chair for the Cannon Ball. To be honest, nothing was going to take my mind off those things completely, but the prospect of landing my first client might at least mitigate the stench of failure that had begun to cling to me at Roz's luncheon yesterday.

My mom had always told me that any job worth doing was worth doing well. This sentiment had seen her through years of under-appreciated service to Roz's father, and it had helped me to graduate *magna cum laude* from Vanderbilt. But when I thought about the prospect of chairing the transportation committee for the Cannon Ball, I couldn't work up much enthusiasm for my old aphorism. Especially not as, one by one, the women Roz had named to my committee called to tell me they wouldn't be able to help this year after all.

"I'm having a root canal," one said. I decided not to point out that a root canal generally didn't put one on the disabled list for six months. We both knew the score. The Cannon Ball was the most prestigious event of the Nashville social season, and, as in real estate, the ball hierarchy was all about location, location, location. The transportation committee was to the Cannon Ball as the septic tank was to a house up for sale—important, but no one wanted to actually be responsible for it.

Another woman who resigned from the committee within forty-eight hours of the luncheon said she was leaving town. I might have believed her, if I hadn't heard later that day from Linda that the same woman had asked to be transferred to a different committee. One by one, they all fled until I was the only one left. The sole inhabitant of my fiefdom.

"What are you going to do?" Linda asked at our next Red Hat meeting. It was Saturday night again, exactly a week since the first time I'd met my new friends. This time we were meeting at Grace's house, the spade-shaped arch entirely appropriate to the gardening tyrant who had been working me like a galley slave in my own backyard for the last few days.

"I don't know." It was difficult not to sound pathetic even though the transportation committee's tasks were fairly routine. Hire a valet service and security officers to keep an eye on all the Mercedes and BMWs. Arrange for shuttle buses to ferry the guests from the parking lot at the entrance of the botanical garden to the grand old mansion-turned-museum where the ball was held. It wasn't brain surgery, but it was also a lot of details for one person to manage.

"It would serve Roz right if all the guests had to hike from the parking lot to the marquee," Linda snapped. "People would remember it happened on her watch."

"Yes, but they'd also remember I was the one who dropped the ball, so to speak. I'm sure Roz would be happy to remind everyone in the country club set of just who had been responsible for the failure. I'll figure out something."

I was also still waiting for Henri to return my call. Jane had been nudging me all week to call him again, telling me that a good businesswoman had to be persistent, but, once more, my southern upbringing made me balk at behavior that might be construed as pushy.

"Tonight, we start teaching you how to bid," Grace said, frowning at Linda and me so that we dropped our discussion of the Cannon Ball and focused on the game at hand. I still didn't own a red hat, so Grace had lent me a perky crimson beret in honor of the possibility of securing Henri as my first client.

"The important thing about bidding," Grace said, "is that you have to do it in a neutral, dispassionate way. No inflection, no emotion. And no extra words."

"No sending signals," Jane added. "That's a huge no-no."

Frankly, I was relieved to find a place where subtext wasn't allowed. "Okay, I can do that."

"Opening bids are the way you start a conversation with your partner to try and find your eight-card fit," Grace explained.

"Eight-card fit. Right." I remembered that from the last meeting. It put the odds in your favor, because if you and your partner had eight of the thirteen trump cards, you held the advantage.

"The suits have a ranking among themselves, too," Grace added.

"Rank?"

"Spades are the highest, then hearts. Those are the major suits. Diamonds are third, and clubs come in fourth. Those two are the minor suits."

"Count the number of high card points in your hand," Grace said. "Do you remember how to do that? Aces are four, kings three, etcetera."

"I remember."

"The dealer gets to bid first," Grace said. "You need to have twelve or more high card points to open. If you don't have enough points, then you pass."

Okay, passing I could handle. It's what I'd wanted to do with that phone call to Henri today, before I'd summoned the spectre of my mother and, thus, my courage. I looked down at the cards in my hand and counted the points. Fourteen. Rats. I would have to bid something. But what?

"Remember to put length before strength," Linda advised me.

"Meaning what?"

"In bridge," Linda said, "it's not just about high cards. You want to have lots of cards from one suit."

I looked down at the cards in my hand. I had the ace, king, and queen of clubs in my hand, but then I also had the ace and jack of hearts and three medium hearts. "Length over strength, hm?" It sounded wrong to me, but these ladies had been playing for a long time. "Okay, one heart."

"Good," said Grace. "You don't want to open at the two level unless you have more than twenty points."

"You can open at the two level?"

"Only with an extraordinary hand. We'll cross that bridge when we come to it. For now, let's just concentrate on the basics."

Grace collected the cards, took the second deck Jane had shuffled, and dealt once more. "We'll just keep dealing new rounds so you can get the feel for opening bids."

We covered more ground that night in my introduction to the intricacies of bidding. It was like learning pig Latin or Morse code. More talk of distribution, balanced and unbalanced hands. Eventually I got so confused that they had to make me a chart, which helped. But by the end of the evening,

I was discouraged. They'd said learning to play bridge was simple, but so far I couldn't agree. This process was turning out to be strewn with as many minefields as the Belle Meade social scene. I said as much to Linda when we took a break to eat more of Jane's delicious pound cake. Tonight it was topped with strawberries and real whipped cream.

"Yes, but you learned how to maneuver in that social circle," Linda said, "and you'll learn this, too. It just takes some time to absorb all the information."

She had a point there. I'd put a foot wrong several times when Jim and I had first begun to make our mark socially. Eventually, though, I'd learned who had been married to whom, who wasn't speaking to whom, and who had been sleeping with whom. There had come a point when I could make out a seating chart for a charity fund-raiser without creating any combustible mixtures.

"I never knew that bridge was mostly about the bidding."

"Well, whoever wins the bidding gets the contract. They have the power to shape their destiny. Win enough contracts, and you win the game. Win enough games, and you win the rubber."

"Rubber?"

"It's like a set in tennis."

"And the match? How many rubbers is it?"

"That depends. Everyone has to agree at the beginning what you're playing to. Some people like to play forever. Others like to keep it short and sweet."

As overwhelmed as I was by all the rules of bridge, I was starting to take some comfort in them. Their structure was starting to emerge, and with absolutes in my life pretty scarce on the ground, the world of bridge gave me some respite. I was even starting to enjoy the hats.

"Want to try more opening bids?" Grace asked as she cleared away the plates.

"Sure." I hurriedly stuffed the last bite in my mouth. "I need the practice."

Grace smiled benevolently. "It's the only way we learn, dear. The only way."

The next morning found me slightly less melancholy and almost enjoying the solitude of a Sunday morning on my patio. I had a real cup of coffee in hand, not the Sanka from last week's despair, and I was surveying with pride my gardening efforts of the last week. Grace and I had made it about a third of the way around the fence line, and the flower beds were beginning to look at least a little domesticated. When I finished my coffee, I was going to see if I could start the ancient lawn mower I'd inherited from my mother. It had lived for years in our basement, since Jim and I had employed a lawn service. Linda's husband, Bob, had given the old mower the once-over yesterday and pronounced it as good as new. I'd been grateful for Bob's quiet help. The chic and social Linda was married to perhaps the most introverted human being on the planet.

"Bob says the mower will run great," Linda said when they brought it back from his workshop. Bob nodded in confirmation of his assessment. "Just remember not to give it too much gas or it will stall," Linda added. Bob grunted his affirmation of this advice and went back to his workshop.

I was draining the dregs of my coffee when my phone rang, and I traipsed inside to the kitchen to answer it.

"Hello?" I was getting good at leaning against the counter when I talked on the phone. I felt tethered somehow, less lost, with the short cord securing me in place.

"Ellie? It's Jim."

Not again. Were his Sunday morning phone calls going to become a habit?

"Hello, Jim."

"Is this a bad time?"

I stifled a bark of laughter. Did he mean right this moment or this whole phase of my life in general?

"I was about to mow the lawn." I tried to keep my voice as dispassionate as possible.

"Why don't you call our service?" For years, a wiry man by the name of Elijah had done our yard maintenance.

"Because I can't afford to." I wasn't going to beat around the bush. "I think you know why."

"Oh." Now he was as monosyllabic as Linda's husband Bob.

"Did you need something, Jim?"

"Need something?"

"I assume that's why you're calling." Tiffany was definitely taking a toll on his IQ.

"I just. . . ." His voice was suddenly muffled, as if he'd cupped his hand over the receiver. I heard him say, "Okay, okay. I'll ask her," in an irritated tone.

"Just what, Jim?" Good. I hoped she was keeping him on as short a tether as the one on my ancient phone.

"Do you want me to come mow your lawn for you?"

Okay, that was the last thing I'd expected him to say. Evidently Jim was feeling remorse for something.

"I don't think so. I can manage."

"You might have some other things around the house you need help with."

"If I do, I can call someone." Now he was being nice to me? After all the pain he'd caused me over the last nine months?

"I don't mind."

"Jim, what on earth is going on?"

Again, muffled voices in the background. "Nothing."

Nothing. I knew a lot about Jim's *nothings.* They had been his standard response when he was stonewalling me. And then it hit me. Maybe Jim was having a little bit of buyer's remorse. Maybe things with Tiffany and her nubile body weren't panning out quite as he'd hoped. Maybe she didn't fit quite as nicely on the back of his Harley as he'd thought.

At the thought, my own hopes ignited like they'd been struck by a match. My pulse thrummed in my throat. Maybe Jim had finally come out of the sex-induced trance he'd been in.

"You can tell me," I said softly. "Anything."

I couldn't believe how, even after all he'd put me through, I was standing there, phone pressed to my ear, dying to hear him say he'd made a mistake. That he wanted me back.

"It's just that. . . ."

"Yes?"

More whispering, and then Jim shushing someone in the background. "I shouldn't ask you this."

My heart rate tripled, and though I knew I shouldn't, I let myself hope for a return to the familiar. Yes, I should have my pride, but the idea that this whole nightmare might come to an end flooded me with relief. I could pack my things and go home, and while I would be grateful to my new friends for the help they'd offered, I wouldn't need it after all. I felt like I might actually take flight.

"You can ask me anything." I was ready to sacrifice my pride, or whatever else it took, to have my old life back. This new one was too frightening, too overwhelming.

"Well, okay." Jim drew a deep breath. "Tiffany found your mother's wedding dress in the cedar closet in the attic, and she just fell in love with it. Said vintage is the 'in' thing. I know it's a lot to ask, but I just paid Connor and Courtney's tuition, and I can't really afford to buy Tiffany a new wedding dress, so would you mind if she wore it?"

I stood there for several long moments, my mouth opening and closing wordlessly like a fish.

"Ellie? Are you still there?"

"If she so much as lays a finger on that dress, I will personally amputate her hand." The venomous words stung my tongue. "You will put that dress in a box, and you will bring it to my house. Right now." I hadn't known I could sound like Regan from *The Exorcist,* but apparently I could. Trust Tiffany to find the one item I'd accidentally left behind.

"Okay, okay. Don't get your knickers in a twist. I was just asking."

The freshly brewed coffee I'd been enjoying threatened to make a reappearance. I had thought that I was dead to hope. That I'd accepted my new circumstances. And now I saw how little it took to resurrect my fantasies of a remorseful Jim who would come crawling back. Secretly, in my heart of hearts, I'd still believed he might change his mind. Now I knew better. Hope died swiftly and painfully within my chest.

"I have a lawn to mow. You can leave the box on the front porch."

"Okay, okay. You don't have to make a federal case out of it. I was just asking."

"Well, here's my answer." I slammed down the phone. This time, though, I wasn't going to sink to the kitchen floor in tears.

This time, I was going to go mow the damn lawn.

# CHAPTER SEVEN

Length, Not Strength

Being lethal to green things turned out to be an advantage when it came to cutting the grass. Several times I flooded the mower's engine, but after a few false starts, the mower and I came to an understanding. With each strip of grass I cut, I fantasized that I was slicing off one of Jim's body parts. By the time I finished, sweat dripping from every pore, the man was strewn in pieces around the backyard.

I put the mower away, fixed myself a glass

of iced tea, and went to check my front porch. Sure enough, there was a large white box, the one that contained my mother's wedding dress. I hadn't worn it when I married because my mother had wanted me to have something more expensive than the homemade, tea-length frock her mother had sewn for her, but I'd been saving it for Courtney in case she wanted to wear it. The thought of Tiffany in my mother's dress sent shivers of revulsion up my spine all over again.

I was putting the box on the shelf in the top of my closet when the phone rang again. Honestly, if it was Jim, I was going to get the spade Grace had given me, drive to our old house, and commit homicide with it.

"Hello?" The word came out more like a bark than a greeting.

" 'Ello? Is this Eleanor Hall?" The smooth, mellifluous voice dropped the "h"s in the way only a Frenchman could.

"Yes, this is she. Monsieur Paradis?"

"Please, you must call me Henri."

He sounded just like Louis Jourdan in *Gigi,* and his voice was enough to make a woman's stomach flutter and her toes curl.

If sex had a voice, it would sound like Henri Paradis.

"Of course, Henri. I'm delighted to hear from you."

Was that the faintest trace of coquettishness in my voice? I hadn't known I still had any left. I'd thought it had worn away with motherhood and middle age.

"Your friend Jane speaks so highly of you, and I am in great need of your help," Henri practically purred. Or at least, that's how it sounded to my American ears. No wonder French women fell into torrid love affairs the same way I fell into a box of Twinkies.

"What can I assist you with, Henri?"

"Everything, I am afraid. But right now I have one pressing need."

"Yes?"

"I have no one to accompany me to brunch today. Perhaps you would be so kind as to consider joining me? We can become better acquainted, and you will hear my whole tragic story." The irony and self-deprecation in his voice was vastly appealing after my recent conversation with Jim, who lacked both those qualities to an alarming degree.

"Brunch sounds lovely."

"You would not mind meeting me at the restaurant?" He named a favorite haunt of the Belle Meade set, one that I was as familiar with as the back of my hand.

"No, I don't mind meeting you there at all."

"In an hour, then?"

"That would be fine." Fine? I was dripping sweat from head to toe, my hair would require a miracle of biblical proportions to make it even halfway presentable, and I had no idea what I would wear. All those carbs had started to take their toll on my waistline, and as a result I could barely button, snap, or zip any of my clothes. Plus, I was likely to see scores of people I knew at the restaurant. People who had disappeared from my life since the divorce. I wonder if my arrival on the arm of a handsome Frenchman would suddenly render me less invisible.

"Then I shall see you in an hour, Eleanor."

The way my name slid off his tongue sent a shiver down my spine. I hung up the phone, let a goofy smile take over my face, and gave myself a moment to fantasize. A handsome Frenchman, the kind my mother had warned me about all those years ago. Perhaps a little champagne. And all those former friends dying to know who he was. Sometimes the gods were, indeed, kind.

I looked at the clock and realized I didn't have time to stand around mooning over a man I hadn't even met face-to-face. I had a business to launch and a number of former friends' noses to tweak.

Halfway through the drive to the restaurant to meet Henri Paradis, my fantasies dwindled away and the cold reality of what was at stake hit me. I called Jane on my cell phone.

"What do I say?" I wailed in panic. "I don't have a name for my business."

"Play it by ear," Jane advised. "Whatever he needs done, that's what you do. This could be a potentially very lucrative market, Ellie. Foreign businessmen have big expense accounts and no time to learn the ins and outs of life in Nashville. If you can make Henri happy, he'll send his compatriots your way."

I sighed. Did I really have the chutzpah to carry this off? "Okay. You're the Queen of Diamonds, you should know. I'll do it."

Although I wondered if I would have the

nerve. Could any service I provided really be valuable enough for me to make a living off of it? More than two decades of unpaid labor had definitely taken their toll on my sense of worth in the economic marketplace.

"That's my girl." Jane's voice over the phone was warmly reassuring. "Call me as soon as brunch is over. I want the scoop."

"Okay." I clicked the off button on my cell phone just as I pulled into the restaurant parking lot. A valet was waiting to take my car. He opened the door, and muttering a prayer under my breath, I stepped out on faith and my one pair of Stuart Weitzman's.

Fake it 'til you make it. I'd read those words in a self-help book once, and I clung to them now as I mounted the stairs to Alicia's. The restaurant was located in an outbuilding of an old Nashville plantation, and the chef was known for her low country cooking and traditional southern dishes. I wondered who had told Henri about it because this wasn't a place visitors frequented. Alicia's was the territory of Belle Meade matrons, and I'd lunched there more times than I could count. I straightened my spine as I marched up the stairs, preparing myself for this all-important meeting that would be conducted under the noses of some very curious onlookers.

A tall man, dark-haired and graying at the temples, stood just inside the entrance. My pulse picked up at the sight of him. His European-cut dark suit and crisp white shirt reeked of money. I tucked my purse more tightly under my arm and tugged at the jacket of the robin's egg-blue suit. I had decided this was one occasion where it would be better to be overdressed than under. "Monsieur Paradis?"

He turned toward me, and his eyes lit up. Hallelujah, hurray, and thank heavens. When I put my mind to it, I could still turn a head or two. He smiled, revealing a multitude of white teeth, and moved toward me.

"Eleanor?" Tiny laugh lines appeared at the corners of his deliciously chocolate-brown eyes.

"Yes. I'm sorry if I kept you waiting."

I extended my hand, expecting him to shake it, but instead he caught my fingers in his and carried them until they were a mere whisper from his lips. It was like something out of a Pepe Le Pew cartoon, but I'm ashamed to admit that I was putty in his hands. His smile, like his voice on the phone, was a mixture of sex appeal and self-deprecation.

"I am a very fortunate man today, indeed." He drew me forward to air kiss each of my cheeks. Despite my jerky response, he carried it off admirably.

"Please, call me Henri. Are you hungry? Our table is ready." He offered me his arm and escorted me to where the college-age hostess stood waiting, her arms piled with menus and a faint blush on her cheeks. Evidently Henri had already worked his magic here.

The hostess led us to our table, too tongue-tied to do more than motion toward our seats. Henri pulled out my chair for me, and I sat down as daintily as I could, trying hard to look as if men did this for me every day of the week. I probably wasn't any better at that than I was at air kissing, but I managed to stay on the chair instead of keeling over onto the floor.

The hostess handed us our menus and fled. The buzz of conversation had subsided as we walked across the room, but it now returned in greater force. A few heads, some that I had seen at the luncheon at Roz's house, swiveled our way. Others, topped with Red Hats—Alice's was a favorite, now that I thought about it—cast appreciative looks at my companion.

Henri laid aside his menu with barely a glance and focused his dark eyes on me. That kind of focused attention was the stuff that dreams, and reputations, were made of, and even a bitter divorcée like me couldn't remain immune to his charms. I was sure he treated all women like this, whether they were nine or ninety, but his complete focus on me and the sexual admiration in his eyes was like Gilead's balm to my wounded ego. If my life was going to morph from one cliché to another, the amorous Frenchman wasn't a bad way to go.

"And so, Eleanor, we have met at last."

I might as well have been the only woman in the room. "Yes. I'm glad you called."

"If I had known how beautiful you were, I would not have waited four days." He frowned, looking as tragic as any Frenchman ever had. "Four days, lost. I will never forgive myself."

Okay, I knew he was piling it on thick, but when you've spent your morning having your ex-husband ask if his tramp of a fiancée can wear your mother's wedding dress and mowing your own lawn for the first time, you're not in a position to turn away even the most practiced of ego-stroking compliments. Only I wasn't so sure he was feeding me a line. To my surprise, he seemed pretty sincere.

"Perhaps we can make up for the lost time." Again, I found the flirtatious words springing naturally—and disconcertingly—to my lips.

Henri smiled, and a dimple appeared at the corner of his mouth, heaven help me. "Perhaps so."

A waitress appeared at the table to take our order, and I looked away from Henri long enough to order a glass of wine and a salad.

"Only a salad? *Non, ma chère.* That will not do. You must eat more than that."

I could hardly tell him that eating was practically all I had done for the last nine months. "Really, that's more than enough."

But Henri was not to be deterred. By the time the waitress left the table, he had ordered a crab cake appetizer for me and the jambalaya entrée to follow the salad. If Jim had ever tried something so high-handed, I would have clubbed him over the head. But coming from the sexy Frenchman, I decided to be flattered instead of insulted. Plus, I really loved Alicia's jambalaya.

"And now we will talk business," he said when the waitress brought a bottle—not a glass—of wine to our table. He'd counter-manded that part of my order as well. But when I saw the label on the bottle, I swallowed my protest. It would be a long time before I ever had a chance to enjoy a Pouilly Fuisse again.

"How long have you been in Nashville?"

"Only long enough to unpack my suit-case." He smiled sadly, and a real sense of loneliness emanated from him. "Jane has found me a wonderful apartment," he said the word the French way, rolling out the syllables, "but it is too desolate. No furniture. Nothing. Not even a bottle of Perrier in the refrigerator."

"So you need a decorator? And the kitchen to be stocked?" I was trying my best to keep things on a professional level, but when I looked at Henri and felt that little and awareness. Okay, I felt a lot more than a twinge.

"That shouldn't be a problem. I can draw up a sample menu for the hors d'oeuvres, and you can tell me what wines you prefer."

"*Bien.*" He lifted his glass. "A toast, then, to our new partnership."

"To our partnership." I lifted my own glass and refrained, just in time, from trying to clink it against his in an American-style toast.

"I think it will be a very beautiful one," Henri said, and I could have happily drowned in the combination of the look in his eyes and the Pouilly Fuisse.

More than a few of the people to whom I'd been rendered invisible after my divorce stopped by my table at Alicia's before Henri and I left. I both hated and reveled in that phenomenon. Women had come a long way in my lifetime, but the validation of a handsome, rich man at your side was still a ticket to ride in just about any social circle, especially mine.

The only thing that worried me, as Henri waited with me for the valet to bring my car

zing of electricity leap between us, profes
sional was the last thing I wanted to be.

He must have felt it too, because he rarely
took his eyes off my face. "Is that something you can help me with?"

Well, I could certainly stock a kitchen. And
I'd learned enough over the years working
with a variety of decorators on my own
home that I could do a passable job of setting up Henri's apartment. I might not be the
world's best chef or decorator or party plan-
ner, but I was reasonably skilled at a variety
of things. *Length, not strength.* The memory
of Grace's words gave me courage.

"That sounds very doable."

"Doable?" He laughed. "You Americans,
you make up words at the drop of a hat."

I couldn't decide if his expression reflected amusement or criticism. I decided to
assume it was the former. "What else do
you need?"

"I am hosting a group of clients for cocktails at my office next week, and I need
someone to coordinate the food and drink
as well as be my hostess." His eyes traveled
over my suit. Or, more precisely, my body
beneath my suit. I felt a twinge of attraction

around, was that we hadn't discussed my fees. Or any of the practical details, really, of what I was going to do for him. As the appetizer had slipped away to the salad, and the entrée had succeeded it, he had directed the conversation to more social channels. He had managed to elicit far more personal information from me than I had from him. The temptation to tell more than I should about the last nine months of my life had been overwhelming. The whole story had tumbled out—Tiffany, the house on Woodlawn Avenue, my new bridge group. In return, I had learned only that he, too, was divorced, that he had grown children, and that he spent his summers in Cannes. But I had also been reminded of what it felt like to be attracted to a man and have him respond in kind. The experience had been quite heady.

I spent the rest of Sunday working on the flower beds and e-mailing my son, Connor, who had begun to construct my Web site. I forgot to call Jane to report on my lunch with Henri, so it wasn't long before she tracked me down in the backyard.

"So? How was it?"

I couldn't help the grin that broke out on my face. "He's quite something, isn't he?"

Jane whooped, a big sound for such a little person. "I told you. Did he just sweep you off your feet?"

I brushed the dirt off my old khakis and slipped off my gardening gloves. "Well, I managed to stay upright. But you were right about him being so attractive."

"Honey, that man's not attractive. He's *edible*."

We giggled like a couple of schoolgirls, and then Jane sighed. "So, what about the business part of brunch?"

"He wants me to decorate his apartment, stock his kitchen, and host a cocktail party for him."

"Excellent. And he agreed to your fees?"

"We didn't exactly talk about that."

Her smile fell. "So you didn't close the deal."

"Well, not in the strictest sense. But I'm sure it will be fine."

"Ellie, the one thing you have to learn as a businesswoman is not to put your faith in anything but a signed contract. No matter how sexy the client is."

"I didn't want to be rude. We were having such a nice time."

"Then you need to send him an estimate for your services. Have him sign it. You need something on paper."

Jane was right, and I knew it. "I lost my nerve."

We started back toward the house. "I'll help you pull something together. You can fax it to his office."

"Thanks." Assertiveness might not be my strength, but maybe my willingness to work hard could overcome that. *Length, not strength.* "I appreciate it."

"Don't worry." Jane opened the back door for me and we stepped inside. "Pretty soon closing a deal will be second nature to you."

I hoped she was right. Because I was only beginning to realize how much I had relied on Jim to play the heavy, whether it was with the lawn service or the children. I was going to have to learn to do the mop-up work myself.

"Have you come up with a name yet? For the business?"

"No. I don't think Rent-A-Wife has quite the caché I was hoping for. What do you call a service that's just doing what the better half usually does?"

Jane's eyes lit up. "That's it!"

"What's it?"

"Your Better Half. That's perfect."

I said it to myself a couple of times, letting the words roll over my tongue. It did capture what service I could offer, and while it implied intimacy, it didn't have any awkward sexual overtones.

"Your Better Half it is, then." Suddenly, it all seemed very real in a way it hadn't before. I was going into business for myself, and I had an actual client requesting my services. For the first time, I began to believe this might actually work.

Perhaps there might be life after Jim after all.

 **CHAPTER EIGHT**

Overcalling

The number of zeroes in the total estimate for my services that Jane helped me draft was enough to make my head spin.

"Don't get too excited." Jane had pulled out a calculator and was punching in several numbers. "The IRS gets its share, and then there's Social Security. True, you can deduct a lot of expenses, but you'll be more than earning that money."

The phone rang, and I went into the

kitchen to answer it while Jane continued to work on the financial angle. "Hello?"

"Ellie, it's Roz."

Her voice was about the last one I ever expected to hear coming through my phone line. I tucked the receiver into the crook of my neck and leaned one hip against the kitchen cabinet.

"Hello, Roz." I tried to keep my tone as unemotional as possible. To show weakness would be to invite her to sink her fangs even further into me. "What's up?"

"We seem to be having a little problem with your committee. Or lack thereof."

I studied the knotty pine of my ancient cabinets. Maybe I could paint them. "Yes, they do seem to be dropping like flies, don't they?"

"Ellie, let's not beat around the bush. No one wants to work with you. I think it would be best if you resigned from the planning committee."

She wouldn't outright kick me off the committee. No, that might make her look bad. Overt acts of aggression were frowned upon in 37205. A stiletto in the back was much more the thing. Besides, if she kicked me off the committee, she wouldn't have the satisfaction of seeing me resign.

"I'm perfectly willing to proceed on my own," I said, taking plates from the dish drainer and returning them to the cabinet. Maybe I could even afford a dishwasher one day.

"Don't be ridiculous," Roz snapped. "Transportation is a lot of work, and if it doesn't go well, the whole event will be ruined. I'm not willing to risk it."

"You won't be risking anything. I'll take care of it."

"Just like you took care of your husband?"

My fingers tightened around the last plate. That was a low blow, even for Roz. But given our history, I knew why she leveled it at me.

"I don't think Jim has anything to do with this." Only when it came down to my feud with Roz, Jim had quite a lot to do with it, actually.

"Look, Ellie, I'm only saying this for your own good. Spare yourself the humiliation and resign now."

"I'm not going to do it." I set the last plate on top of the others with a snap.

"Then you'll regret it."

"Are you threatening me?" I laughed. "What are you going to do to me, Roz, that hasn't already been done?"

"You're only making this harder for everyone. The rest of the committee will just have to pick up the pieces when you fail."

"I'm not going to fail."

"I lack your confidence."

My gaze fell on the box containing my mother's wedding dress that I had set on the little café table in the kitchen. The sight of it sent a thousand memories shooting through my mind. My mother, exhausted from a long day of seeing patients, standing at the ironing board, pressing my uniform skirt into knifelike pleats. The drawn expression around her mouth each time she balanced her checkbook. And the look of pride on her face when I had been named salutatorian of the senior class. Roz had graduated in the bottom quarter. My mother had been no stranger to hard work, and neither was I. And I wasn't going to let Roz Crowley take away my last connection to my old life.

"I think my track record speaks for itself. I've put in my time on more than a few Cannon Ball committees over the last few years.

If you have nothing else to say, I'm going to hang up now."

"Don't think this is over, Ellie."

"It won't be over until I finish the job, Roz."

She hung up before I had the chance to do it first.

"Who was that?" Jane called from the dining room.

"The enemy," I said, half-laughing but scared, too. Because Roz was right. Arranging all the transportation by myself was going to be a bear of a job, and the consequences were dire if I failed.

Jane appeared in the kitchen doorway. "Anything I can help with?"

"Thanks," I said. "But I think this one calls for the Queen of Clubs."

"You have to overcall her," Linda said when I repeated my conversation with Roz. Jane had gone home, leaving behind a budget to finalize for Your Better Half, and I had walked over to Linda's house to get her advice about how to handle Roz. Linda was in the kitchen chopping vegetables for soup, and so I pulled up a stool to the bar that separated the kitchen from the breakfast room and plopped down.

"I have to what?"

"Overcall her."

"What does that mean?"

"In bridge, when your opponent opens the bidding, you don't want her and her partner to just run off with the contract. Especially not if you have decent cards yourself."

"Okay." I could sort of see the analogy, but I wasn't sure where Linda was going with this.

"Let's say your opponent opens 1♦. If you have enough high card points that you would have opened the bidding yourself, then you overcall her by bidding something higher."

"Like 1♥ or 1♠?" I said, remembering that spades and hearts outranked diamonds.

"Exactly. If you wanted to bid clubs, because that was your longest suit, then you'd have to jump to the two level."

"So how do I overcall Roz?"

"I think you already did. She tried to get you to resign, and instead of passing and letting her have her way, you overcalled her."

"Yeah, but I'm not sure my hand was strong enough to open. What if I can't pull this transportation thing off?"

Linda smiled and pulled an onion toward her, which she proceeded to chop with the same efficiency she demonstrated dealing cards. "You, my friend, are in luck. Because you happen to be looking at a former chair of the transportation committee for the Cannon Ball."

"You?" I had known Linda by reputation long before I'd met her, and with her social connections, I couldn't imagine anyone had ever dared to give her the transportation assignment. The preparations for the Cannon Ball were so Byzantine that you couldn't always keep up with who had done what.

"Yep. Before your time. So I can feel your pain." She paused to wipe the onion tears from her eyes.

I was still trying to absorb this improbable information. "So what did you do?"

"I made sure that the transportation was the most memorable part of the Cannon Ball that year."

Ten years ago had been long before I'd managed to work my way onto the guest list, much less the planning committee.

"Isn't it just a matter of making sure there are enough valet attendants and shuttle buses?"

"It could be. It usually is." She sniffed and then paused to wipe her streaming eyes with a dish towel. "But I came up with something a little different that year. Limousines."

"Instead of the shuttle buses?"

"The chair of the ball nearly had a coronary at the cost, but we had an open bar in the limousines. Made for the happiest ballgoers ever."

"That's brilliant."

"That's an overcall."

"Sounds more like trumping someone's ace to me."

Linda stopped chopping for a moment and smiled in fond remembrance. "It was one of my better hands."

"I could use some high card points of my own right now."

"Remember, length, not strength."

"Whatever that means in this situation."

"You'll figure it out." Linda set down her knife and went to the sink to rinse her hands. "And we're all here to help you."

The next morning, after I'd made a run to

Office Depot to buy a fax machine, I sent my estimate to Henri's office. I had planned to spend the rest of the day digging up more weeds with Grace, when the phone rang.

"Eleanor? Henri." He sounded a little miffed, and my pulse shot up. Had I offended him by sending the estimate?

"Good morning. You got my fax?"

"A piece of paper is not the same as hearing your voice," Henri scolded, but I could tell from his tone he was flirting with me rather than expressing annoyance. "Perhaps we could meet for lunch at my apartment? Then you can see the work that is to be done. And I can give you a key and whatever else you require."

At this point, I had to wonder if everything a Frenchman said came out sounding like a prelude to taking a woman to bed. I mean, if one of Jim's business colleagues had uttered the same words, would they have made me go a little weak in the knees?

"Lunch sounds fine." It sounded more than fine, actually, but I'd decided to take a cue from my new bridge group and not send any signals during the bidding phase. Especially when I wasn't sure whether Henri was making romantic overtures to me or just being French.

"One o'clock?"

"I can be there. What's the address?"

He told me, and I had to acknowledge that Jane was right. His apartment was in an exclusive historic building on Harding Road—more of a co-op than an apartment—and though it wasn't too far from Woodlawn Avenue in terms of distance, it was a world away in terms of price range.

"I'll see you then." Once more, I set off for my bedroom in a mad scramble to find something to wear, and this time, I couldn't rely on the robin's egg-blue suit.

It had been so many years since I'd had to interpret a man's romantic intentions that I was really out of practice, so as I knocked on the door of Henri's apartment and waited for him to answer, I could feel little drops of perspiration beading on my forehead. Over time, as Jim and I had settled into that comfortable routine/rut so common to married couples, we'd developed our own shorthand for signaling whether one or both of us was interested in getting amorous.

"Want to lose some laundry?" Jim would say with a mock leer. Or "Hey, babe, want to get lucky?" I'd ask with atypical raunchiness. It was as if both of us were protecting ourselves by hiding behind a façade of humor. How odd that two people who had been married for decades felt the need to protect their egos so carefully. But we had felt that need to cushion the sting of rejection, and if I were honest with myself, I could admit that Tiffany hadn't been the problem. She was the solution Jim found to insulate himself from the pressures and problems of a middle-aged marriage.

Was Henri my solution? Just as that thought occurred to me, the man in question opened the door. Today, he wore a polo shirt and khakis, but casual attire made him no less appealing. I'd forgotten how tall he was. Or just how attractive the light sprinkling of gray at his temples made him look.

Again, his face lit up at the sight of me, just as it had at the restaurant. "Eleanor."

This was business, I reminded myself. Your Better Half's maiden voyage. I needed to keep focused on my upcoming house payment, not the knots in my stomach.

I had done my best as far as my appearance went, pulling out a pair of silky gabardine trousers and a cashmere sweater. Again, he kissed the air near each of my cheeks. Only this time, when he pulled back, his lips lightly grazed my temple, and I wasn't sure whether he had done it accidentally or on purpose. Either way, it sent a decidedly delicious tingle up my spine.

"Hello," I murmured, suddenly shy. While Tiffany might have only been a symptom of the problems in my marriage, she was the root cause of the sudden uncertainty that flooded my chest. Who was I kidding, thinking that Henri had any interest in me other than as an employee? I had seen him charm the hostess at Alicia's, and he had clearly used that same charisma on Jane. Any woman who moved within range would be pelted with the same savoir faire. I needed to get over myself, as Courtney would have said.

"Please, come inside." Henri stepped back and motioned me through the door.

I followed Henri into the empty apartment and just managed to stifle a gasp of wonder. The high ceilings and gorgeous hardwood floors were positively palatial. They were complemented by enormous windows that let in copious amounts of light. The combination living and dining area featured a beautiful marble mantelpiece beneath which gas logs burned. And though there was no furniture in sight, a small blanket had been spread across the hardwood in front of the fireplace. An elegant picnic, complete with china and crystal, occupied the space at the center of the blanket. I recognized brie, a long baguette, a bowl of grapes and oranges, and a bottle of wine chilling in a silver bucket.

"It's beautiful. How thoughtful."

Okay. So maybe I might have been wrong about Henri viewing me as just another employee. Unless he often sat around on the floor enjoying a romantic picnic with his business associates. Once more, my pulse rate accelerated.

"Would you like to see the apartment before we eat?" he asked, and I nodded in agreement.

"The kitchen is through here," he said, placing a hand at my back and leading me through an archway. I breathed a sigh of relief as we moved away from the picnic blanket and its romantic overtones.

The kitchen was, of course, state of the

art and designed to make anyone with the slightest culinary bent pea green with envy. By the time I started opening and shutting cabinets to get a feel for it, I was practically chartreuse.

"Do you want to fully stock it, or just cover the basics?" I was trying, with some difficulty, to maintain a professional demeanor since Henri followed far more closely on my heels than one would expect from your average employer. His nearness set off a thousand alarm bells in my head, but since it also made my skin tingle with anticipation, I moved slowly so he could keep up.

How long had it been since I'd felt like this? I had to admit, even if it was only to myself, that I hadn't trembled with aware-ness of a man like this in a very, very long time.

"Did you want to host the cocktail party here?" I continued to move around the kitchen, peeking into all the nooks and crannies as Henri moved with me.

"Yes. Would it be possible to do so in two weeks' time?"

I turned to look at him, which proved to be a mistake. I could see in his eyes that he was clearly stalking me, albeit in a very sexy manner. If Jim had followed me around the house like that, I would have told him to knock it off.

"Two weeks will be tight, but I can do it." I swallowed hard, both to get myself under control and to work up the courage to ask a difficult question. "Of course, it would make things go more quickly if I could charge the purchases directly to you instead of having to invoice them."

The truth was that my new credit card limit couldn't withstand the demands of decorating this kind of apartment, much less stocking the kitchen or throwing a cocktail party.

"Bien sur," Henri said, and then he moved in a little closer. "I will give you whatever you need."

I knew it was rather like a scene from a movie where the fading housewife succumbs to the charms of a practiced roué, but when your pulse is pounding in your ears and you feel alive for the first time in nine months, you don't stop to analyze the situation.

"I'll just make a list—" I fumbled in my purse for the pen and notebook I'd put there earlier in hopes of pulling them out with professional efficiency.

Henri took the pen and notebook from my hands and set them on the kitchen counter. "Later, *ma chère.*"

"Later?" I croaked.

"Yes. First. . . ." His voice trailed off.

"First?" I sounded like a bad echo, and all I could think was that I hadn't been kissed by anyone other than Jim in almost thirty years. What if I'd forgotten how to do it?

"First," said Henri, bending his head toward mine and lowering his voice to a whisper, "we must eat."

And then he smiled, smiled in a way that told me he both knew what I had been expecting and that he intended to fulfill that expectation. Just not quite yet.

I was putty in his hands. What right-thinking woman—or *non*-thinking as the case might be—wouldn't have been? He led me back to the living room and we settled in on the picnic blanket. Before I knew what was happening, I had a goblet of champagne in my hand and an array of delectable tidbits on a plate in my lap.

"Try this," Henri urged as he spread Brie on a chunk of the baguette and offered it to me. His fingers brushed mine as he handed me the bread, and I almost jumped out of my skin.

"Okay."

The same thing happened when he refilled my champagne flute, his fingers curling around mine where they grasped the stem of the glass as he poured. Just when I thought I might spontaneously combust, Henri shifted the mood and began to tell me amusing stories of his experiences since coming to Nashville. He leaned slightly away from me as he spoke, and I was both thankful for and annoyed at the distance.

We worked our way through the bread, cheese, fruit, and, most importantly, the champagne. Then Henri excused himself to the kitchen and returned bearing a plate of tiny lemon tarts and a thermos of coffee. For the first time in months, I felt replete, as if every need had been satisfied, a feeling that all those months of binging my way through the kitchen hadn't been able to give me. And though the fat and carbs that comprised Henri's picnic were more elegant than my usual fare of Twinkies and Krispy Kremes, the only real difference was the company in which I'd consumed them—my own vs. that of Henri.

And so when we had finished the meal and I leaned forward to begin stacking all the plates and dishes, I was both unprepared for and yet expecting what happened next. Suddenly Henri's mouth was inches from my own, and then his lips were against mine.

Liquid warmth washed over me, and I didn't feel fifty anymore. No, I was as giddy as a teenager in the throes of puppy love, although the way Henri kissed me was far from innocent. The taste, the texture, and the sensations had me grasping his shoulders to keep myself from floating away on a cloud of pure joy.

How could I have let myself forget what this was like? The warmth of another person's lips, the gentle yet firm pressure that made it difficult to breathe. The taste of wine and fruit on a man's breath that seemed to connect me to the very earth from which they came.

"So beautiful," Henri murmured when we came up for air. He stroked my cheek with his palm, and it was all I could do not to turn my head and nuzzle it. I'd thought that at age fifty I'd be long past such feelings, such experiences. Apparently, I'd been wrong.

And I'd never been so glad to be wrong in my whole life.

"Thank you." I could feel myself blushing like a schoolgirl.

"It embarrasses you, my appreciation for your beauty," he whispered, moving his lips close to my ear to say the words, and the touch of his breath on my ear was nearly my undoing.

"Yes. No. I mean—"

"You American women, you doubt yourselves too much. A Frenchwoman, she takes admiration as her due. But for you . . ." He broke off to explore my neck with his lips. Clearly I had died and gone to heaven. My suffering over the last nine months was finally being rewarded.

"It's not that we doubt—" I tried to object to his characterization, but I'd always been particularly sensitive to a man's lips right where my neck curved into my shoulder. Henri honed in on that vulnerability like a heat-seeking missile.

I hadn't seriously made out with a man since the days Jim and I used to steam up the windows of his Mustang in college, but Henri was clearly open to helping me make up for lost time. And so I let him.

Much, much later, long after any reasonable-length business lunch would have been over, I was curled up in Henri's arms, completely oblivious to the unforgiving hardwood floor beneath me, and we were both breathing heavily. To my surprise, and relief, Henri hadn't tried to push me past the point of some very heady kisses.

"I think I've violated about a million professional standards," I said, because once the kissing had stopped, I'd been flooded with worry. I'd heard so many horror stories about mixing business with pleasure, and yet I'd been as vulnerable to it as anyone.

"Hm," Henri said, continuing to stroke my hair. I hadn't felt cherished in such a long time that the simple brush of his fingers against my scalp brought a sting of tears to my eyes.

"I'm hoping this isn't your normal business lunch." I decided humor might be the best way to ease out of the situation. "Or is this just part of your new employee orientation?"

Henri stiffened. Oops. I should have kept my mouth closed. "What are you saying, Ellie?"

I sighed. "Sorry. I'm just thinking that I

should have kept things on a more professional level."

"You are sorry for what happened?" He looked as if the mere possibility wounded him to the core. Only I didn't think it was an act. He looked truly hurt at my regret.

"I'm not sure I can be your employee and . . ." My voice trailed off, because I wasn't quite sure what to call what had just happened. "Your whatever this is."

"Then you're fired." Henri smiled, and my insides did another somersault. And another. And another.

And that's when I knew I was in deep trouble.

 **CHAPTER NINE**

Don't Send a Boy To Do a Man's Job

"Fired?" My voice squeaked like a boy going through puberty. "You're firing me?"

"If you insist that I choose, then yes, I would fire you immediately. I can always hire someone else to help me with the apartment," he moved his lips close to my ear again, "but who else could have made this meal so . . . enjoyable?" He drew out the syllables of the last word as if pronouncing them in French—*en-joy-ah-bleh.* Emphasis on the "ah."

"Oh."

"So, should I fire you? Would that make your American sense of propriety feel better?" Henri smiled.

Okay, the bottom line was I didn't want Henri to fire me. I couldn't afford it. Literally. "No, I don't think you should fire me."

"Good." He playfully tapped the end of my nose with the tip of his finger. "Because I have never found it to be a problem to mix business with pleasure."

Maybe I was being too provincial. Too American. In which case, I could pretend to be just as sophisticated as any French-woman on the planet. *Pretend* being the operative word of course.

"Back to work, then," I said, tapping the end of his nose in return. I shifted to my knees and stood up. "I'll just get my pen and notepad." I turned to walk across the room to the kitchen where Henri had tossed those two items on the counter. As I went, I was aware of his gaze firmly and appreciatively fixed on my derriere.

Take that, Jim, I said to myself, and I put a bit of extra swing in my hips as I walked away.

*   *   *

Should I be ashamed to say that from that point, not a day went by that I didn't see Henri? Sometimes it was business—meeting him at an antique store to have him choose from several beautiful armoires or rendezvousing at a local carpet warehouse to look at gorgeous Persian rugs for his living room.

Other times, we would rendezvous in the true sense of the word. He took me to dinner at Mario's and The Wild Boar, and I worked harder than ever pulling weeds in my backyard to counteract the pâté and crème brulée. And even though new furniture was delivered to his apartment each day, we continued to enjoy picnics in front of the fireplace whenever our schedules allowed. He worked long hours, and I was beginning to add some other clients. Small jobs, to be sure. A wealthy, elderly widow who needed someone to take her shopping. An absentminded Vanderbilt professor with a genius IQ who couldn't remember to pay his bills on time. They weren't generating an overwhelming amount of income, but it was a start.

As caught up as I was in the double satisfaction of doing good work and being thoroughly romanced, I still had time for self-doubt. One evening, as Henri and I were leaving a performance of the Nashville Symphony hand in hand, we were crossing an open plaza downtown when I couldn't keep myself from asking the question that had been bothering me since that first picnic.

"Why me, Henri?" I asked quietly, half-hoping the whooshing of the fountain in the middle of the plaza would drown out my words. I was a fool to rock a boat while I was so desperately clinging to the sides.

"Because Jane recommended you, *bien sur.*" But his eyes twinkled so that I knew he was teasing me.

"You know what I mean."

And then he stopped, turned me toward him, and put his fingers beneath my chin, lifting my eyes to his. "You truly do not know?"

I shook my head and would have looked away, embarrassed, but his fingers held my chin in place.

"To begin with, you are very beautiful."

I tried to shake my head in denial, but he leaned forward and kissed me softly on the lips.

"I'm middle-aged," I protested.

"And that means you cannot be beauti-ful?"

Well, he had me there. Because here in America, that pretty much summed it up. Evidently the men in France hadn't gotten the memo.

"You are also intelligent," he added, kiss-ing my forehead. "And compassionate." He kissed my cheek. "And you have taken pity on me, a stranger in a strange land." He kissed the tip of my nose. "How could I do anything but adore you?"

And despite my misgivings, I believed him. His eyes, his voice, his touch all oozed sincerity. In a good way.

"Perhaps," he said, "it would be better to ask why a woman like you would take pity on a pathetic specimen like myself."

And then he kissed me in earnest. The fresh air of a cool spring night bathed my heated cheeks, and I allowed myself to feel the happiness that poured over me like wa-ter from the fountain next to us.

"You've been doing what?" Jane's jaw dropped, practically brushing my hardwood floor, where the four of us sat around my dining room table at our next chapter meeting, the ever-present red hats in place and lots of munchies on hand.

"We're having a bit of a . . . well . . . fling, I guess." I was blushing to the roots of my hair. I had managed to keep the level of my involvement with Henri to myself for two whole weeks—fourteen days of amazing kisses and the ego-building attentions of an incredibly sexy man. Whenever I felt a Twinkie twinge, I pictured Henri, and the urge to binge quickly receded.

The cocktail party the night before had been a smashing success. I'd found an amazing little black dress on the 75 percent off rack at Dillard's, and the shrimp puffs and caviar had been crowd pleasers. As I circled the room, directing the two waiters I'd hired for the evening and encouraging the bartender to practice liberality, I'd taken great satisfaction in the evening's success. Henri had lavished praise on me in front of his colleagues with as much enthusiasm as he kissed me with when he followed me into the powder room. For a woman who'd been a certified couch potato a few weeks before, I'd undergone a serious transformation. I'd charmed and satisfied every guest, pulling off an elegant gathering of fifty of Nashville's top business people.

And over the course of those two weeks, even Jim's increasingly frequent phone calls couldn't perturb me for more than an hour or two.

At first, I had put the calls down to a need to rub my nose in his happiness with Tiffany, but over the last few days, I'd begun to wonder if my assessment was correct. Especially when the last time he'd called, he'd wanted to know how to wash delicates. In twenty-plus years of marriage, Jim had never expressed the slightest interest in washing anything, delicate or otherwise.

"Are you sure that's wise?" Linda asked, pulling me back to the here and now. "Dating Henri?" For the first time, the Queens of Woodlawn Avenue were meeting at my house, and in honor of the occasion, I'd bought my first red hat. It was a 1920s-style cloche, its turned-up brim anchored by a purple ribbon rosette. "You know what they say about mixing business with pleasure." Linda frowned and her green eyes looked troubled.

I'd waited until we were in the middle of a

hand to drop my bombshell. Grace and I had lost the bidding to Linda and Jane, but halfway through the hand, Grace had the lead. She slid an eight of hearts into the middle of the table. Jane reached over and pulled a ten from Linda's dummy. I looked at the cards in my hand, completely void in hearts, and pondered which of my trump suit to play. Excited at the prospect of an extra winner, I pulled a five of spades from my hand and slid it on top of the other cards.

Grace frowned. Not a good sign. Then Jane pulled a card from her hand and threw it on the pile. "Don't send a boy to do a man's job," she said as her king of spades trumped my little five.

Shoot.

Grace didn't look too happy with me. "Don't send a boy to do a man's job," she repeated. "That means, don't underplay your cards, thinking you can squeak out an extra winner. If you're going to take the trick, do it with authority. Otherwise you let your partner down. Next time play a higher card."

Jane nodded in agreement. "Don't be afraid to use your power."

Don't be afraid to use your power. Her words coalesced in my brain and wouldn't leave, even after the bridge game was over and the other Queens of Woodlawn Avenue had long departed.

I was still wrestling with the implication of those words later that night. Curled up in bed in an old pair of flannel pajamas, I'd taken a wooden box from its place of honor on my nightstand, opened the lid, and lifted out its contents piece by piece.

I'd made the memory box at some Amway-style party where one of my former Belle Meade friends had been hawking the latest distraction/activity for bored house-wives and stay-at-home moms. Being me, I'd not been satisfied with a slapdash job. No, my memory box, with *Ellie & Jim* written in elegant calligraphy across the top, had been a flipping work of art. A monument to a marriage that was dying right under my unknowing nose.

The box was full of mementos. Intimate things. Bits and pieces of my life that now lay strewn across my bedspread. A scrap of lace from the negligee I'd worn on my hon-eymoon. Ticket stubs from plays and movies we'd enjoyed. Little notes Jim had written me over the years. *To My Dearest El-lie. With all my love, Jim.* A remnant of love from happier times. The only use I'd found for these mementos over the past nine months had been as instruments of self-torture. Over and over again, I'd sifted through the contents of the memory box just as I was doing now.

And then the phone rang.

"Hello?"

"It's me."

My pulse shouldn't still leap at the sound of his voice. I decided to attribute my reaction to the maudlin stroll down memory lane.

"What do you want, Jim?" Too bad I couldn't keep the asperity out of my voice. I wanted to sound cool and distant.

"Did you get the check I sent?"

"Yes, thanks." I wasn't going to praise him for alimony that was fourteen days overdue. I had deposited it in the bank with a sigh of relief, grateful for the small cushion it provided.

"How's your business going?"

"Fine, thanks." I didn't say anything else, because somehow the combination of his voice and the sight of all those mementos lying on the bed tied my tongue. Jim was silent for a long moment, too.

"Well, I guess that's all I really wanted. To make sure you got the check."

"Okay." Two syllables I could barely force past the sudden constriction in my throat.

Another silence.

"Okay, well, good-night, Ellie."

"Good-night, Jim." I hung up the phone, and, darn it, tears sprang to my eyes. That old hurt welled up in my chest, and it was like the last two weeks had never happened. I was the same, pitiful wreck that Jim had walked out on all those months ago.

And then suddenly Grace's words ran through my mind again. *Don't give your power away.*

I wiped away the tears with the back of my hand and took a deep breath. Then I picked up the phone and, stabbing at the buttons, dialed my old number.

"Ellie?" Jim had apparently looked at his Caller ID because he didn't bother to say "hello." "Is anything wrong?"

"I want you to quit calling me."

"What?"

"I don't know why you're doing it, but I want you to quit calling me. If you want to know if a check has arrived, send me an e-mail. If you need to know how to wash Tiffany's lingerie, ask her. And for heaven's sake, Jim, if you're lonely, don't drink and dial. Go find your little floozie and bother her. But quit calling me."

The words rushed out in a torrent, and with them came a feeling of relief. A cleansing.

"You don't have to be nasty about it," Jim snapped. "I was just trying to be nice."

Only he wasn't. Trying to be nice, that was. "You can't eat your cake and have it too, Jim. We're done. You made sure of that. So quit calling me."

"Are you seeing someone?"

Two weeks ago, the jealousy in his voice would have thrilled me to the core. Now, it left me tired and exasperated. "That's none of your business." I began to stuff the mementos back into the memory box.

"You *are* seeing someone."

"Jim, even if I'm dating, you're about to get *married,* for pete's sake. What does it matter if I have a boyfriend?"

"Who is it?"

"I'm hanging up now, Jim. Go talk to

Tiffany if you need your masculinity rein-
forced."

"She's at work," he snapped, and the
words stung. He'd only called because his
hootchie mama was off plying her wares for
minimum wage plus tips to a bunch of sali-
vating Neanderthals just like him.

"Lucky her." I slammed down the phone,
closed the lid of the memory box with a
snap, and returned it to the bedside table. I
flicked off the lamp.

And then I lay sleepless in the dark for a
very long time.

I spent the next week putting the finishing
touches on Henri's apartment and attending
a couple of Red Hat events. Henri worked
late every night, so I didn't see him at all. Instead, I cooked gourmet meals that I left in
Tupperware containers in the refrigerator for
him to heat up when he got home. And in
his absence, doubt took root in my mind like
all the weeds I was pulling from my flower
beds. Who was I kidding, carrying on with
Henri like a twenty-something in love for the
first time? Henri's attentions might be a
balm, but the wound beneath was still there,

still fresh. And I found myself wishing in my darker moments that Jim would start drinking and dialing again.

Jane passed along leads for more clients, but with all I was doing for Henri and the few others I'd already acquired, I didn't have time to follow up on them. I even splurged on a visit to the salon to have my highlights brought up to date.

That's where I ran into Roz.

There I was, trapped under a heat lamp with enough aluminum foil residing on my head to make me look like an extraterrestrial. I was flipping through the pages of the latest French *Vogue* I'd picked up at the bookstore, hoping to pick up some tips on being less American and more confident, when one of the stylists brought someone to the chair next to me. I looked up and saw Roz.

"Ellie!" She smiled in that feral way of hers, the one that told you she was the kind of woman who would eat her young. In this case, though, it looked like she was willing to settle for me.

"Hello, Roz."

"Ellie. I'm so glad I ran into you. I have big news." She said it in such a way that I knew it wasn't going to be very pleasant news, whatever it was. At least not for me.

"About the Cannon Ball?"

"Yes. Very exciting. We've changed the date."

My head popped up and banged against the heat lamp. Pain spread across my scalp, aided by the conducting properties of the foil.

"Will it be later in the fall?"

Roz's smile revealed her extra-sharp canine teeth. It was a wonder, with all the cosmetic dentistry she'd had, that someone hadn't filed those fangs down.

"No, actually. We've been hoping for ages to move it to the summer, but the museum couldn't accommodate us. Now they can, though."

Summer? I wanted to leap out of my chair, but I'd already banged my head against the heat lamp once. "So we're talking what— July?" I asked hopefully.

Roz shook her head. "Oh, no. Too hot then. No, we're the first Saturday in June. Only a few weeks away."

My head started to swim. No way. There was no way the committees, any of the committees, could pull that off.

And then I saw the gleam in Roz's eye, and I realized the truth. She had done whatever was necessary to change the date merely to inflict suffering on me, and she didn't care who else got caught in the line of fire.

"The date change shouldn't present that big of a problem. You're on top of it, aren't you?"

"I am." When had I become such a glib liar? "No, the change won't be a problem."

We both knew the truth, though, and Roz just sat there, smiling, basking in her triumph. I had thought she would be satisfied with humiliating me with the transportation assignment and then watching as my committee deserted. But apparently that wasn't enough to satisfy her blood lust.

Thankfully, at that moment, my stylist appeared to take me away to the shampoo room so she could remove the foil and rinse out my hair. I managed to avoid Roz until I left the salon, highlights glowing golden in the sunlight, but I couldn't so easily escape the sound of the ominous, rapidly ticking clock my old nemesis had planted in my brain.

*   *   *

By Friday night, I was desperate for my Henri "fix," so I put on a new silk dress that I really couldn't afford and headed for his apartment. Since I had my own key, I could let myself in. He'd called earlier in the day, distracted and harried, but at least he asked if I would join him for dinner at his apartment. I hadn't even minded when he wanted to know if I'd be willing to cook the meal.

A romantic evening, tête-à-tête, was just what the doctor ordered, so to speak. No Jim. No Roz. No worry about whether Your Better Half would turn out to be more than a one-hit wonder and no talk of bridge or red hats. Just a delicious meal and Henri's even more delicious attentions.

He turned up an hour late, by which time I'd reheated the *beouf bourgignon* to the point of disintegration. If Jim had kept me waiting like that I would have been livid, but since I was waiting for the mouth-watering Henri the delay only served to heighten my already fevered state of anticipation.

"Ma chère," he purred when he came through the door, dropping his briefcase with a thud and sweeping me into his embrace. Then there was no conversation at all

for a nice long time. Finally, when we came up for air, I could return his greeting.

"How was your day?" I took him by the hand and led him to the kitchen so I could serve the meal. His fingers threaded through mine as we went, and a warm glow took over for the hunger pangs that had been gnawing my stomach. I'd forgotten how sensual merely holding hands could be.

"My day? *Horrible,*" Henri said. "I will never understand you Americans."

I hid my wince. At times, Henri's contempt for the good old US of A and its inhabitants rubbed me the wrong way. But then he would kiss me and I'd forget all about it.

"Maybe this will help." I picked up the plates of food. "Grab the wine," I said and led him back to the dining room.

I'd set the table with a pristine linen cloth and tall tapers in the silver candlesticks my mother had given to Jim and me for our twenty-fifth anniversary shortly before her death. I lit the candles while Henri poured the wine.

"This is what a man dreams of when he is trapped in an office all day with imbeciles." Henri leaned over to kiss me when he handed me my glass of wine.

Okay, so he was arrogant, but he was also the most amazing kisser. He pulled out my chair for me—a courtesy Jim had rarely performed—and we sat down to eat. As the stresses of his day melted away, Henri turned on the charm and easily ensnared me.

Dinner gave way to an aperitif on the new leather couch in front of the fireplace. I slipped off my shoes and curled up next to him. His arm slid comfortably around my shoulders.

"You are an extraordinarily amazing woman," he murmured in my ear. He was quite the ear-murmurer, Henri, and it would have seemed a little slick if it hadn't been so darn effective.

"You're not so bad yourself."

"Not so bad?" He arched one eyebrow. "I can see that I must improve your opinion of me."

And he did. First on the couch, and then later when we moved to the bedroom. I'd bought the enormous four-poster bed for him with less than pure intentions, I must admit. The sheets were six hundred count cotton, so luxurious they might as well have been silk. And the small stereo system surrounded us with soft jazz.

All in all, I'd set the scene for my own seduction. And to my delight, Henri definitely wasn't a boy sent to do a man's job.

Over the years of my marriage, I'd gradually forgotten how exciting making love for the first time could be, but I'd also forgotten the awkwardness of the morning after. The night before, I'd been emboldened by the wine and the firelight. In the cold, harsh light of Saturday morning, though, I faced the reality of being a middle-aged woman who'd taken a new lover.

"Eleanor?" Henri mumbled sleepily when I slipped from the luxurious bed, taking the flat sheet with me so that I could conceal myself for the trek to the bathroom. The ravages of time and gravity on my figure could be camouflaged in the dark, but nothing short of a burka could cover them in the glaring light of day.

"Be right back." My dash for the bathroom was hampered by the constricting wrap of the sheet. I looked over my shoulder when I reached the bathroom door to find Henri smiling at me with his usual combination of sensual interest and amusement.

The bathroom was a veritable hall of mirrors, so I clutched the sheet as I moved to the vanity and leaned closer to examine my reflection. My face looked the same as always—the crow's feet flowing from the corners of my eyes, little red splotches here and there across my cheeks and brow where I'd once had smooth, even skin tone. My face was no different from that of any fifty-year-old woman. I was disappointed, because I would have thought something as amazing as the night before would have shown up in the mirror.

"What are you doing in there?" Henri called.

I jerked back from my reflection. "Nothing."

"Well then hurry and come back to bed." His voice promised another round of sensual pleasure. And, strangely, where I should have been excited at the prospect, a vague sense of disappointment lodged in my stomach. Why? After months of depression in the wake of Jim's departure, things were finally going my way. I should be on top of the world. So why did I feel so sad?

I hadn't been naïve about where my relationship with Henri was headed. I'd packed a small tote bag with morning-after essentials and stashed them in the cupboard underneath the sink the night before. Quickly, I brushed my teeth and ran a wide-toothed comb through my hair, leaving it tousled but tangle-free. Undereye concealer or other tricks of the trade would have to wait. I hitched the sheet up a little higher over my breasts and returned to the bedroom.

Henri was leaning against the mound of pillows he'd piled against the headboard. He smiled lazily and patted the mattress next to him. "Come back to bed."

And I did. But I brought with me the knowledge that part of me was disappointed it wasn't Jim looking at me beneath heavy-lidded eyes and welcoming me into his arms with a deep, lingering kiss, the way he would have once upon a time.

Sometimes, even at a time like this, you couldn't do anything but miss the boy you'd fallen in love with, even when he failed at being the man you'd thought him to be.

CHAPTER TEN

An Unmarked Knave

I left Henri's late Saturday morning after fixing a cheese omelet for the two of us and jotting down a list of what he needed done during the next week. If it hadn't been for the invoices for my work hours that I sent him on a regular basis, I'd have felt almost married to the man, our relationship was so domestic.

It felt good to be headed back to my house after the emotional highs and lows of the last twenty-four hours, although when I pulled into the driveway I hoped that none of the Queens of Woodlawn Avenue noticed I hadn't come home last night. I was confused enough about this new development to want to keep it to myself until I'd had a chance to sort it out.

My life had gotten so busy that there was no shortage of tasks I should have attended to, but I ignored them and instead headed for the backyard with my gardening tools in hand. Grace's influence was growing more evident in the flower beds that lined the privacy fence where it enclosed the yard. Little by little, I was reclaiming the wilderness.

I'd been digging up weeds in the back flower bed along the fence for about an hour when I decided that the whole bed really needed turning over. I traipsed over to the ramshackle detached garage to fetch my shovel.

I had dug pretty deep in the flower bed when the shovel hit something hard. A crack like a popgun nearly sent me straight out of my gardening clogs. With the edge of the shovel, I scraped back the loose dirt to discover the source of the sound.

Scattered white sticks tumbled this way and that. And then my stomach dropped to my aforementioned clogs when I realized that those little white things weren't sticks. Or roots. Or anything else you'd expect to find when you dug a hole in your backyard.

They were fragments of bone.

Great. I had dug up old Flossie's dog or cat, the remnants of that first Queen of Hearts' beloved family pet.

At least, I thought it was a family pet. Until I scraped away more dirt and saw the very distinct shape of a human tibia, along with a metatarsal or two. A little more scraping revealed some vertebrae. Connected to a human skull.

Grace said later that my scream took ten years off her life. She called 911, thinking I'd been attacked by one of the transients who sometimes roamed the neighborhood looking for odd jobs. The next thing I knew, two armed Metro patrol officers appeared around the corner of the house, Grace hard on their heels and brandishing a baseball bat.

"Ma'am? You okay?" the first officer asked. He was young, not much older than my son Connor, and he had the freshly scrubbed look of someone who hadn't been beaten down by life—at least, not yet. The second officer, older, harder, and more cynical-looking, ducked into the garage in pursuit of my phantom attacker.

"No. In there," I said, pointing with a trembling finger toward the hole. The young officer stepped into the flower bed and looked down.

"Holy crap."

I couldn't have agreed more.

"What is it?" Grace asked, coming to peer over my shoulder. "Are you okay, Ellie?" And then she gasped when she, too, saw what was in the hole.

Officer McFarland, according to the name on his badge, reached for the radio at his belt. "I'd better get crime scene over here." His dark eyes bore into mine. "Ma'am, do you have any idea who this is?"

I shook my head, throat too dry to speak.

Grace peered into the hole again. "What's that in there with him?"

"Where?" I asked.

Officer McFarland stepped up beside me and looked down. "It looks like hair." He pulled out his billy club, stuck it into the hole, and fished out the object. A matted clump of brown emerged, and when he flipped it over onto the ground, you could

see some sort of material or netting underneath.

"It's a toupee," he said.

"Marvin Etherington," Grace said in a
matter-of-fact tone. "I'd recognize that bad
toupee anywhere."

"Who?" the officer and I asked simultaneously.

"Flossie's husband. Marvin Etherington.
He ran off in 1947. At least, that's what
Flossie always said. She had him declared
legally dead and collected the insurance
money. And he wore the world's worst
toupee."

"Are you sure?" I asked.

"How many other missing men with bad
toupees would be buried in your flower bed?"
Grace's papery cheek had gone pink beneath
its veneer of pancake makeup and face powder. She meant to appear calm, but her high
color revealed her distress. I guessed it would
have been rather disconcerting to come face-
to-face with the bones—and toupee—of a
deceased former neighbor.

Officer McFarland pulled out a small spi-
ral notebook and began jotting things down.
"He disappeared in '47, you say?"

Grace nodded. "It took a while, but

Flossie had him declared dead. Legally dead. She collected enough life insurance money to put the girls through college without having to go back to work."

The officer scowled. "Where can I find this Flossie?"

Grace snorted, some of the tension in her face receding. "Mount Olivet Cemetery. In the family plot." She winked at me. "If you want to interview her, I'd be happy to go along for the ride."

Officer McFarland didn't appreciate Grace's flippant reply as much as I did. I also suspected it was her way of dealing with the shock. "That won't be necessary, ma'am," he scowled. "If you ladies would just wait in the house, I'll do my job."

"Yes, officer," I said in my most placating tone, the one I'd cultivated for the days when Jim came home from a fifteen-hour day in surgery. If there was one thing I knew how to handle, it was a fussy man.

Grace balked at being ordered around by someone fifty years her junior, but before Officer McFarland could take exception to a senior citizen with no respect for his authority, I hustled her away. I wanted to know a lot more about the late Marvin Etherington and how in the world he wound up in my flower bed.

Within a short time, the crime scene unit rolled up in front of my house. Young Officer McFarland called me outside again to ask me more questions, so it was some time before I could corner Grace and find out more about the first Queen of Hearts. The crime scene people dug a pit the size of Cleveland in my backyard, but eventually they recovered all of Marvin Etherington's various bits. I know that because I'd done my time in dissection lab while in nursing school at Vanderbilt. On more than one occasion, I'd carried a bunch of bones in an unassuming paisley print bag from the lab to my dorm room for further study. So as I watched the forensic pathologist lay out Marvin's remains on a tarp, I could tell he was all there. And it didn't take a trained eye to see the hole in the back of his skull. Whoever had done him in must have hit him so hard that, ironically, he'd probably never felt it.

When I returned to the house, Grace was running the dust mop around the scarred hardwood floor of my dining room. The Queens of Woodlawn Avenue certainly weren't hesitant to make themselves at home in one another's houses.

"Did they find all of him?" Grace asked as she swept the lint and dirt into the dustbin.

"Everything except the missing part from the back of his head." I slumped into one of the dining room chairs. "Not much doubt about how he died."

Grace pulled out the chair next to me and sat down. "Don't judge Flossie too harshly. Marvin was a trial to her. Always staying out late, carrying on with other women."

"Oh, I'm not judging her," I assured Grace, thinking of Jim's last phone call. I knew too well how Flossie must have felt. "But wouldn't divorce have been less risky?"

Grace frowned. "Not back then. Women didn't have as many rights, or any assurance they'd get custody of the children. Not like you young things today."

"Well, I can sympathize with her murderous intent."

Grace patted my hand. "You're lucky. You have choices."

I tried to return her smile, but the truth was, I didn't feel lucky. I felt screwed over.

And none of this had been my choice. My husband, my house, my seat in the dining room at the country club now belonged to another woman whose only claim to fame was that her breasts had yet to sag.

"When the police are done, we'll have our bridge night," Grace said.

"Bridge night? Grace, how on earth am I supposed to play bridge? They've just found a murdered man in my back flower bed."

She looked genuinely puzzled. "Marvin Etherington's been dead a long time. And you didn't kill him. Why should that keep you from going on with your life?"

I looked at her, mouth agape.

About that time, Officer McFarland knocked on the front door yet again, and when I answered he politely thanked me for putting up with all the hoopla. "We'll send someone back to fill up the hole."

"You don't have to do that," I assured him. "I can take care of it."

"You're sure?"

"Yes." And I was.

Because it had occurred to me during my conversation with Grace that if my life was going to move forward, it might be a good idea to bury some dead bodies of my own in that big hole in the backyard.

Okay, I wasn't literally going to bury a body, although the thought of Jim laid out in that hole had a certain appeal. No, I wasn't going to give Officer McFarland a reason to come back. What I was going to lay to rest were more like symbols. Tokens. Mementos. Things I was done with. Not things my kids would want some day, like our wedding photos or the picture of the whole family made on the cruise ship on our twentieth anniversary a few years ago. I wanted Connor and Courtney to have some happy memories of their parents' marriage.

"Why don't you take a shower and get ready for the bridge game?" Grace said when I'd closed the door on Officer McFarland.

"I'll change in a minute. First, I've got to do something."

I went to my bedroom and took the memory box off my nightstand. I wanted to do this before I lost my nerve. When I came back through the living room, Grace got up from the couch and followed me into the backyard.

"Ellie? What are you doing?"

"Burying my husband," I said. "Just like Flossie did."

The shovel was still lying next to the hole, and when I saw the size of the yawning cavern along my back fence, I almost regretted not taking the officer up on his offer of help.

"Ellie, you can't fill that whole thing in by yourself."

"Yes, I can." I had no idea if I really could. Ironically, I could have really used Jim's Bowflexed-honed biceps at a time like this. Without further ado, I dropped the box into the hole. It landed with a satisfying thud.

"Are you sure about this?" Grace's words were cautious, but she had a smile on her face. A smile that said she understood the symbolism perfectly.

"Remind me to thank Flossie in my prayers for the inspiration."

We both laughed, and I picked up my shovel and began to scoop dirt into the hole. The thick clods that fell on the box echoed like the ones I'd heard at funerals when the gravediggers started to cover the coffins.

By the time I had the hole half-filled, I was sweating and blisters had formed on both hands. By the time the hole was completely full, my hair was plastered to my head with sweat and I was starting to smell about as rank as the compost heap at the other end of the flower bed. Grace had left long before since she was hosting the Queens that night and needed to attend to her hostess duties. The only sounds in the backyard were my own labored breathing and the slice and whoosh of the shovel as it conveyed the dirt.

Finally, I threw down the shovel and sank into a heap on top of the mound of dirt, exhausted. My earlier elation had slipped away under the physical strain of filling the hole, and I just felt spent. But I had done it. I had taken my life with Jim and given it the funeral it deserved.

Now I just had to conquer the urge to pick up the shovel in my blistered and bloody hands and start digging it back up.

 **CHAPTER ELEVEN**

Vulnerable

If someone had told me a month ago that by the end of April I'd have launched my own business, taken a lover, joined the Red Hat Society, been named the chair of a nearly non-existent committee for the Cannon Ball *and* found a dead body in my backyard, I would have laughed.

I wasn't laughing now, though.

I dragged my aching body to Jane's house that night with little enthusiasm for red hats or bridge lessons or even for Linda's delectable lemon tarts. Per usual, though, the Queens of Woodlawn Avenue refused to let me wallow—or even take a breather for that matter.

Tonight, they intended to teach me how to keep score. I had watched the rest of them scribble down numbers in the "we" and "they" columns, above and below seemingly arbitrary lines, and it was all Greek to me. And I wouldn't have minded it staying that way.

The other Queens, though, were determined.

"To make game, you have to score a hundred points. The first team to win two games takes the rubber."

Okay, I could wrap my brain around that much, but things became much foggier when they started talking about bonus points, part-scores, and the difference between the numbers above and below the line.

"Let's say you make game," Linda said, writing down *100* below the line. "Then you're vulnerable."

"Vulnerable? What does that mean?"

"It means you're halfway there," Grace said. "But you're also in more danger."

"Why would it be more dangerous to be ahead?"

"Because the penalties for not making your contract are doubled."

"That hardly seems fair. If you're ahead, you shouldn't be penalized twice as much for getting set."

Jane laughed. "Whoever said bridge was fair? It's a lot like life. The bigger they are, the harder they fall."

"It's like raising the stakes in poker," Grace said. "The more you wager, the more you win."

"It still doesn't seem right." After all I'd been through in the last month, I was in a frame of mind to be rewarded for the risks I'd taken, not penalized.

"Look on the bright side." Linda smiled encouragingly. "If you're vulnerable and you win the next contract, then you win the rubber."

"Just remember not to overbid when you're vulnerable," Jane advised. "By the same token, you can be a little more aggressive when you're not."

It was the weirdest definition of vulnerable that I'd ever heard, but it also made a strange sort of sense. At least it did to me.

I'd thought I was ahead in my life until Jim had dropped the Tiffany bomb, and I'd suddenly discovered just how very vulnerable I was.

Keeping score, I learned that evening, wasn't any more straightforward in bridge than it was in real life.

Henri turned out to be as demanding a client as he was a lover, which was saying something on both counts. I spent the next week running back and forth between his office, his apartment, and my house. I was faxing him invoices at a furious pace as my billable hours piled up, but to my consternation, none of them seemed to be getting paid.

"Not to worry, *ma chère,*" Henri would purr. "The accounting department is a bunch of Italians who take a break every time the wind shifts directions."

Which was all fine and good except that my mortgage company did not operate on the same leisurely schedule.

"Could you light a fire under them?" I asked Henri one night as we turned out the lights and slid into bed. I was spending more nights at his apartment than at my house. He made a very naughty remark about where else he would like to light a fire, and I forgot all about the unpaid invoices.

Between assignments for Henri and my handful of other clients, I struggled to salvage the transportation for the Cannon Ball as the approaching deadline loomed.

"Vanderbilt Valets," the man at the parking service said when he answered the phone.

"Yes, my name is Ellie Hall, and I'm with the Cannon Ball. I understand you handled the parking for last year's event."

"Yes."

Okay, he wasn't very forthcoming, which I took for a bad sign.

"I'd like to book you for this year's event."

"I'm afraid that won't be possible."

"But you don't even know the dates."

"It wouldn't matter."

I tried to remember if I'd heard anything about last year's transportation for the ball—some fiasco or disaster—but nothing came to mind.

"Was there a problem?"

"Lady, we're still waiting on the last payment on your bill."

"Oh." Roz, of course, had failed to mention that little tidbit of information. "Are you sure you won't reconsider?"

"I've got plenty of paying clients, ma'am. I'll stick with those."

The next two services I called were already booked.

"Geez, for a big charity event like that, you've got to book six months in advance. A year even."

And that was the moment when I realized just how much trouble I was in as the chair and lone member of the transportation committee.

"What am I going to do?" I wailed to Linda. We met for lunch at The Picnic Café so I could drown my sorrows in iced tea and their fabulous chicken salad.

"I can't believe Roz did this," Linda commiserated. "What a rotten trick."

The Picnic Café was always packed with "ladies who lunch," and today was no exception. I scanned the close-set tables around us, their blue and white–checked tablecloths practically touching they were crammed in so tightly. A good portion of the tables featured clusters of my new red-hatted sisters. Just as newly pregnant women suddenly see other expectant mothers wherever they go, I had suddenly become aware of all the Red Hat women in the world. Overhead, the unforgiving fluorescent lights reminded patrons that they were, in fact, eating on one side of a drug store. Fortunately, the culinary delights of the café more than made up for the mostly sterile ambience.

"I won't let her win." I attacked my chicken salad with my fork. "There's got to be another way."

"You didn't have any luck with the shuttle buses either?" Jane sipped her ice tea.

"Nope. They're all reserved for some country music festival."

"So what are you going to do?"

I looked at her, stricken. "I was hoping you would have some ideas."

Linda used her fork to push her chicken salad around on her plate. "You know what this is like, don't you?"

"What do you mean?"

"It's just like when you're vulnerable in bridge. The way we showed you the other night."

"What do you mean?"

"Look, Ellie, all things considered, you're way ahead. You've accomplished so much in the last month. But that also means the stakes are higher, and your opponents won't be above doing some stinky bidding."

"Stinky bidding?"

"When your opponent is vulnerable, sometimes you bid high enough to get the contract even when you know you can't make it."

"That doesn't make sense."

"Think about it. Even if you go set, that's far better than allowing your opponent to make the second contract and win the rubber."

"Seems counterproductive to me."

"It keeps you in the game. That's what Roz is trying to do. Set herself just so you can't win."

"I guess that makes sense in a weird sort of way." I sipped my tea thoughtfully. "So, what do you do when your opponent engages in stinky bidding?"

"You have to decide if you're going to let them get away with it. And you have to remember that when you're vulnerable, it's very important not to overbid."

My head was starting to spin, and not from the caffeine and two packets of Splenda in my iced tea.

"So I should be aggressive but not too aggressive?"

"Exactly."

"But what does that mean in this situation?"

Linda sighed. "I have no idea."

And so I had yet another sin to chalk up against Roz, because after that bewildering conversation, I couldn't properly enjoy my chicken salad, and my loss of appetite had nothing to do with the lack of ambience.

Friday afternoon, I was in the process of covering up the evidence of the hole in the backyard with scores of impatiens (it was a rather shady part of the backyard, and Grace had informed me that impatiens adored shade), when Officer McFarland made a return appearance. I was glad Grace had only come by to inspect my handiwork and then returned to her own home, because she and Officer McFarland were clearly like oil and water. So I was alone in the backyard when he appeared from around the side of the house.

"Afternoon, Miz Hall." He looked even younger than he had last week.

"Hello, Officer." I set an impatien into its

hole, pressed the earth firmly around it, and used the watering can at my side to give it a nice long drink. Frankly, I could have used a nice long drink myself, but I knew from watching all those episodes of *Law and Order* not to offer an on-duty officer an alcoholic beverage. "What can I do for you?"

"I wanted to ask you a few more questions about the Etheringtons." He drew a small notebook and pen out of his shirt pocket.

"Has the case not been turned over to the homicide unit?"

"I just had a few more questions for my report." He smiled at me, and it was a long moment before I realized it was more than just a friendly expression. Perhaps what tipped me off was the way his eyes traveled up and down my body, lingering far too long for comfort between my waist and neck.

Okay, this man was young enough to be my son, and though I had enough vanity to feel flattered, I also found his attentions somewhat disturbing. I certainly hoped that Connor wasn't going around ogling middle-aged women in this fashion. The mere thought was enough to sour my stomach.

"What did you need to know?" I resisted

the urge to clutch the watering can to my chest. Better to play dumb and/or oblivious. That had always served me well at the country club when some other woman's drunken husband started to come on to me.

"Mrs. Davenport seemed to know an awful lot about the Etheringtons' marital difficulties."

"Mrs. Davenport?"

"Mrs. Grace Davenport."

"You don't think Grace had something to do with Marvin Etherington's death? That's ridiculous."

"She didn't seem upset when you dug up his remains."

"She's almost eighty. With all she's seen in her lifetime, I don't think much of anything upsets her."

"What I mean is, she didn't seem very surprised that you found Mr. Etherington in your flower bed. If he was a player, like Mrs. Davenport said, maybe she was one of his . . ."

"One of his what?" My disbelief gave way to anger. "You think Grace was involved with Marvin Etherington?"

"Anything's possible."

"Grace was happily married. Three times, I might add."

"Three times? That's a lot of divorces."

"She didn't divorce. She was widowed."

"All three times?" He raised an eyebrow.

Shoot. I was just digging a deeper hole, so to speak.

"I'm sure if you ask Grace, she'd be glad to give you details about their illnesses."

"I will. Thanks for the tip."

"Wait a minute! That wasn't a tip. You're taking this the wrong way."

"I appreciate you being so cooperative in the investigation, Miz Hall." He grinned again, only this time it definitely veered into leering territory. "I shouldn't have to bother you again." Although his tone made it clear he'd be more than happy to bother me.

What was happening? I hadn't meant to implicate Grace in any way—the thought had never crossed my mind—and I certainly didn't have any intention of seducing a police officer half my age.

I clutched the watering can across my chest. "I'm sure Grace had nothing to do with Marvin's death."

"Sure. Sure." He flipped his notebook closed and tucked it back in his pocket.

"But if you think of anything else, or if you need me for anything . . ." His voice trailed off suggestively. "A woman alone should be careful."

Evidently. And the thing she needed to be careful of was the Metro Police.

"I'm sure I'll be fine." I just wanted him to leave so I could make a beeline to Grace's house and let her know what was going on. It was ridiculous to think her calm response to the discovery of Marvin Etherington's remains meant that she had anything to do with his death. I told her as much a few minutes later when I found her in her own backyard, planting impatiens just as I'd been doing.

"Some people will tell you it's too early for annuals," she said after she'd stood to greet me. I'd wanted to spill the beans the moment I saw her, but the sight of her frail frame bent over her plants stopped me short. She looked incredibly vulnerable, although I knew she must be as tough as shoe leather to have survived the loss of three husbands. "But I don't believe in waiting until after Mother's Day." She flashed me a smile. "After all, I might not still be here then."

"Don't say that," I said, alarmed. Grace raised her eyebrows at my agitation.

"Ellie, dear, is something wrong?"

"Officer McFarland was just at my house." I looked down at the grass beneath my feet, unable to look her in the eye.

"Did they find out who killed Marvin?"

"No. But he does have at least one suspect." I forced myself to look up at her.

"Really?" Grace's eyes widened in surprise. "After all this time? Who is it?"

I swallowed. "It's you, Grace."

"Me?"

Around us, bees buzzed in the flowers.

"He thinks you had something to do with Marvin's death."

I was prepared for her to be shocked, horrified, scared. Instead, she burst into laughter.

"He thinks I killed Marvin Etherington?"

"Because you weren't surprised when I dug him up."

"Ellie, at my age, very little surprises me anymore."

"That's what I told him."

"But he didn't believe you?"

"He's so young—I don't think he gets it yet. Although . . ."

"Although what?"

"He kept staring at my chest."

Grace let out a whoop of laughter and wiped a hand across her damp forehead. "Well, you do have that glow about you."

"Glow? What glow?" I broke out in a sweat as profuse as Grace's.

"The one Henri has put in your cheeks."

I clapped my hands to my evidently glowing cheeks to hide them and blushed furiously. "Is it written all over my face?"

"Of course it is. As well it should be. Otherwise, what's the point?"

"So everyone in Nashville can tell I'm— you know—just by looking at me?"

"No. What I mean is that everyone can see that you're a woman in her prime who's enjoying her life."

Was I? Grace's statement made the ground beneath my feet seem to undulate. I mean, I'd certainly come a long, long way in the last five weeks. I was no longer sitting on my couch consuming vast quantities of snack cakes. But was I enjoying my life? Or was I simply filling it with activity to avoid the underlying problems?

"Wait a minute. Grace, we don't have time

to discuss my love life. We need to get you an attorney."

"Whatever for?"

"Because Officer MacFarland's going to come back. I'm sure of it. Maybe he thinks he can get some notice in the department by solving this old case." I wished we could sit on the lawn chairs a few feet away on the patio.

"Maybe so. But he can't arrest me for something I didn't do."

"Grace, people get arrested for things they didn't do all the time."

She waved a hand as if warding off my words. "You watch too much television."

"I still think you'd better get a lawyer."

"I don't need one. I'm innocent."

I could see it was going to be useless to argue with her. "Well, at least call me if he comes back. You have my cell phone number."

"Okay. Okay." She knelt back down by her flower bed. "Don't you have impatiens to plant?"

"Yes."

"Then go do it."

I knew from my experience with my own mother in the last years of her life that you couldn't help someone without their cooperation. Sometimes you just had to take a step back. So that's what I did with Grace.

"Okay, but if you need me, please call."

"I will, dearie." She flashed me a smile. "You're sweet to worry."

Only I didn't feel sweet. I felt guilty. Because the one thing I didn't have the courage to tell Grace was that I was the one who had put the idea that she'd killed Marvin Etherington into Officer McFarland's head.

 **CHAPTER TWELVE**

Doubling and Redoubling

That Saturday afternoon, as I baked Toll-house chocolate chip cookies for the Red Hat meeting that night, I spent as much time angsting over the state of my life as I did sifting flour and transferring baking sheets from the oven to the hot pads on the counter.

"I'm in way over my head," I murmured to no one in particular. Talking to myself was probably another bad sign, as was avoiding Henri's phone calls for the past twenty-four hours, but I was feeling increasingly uncomfortable about the non-response to the invoices I'd been sending to his office. Somewhere in the last few weeks, everything had become so jumbled. Business mixed with pleasure. Social mixed with more personal concerns. On top of it all, I had experienced my first hot flash at the Harris-Teeter the day before. Fortunately, the aroma of baking cookies soothed my soul somewhat.

At least, it did until the phone rang. I picked it up automatically, a reflex action, and regretted it immediately.

"Hello?"

"Ellie? It's Jim."

"I told you two weeks ago to quit calling me."

"I know. But—."

"No buts, Jim. We're done. Leave me alone."

I expected him to respond with some defensive, sarcastic remark. Instead, he whispered, "I'm sorry."

"What?" I could barely hear him as I opened the creaky oven door and pulled out another sheet of cookies. I had made enough to supply a good-sized Girl Scout troop—another sign of how unsettled I was feeling despite the gains I'd made in the last few weeks.

"I'm sorry for the last year. I never meant to hurt you like this."

"Ouch!" The cookie sheet scorched my hand around the edge of the hot pad. I dropped it with a clatter on top of the stove.

"Are you okay?" Jim actually sounded concerned.

"I'm fine." I flipped on the faucet and ran cold water over my hand. "Look, Jim, if you need to assuage your guilt, I'm sure you can get the name of a nice therapist."

"It's not that."

"Then what is it?"

He paused. Then, "Never mind."

"Gladly. Good-bye, Jim." And I slammed down the phone, harder than I'd intended, but it felt good. The last thing I needed right now was another complication, especially in the form of a remorseful ex-husband who I still hadn't exorcised from my heart.

I was still feeling guilty about implicating Grace to Officer McFarland when I arrived at her house that evening, tollhouse cookies in hand.

"There you are." Grace greeted me at the door with a warm smile, and I felt like an amoeba on a flea on a rat. At some point, I was going to have to confess that I'd spilled the beans about her three-time widowhood to the police.

"Sorry I'm late." At the last minute, I hadn't been able to find my hat. Grace would have let me borrow one, but I had begun to feel the need to wear a hat of my own rather than borrow one from the other women.

"The others are already here," Grace said, leading me to the dining room through the spade-shaped arch.

"Hello, ladies." I greeted Linda and Jane, who were already sitting at Grace's dining room table. "So, what am I learning tonight?" I had come to expect that each of our sessions would be the next in my series of bridge lessons, and I was right.

"Doubling and redoubling," Jane said with a smile. "For when things get really wicked."

Since things in my life in general already felt pretty wicked, the topic seemed apropos.

"So what's a double?" I asked as Linda began to deal the cards.

"Remember I told you the other day about stinky bidding?" Linda said.

"Yes," I said, recalling our conversation at the Picnic Café about bidding simply to thwart your opponents.

"Well, instead of stinky bidding to keep your opponents from taking a contract, you let them have it and double them instead."

"So it's a bid?"

"Right. It says, 'I don't think you can make your contract, and if you don't you get double the penalty.'"

"Then what's redouble?"

Jane, who had been sipping decaf from a mug with her real estate logo on it, set her coffee on the table. "If your opponent thinks she can make the contract, she redoubles. She gets even more bonus points if she does succeed."

Near as I could tell, bridge seemed to be more about constantly upping the ante than anything else. In a way, it was nothing but a more refined (and intricate) version of poker.

The other three ladies went on to demonstrate the different kinds of doubles (takeout and penalty), and I grasped the general concept pretty quickly. In a way, it reminded me of my phone call earlier in the day from

Jim. By refusing to let him hook me in to whatever drama he was currently involved in, I was doubling him. Of course, the fact that he kept calling meant he was redoubling. I took a bite of a cookie and savored the chocolate and butter on my tongue.

Clearly, Jim hadn't given up on the game, and I felt a pang at the thought. A pang that I shouldn't be feeling if I'd moved on with Henri.

Doubling and redoubling. Definitely something to think about.

Sunday afternoon, almost two weeks after Roz had announced the date change for the Cannon Ball, I was searching the Internet for other valet parking options when Linda appeared on my doorstep, every brunette hair immaculately in place per usual. I invited her into the living room, but she declined my offer to have a seat. Instead, she crossed her arms and struck a militant pose just inside the doorway.

"I just got a call from Roz."

Great. Hers was the last name I wanted to hear at the moment. I had progressed beyond Nashville to services from Columbia, Bowling Green, and Jackson, all to no avail.

"She wants to replace you as chair of the transportation committee."

Ouch. Now that would be the social equivalent of the coach benching the third-string quarterback and sending the water boy in to replace him.

"Can she do that now?"

"The chair of the ball giveth, and the chair of the ball taketh away."

"Great."

"She also added Jim and his hootchie mama to the guest list."

"She didn't." I sank to the sofa, needing to sit down even if Linda preferred not to.

"What's the deal with you two? Did you steal her high school sweetheart or something?"

I blushed, looked at the mantelpiece, the floor, the ceiling, anywhere but at Linda. Her eyes widened. "You didn't!"

I could only nod, mortified. I'd hoped to keep this particular piece of information from my new friends.

"Okay, maybe I will sit down. This I've got to hear."

And so I had to confess to Linda, over

coffee sipped on opposite ends of my sad sofa, that Roz Crowley (née Smith) did have some justification for the enmity she felt toward me.

"Jim?" Linda said, disbelievingly, distractedly stirring the cream into her coffee. "Jim and Roz were high school sweethearts?"

"I was on scholarship to Harpeth Hall." It still pained me to remember my high school days when I had definitely been a poor relation at the exclusive Nashville girls' school. But my mother wouldn't settle for anything less than the best for her daughter.

"Roz was president of everything and drove her mother's old Mercedes to school. I took the city bus and sat in the back row."

"And Jim? How did he figure in to things?"

"Jim was the star wide receiver at Montgomery Bell Academy." MBA was the boys' equivalent of Harpeth Hall. "He and Roz were an item from freshman year on."

"So what happened?" Linda leaned forward, ready as any woman worth her salt would be for some juicy gossip.

I sighed. "Roz went off to Auburn, and Jim stayed here to go to Vanderbilt. So did I."

"Then you started dating?"

I felt my cheeks heat up again. Although I generally thought of myself as a good person, I had a skeleton or two in my closet (or backyard) just like anyone else.

I sighed and set my half-empty cup on the coffee table. "I believe the old-fashioned expression is 'setting your cap.'"

"You went after him?"

"Like a bee after honey." They say confession is good for the soul, but I'd have preferred to keep my unflattering actions a secret.

"Just because he belonged to Roz?"

I winced. "At first it was because of her. I pledged a sorority, thanks to my mother pulling some strings with mothers of some of her patients, and Jim was in our brother fraternity. I got him to notice me, and then we started dating."

"And Roz found out?"

"Immediately."

"I hope you wallowed in your triumph appropriately."

"Actually, I did something far worse than that."

"What?"

"I fell for him."

"But that's good. Or it was good. You had

twenty-five years of marriage and two great kids."

I glanced at the portraits of Connor and Courtney on the mantelpiece. "And now I have no marriage and my kids have gone off to find lives of their own."

"Do you regret it, marrying Jim?"

The question pierced me to the core, and I answered it honestly. All the Henris in the world couldn't make up for the loss of what Jim and I had once had. "No. No, I never could."

"Because?"

The sadness that I'd been covering up with Henri and Your Better Half and bridge and pulling weeds in the backyard welled up inside of me. "Because I love him."

"Because you *loved* him, you mean," Linda said, emphasizing the past tense.

I shook my head, knowing that the truth wouldn't go away just because I refused to acknowledge it. "That's the hardest part. I do still love him." I grabbed one of the shabby throw pillows next to me and clutched it against my chest.

What could Linda say to that? We were silent for a long moment.

"Do you want him back?"

"No. Yes. I don't know." In the dark of the night, alone in my house and even more so in my bed, I still wanted Jim with an intensity that scared me. And even the thrill of Henri's attentions couldn't change the fact that without Jim, I felt like an emotional amputee.

"Wow," Linda said at last. "I had no idea."

"I'm not sure I did either." I'd worked so hard to convince myself that I was moving forward, when in reality I was simply killing time. Burying a memory box in the backyard wasn't the same thing as letting go.

"So what will you do now?"

I shrugged my shoulders. "I don't know. Roz doubled me with this transportation committee thing."

"So, will you redouble?"

I didn't want to. High stakes games had never been my thing. But somewhere in all of this, I had to find myself again. I had to come to terms with what had happened to my life and move forward. I had to get past Jim.

"Do I have a choice?"

Linda leaned over and patted my knee. "Good girl. I have faith in you. And we're all here to help."

"Thanks." But I would have felt more confident if I'd had a tad more faith in myself than in the surrogate powers of the Queens of Woodlawn Avenue.

I wasn't getting any farther with hiring security for the ball than I had with the valet parking. When I called the next place on my list, the man actually laughed when I told him what I wanted and when.

"For an event that size? With less than a month's notice?"

Well, at least I had given him his chuckle for the day.

The next place handled off-duty security for Metro police officers. Given the number of officers on the force, surely they could help me out.

"I'm afraid we don't have anyone available for that evening," the woman on the other end of the line said in a regretful tone. "Did you have another date in mind?"

Another date? How about the twelfth of never, I wanted to say, but I bit my tongue. It wasn't this woman's fault that my feud with Roz was going to destroy Nashville's most venerable charity benefit.

A third and final call left me scraping my hopes off the floor.

"No way, honey." I could practically hear this woman's gum popping over the phone. "You want a June date, you gotta plan like a bride—at least a year in advance."

I had enough sense to know when I was licked. And when to polish off the rest of the Tollhouse cookies left from Saturday night. I had just poured myself a big glass of milk to wash them down when the doorbell rang.

Great. I was so not in the mood for entertaining.

My ancient front door didn't sport anything as modern as a peephole, and if I tried to peer out the living room window, whoever was on the porch would spot me for sure and I'd be committed to answering the door anyway. So I took a deep breath, cast a last, longing glance at the plate of cookies on the coffee table, and opened the door.

"Afternoon, Miz Hall."

The ever-present Officer McFarland. Was it my imagination, or did he look younger every time I saw him? Although today no hint of a smile played around his lips.

"Hello, Officer."

"Would you mind if I came in?"

What was I going to say to that request? No? Besides, maybe he had come to tell me that he'd struck Grace's name off the list of suspects.

"Please, do." I opened the door wider so he could step inside. "I was just going to have a snack. Would you care for some milk and cookies?"

The mom role was certainly one I could handle. Heaven knew I'd fed similar snacks to Connor's friends enough times over the years to be quite adept at it.

"Milk and cookies?"

"Sometimes you have to go for the comfort food," I said with a forced smile. I could tell he was trying to decide if I was insulting him. "If you don't help me eat them, you'll be responsible for at least a five pound weight gain."

I didn't mean that remark to come out as flirtatious as it sounded, but unfortunately it did sound coquettish and that interested gleam in his eye reappeared.

Rats. All I did was offer the man some milk and cookies.

"I'll just get the milk. Please, have a seat."

I made my escape to the kitchen, took a deep breath before pouring the milk, and then mustered all my sophistication so I could return to the dining room calm and poised.

"Have you uncovered new evidence?" I asked as I set the milk down in front of him. I took a seat on the opposite side of the table, putting as much distance between us as possible. I had to lean over a bit to slide the plate of cookies toward him. "Here. Help yourself."

"Thanks." He scooped up two cookies and took a big bite from the first one. Then he chewed thoughtfully for a moment before nodding in approval. "Nice."

"Thanks." I sipped my milk and waited to see what he had to say. He wiped his mouth with a napkin he'd plucked from the holder on the table and then pulled out his pad and pen from his shirt pocket.

"The ADA has a court order to exhume Mrs. Davenport's late husbands."

"All three of them?" A huge weight crushed my chest. "Is that really necessary?"

"We won't know until we've had new autopsies performed."

My heart ached for Grace, and I wondered if she knew yet. She didn't deserve any of this, and I was the responsible party.

"That seems like a lot of trouble without any proof that Grace had a part in Marvin's death."

"We have some evidence that she and Mr. Etherington were romantically involved."

I choked on the bite of cookie I was swallowing and had to stop and cough before I could clear my throat and speak. "What kind of evidence?"

"I talked to some of his co-workers from that time. They all said he was carrying on with a married woman, a neighbor, and that his wife was livid about it."

I looked at the half-eaten cookie on the napkin in front of me and bile rose in my throat.

"But Grace and Flossie were best friends. She would never have slept with Marvin."

"People do strange things, Miz Hall. Act in ways you'd never suspect."

Well, I couldn't argue with him there, given my recent experience, not only with my husband's defection for a Hooters waitress but also my own relationship with Henri.

"What about other neighbors? There had to have been a number of married women on this street at that time."

"I'm checking into that."

He certainly was being thorough just for the sake of an incident report. "Couldn't you do that before you dig up Grace's husbands?"

He paused, a cookie halfway to his mouth. "Are you asking me for a favor?"

My pulse skyrocketed. What was he going to do—arrest me for attempted bribery by tollhouse cookie?

"No, not a favor."

He smiled, then, for the first time. "That's a shame. I wouldn't mind you owing me."

"Why?" I asked the question before I could stop myself.

"Miz Hall . . . Ellie . . ." And then he blushed. Actually blushed. "I know I'm not . . ." His voice trailed away. "That is, I was wondering . . ."

"Yes?" Did he want me to go undercover? Wear a wire and lure my friend into a confession?

"I was wondering if you would have dinner with me sometime."

"Oh." I jerked back, and my hand bumped the glass of milk on the table. It sloshed over the top. "I'm old enough to be your mother," I said, dabbing at the spilled milk with a napkin.

He blushed even more. "That's not a problem for me."

A light bulb went off in my head. I'd heard about young men with a penchant for older women. I'd even seen it on TV and read about it in books. But, honest truth, I never, ever thought I'd be on the receiving end of it.

"Um . . . well, I'm actually seeing some- one right now." Thank God for Henri, even if I hadn't actually seen him much in the last few days.

"Oh." He looked like a crestfallen adoles- cent who'd just had the girl of his dreams turn down an invitation to the prom. I felt sorry for him. I also felt a little grossed out, too, as Courtney would have said. And, se- cretly, a part of me was very flattered, even if his attraction to me was only slightly less creepy than a shoe fetish.

Only why did it have to be that a younger man liking older women was weird? I mean, look at Jim and Tiffany. A younger woman throwing herself at him probably earned him a lot of "atta boys" and pats on the back in the locker room at the country club.

Just then, Officer McFarland's eye landed on the pad of paper I'd been scribbling on while I searched for private security for the ball.

"What's this?" He frowned. "Is someone bothering you? You need protection?"

The way he bristled on my behalf was actually quite sweet, although the only person I needed protection from at the moment was quite possibly Officer McFarland himself.

"No, I'm trying to line up some security officers for a charity event, but I'm not having much luck."

"Why not?"

I wiped the table again, even though the spilled milk was long gone. "The date got moved forward six months. It's only a few weeks away, and everyone's booked."

"When is it?"

I told him.

"Maybe I could help you with that."

My pulse shot up again. Relief mixed with triumph mixed with wariness. "Really? How?"

"I know some guys who might be willing to pull an extra shift. How many officers would you need?"

I told him, and he nodded. "Tell you what,

you have dinner with me and I'll get you the security detail."

Okay, we were both on pretty shaky ethical ground here, and there was the possibility I might wind up in some stalking situation that would one day become a Lifetime movie, but what choice did I have?

"As long as you know it's only dinner. And only once," I said in my best scolding-mother tones.

He grinned. "Until I convince you to change your mind about that."

His smile wasn't wolfish or disturbing, just filled with the confidence of someone who hadn't fully been squashed by the realities of adulthood. Shoot, if a cute, younger man wanted to buy me dinner, and I got security officers for the Cannon Ball out of the deal, what could it hurt?

CHAPTER THIRTEEN

Kibitzers

That Saturday night at the regular Queens of Woodlawn Avenue meeting, we had a surprise guest. We met at Jane's house, and her sister was visiting from out of town. Which wouldn't have been a problem, except that her sister—when she wasn't one of the foursome—liked to sit beside me and give me helpful advice.

"No, that's not what you should say to your partner's short club." Elaine was as tiny as Jane, but her hair was jet black rather than blonde and she wore an excessive amount of red lipstick.

"Short club?"

"A 1♣ opening bid means that your partner has a really strong hand, but it's spread over several suits. She has a lot of strength, but no length."

"What am I supposed to do?" The more I learned about bridge, the less I felt like I knew. It was a pretty good metaphor for my life at that moment, actually.

By this point, Grace and Linda were frowning deeply, clearly disturbed to have the bidding process—which was supposed to be entirely neutral—laid out in such explicit terms now that I'd passed the rudimentary stage.

I heard Jane mumble something under her breath. Her sister's spine went ramrod straight. "Did you have something to say, Jane?"

Growing up as an only child, I'd often wished for a sister. But since the tension between these two sisters could be cut with a fairly dull butter knife, my lone child status didn't seem so bad at the moment.

Jane just glared at her. "I said that we don't need a kibitzer."

You'd have thought that Jane had called her a name not used in polite circles.

"Fine." Elaine leaped to her feet and stalked from the dining room through the diamond-shaped arch. A moment later, I heard a door in the back of the house slam.

"Thank heavens," Grace said. "I thought I was going to have to whack her on the head with something."

Jane and Linda laughed, and I pretended to. Because Officer McFarland and his suspicions about Grace were never far from my thoughts.

"So, really, what do I do about the short club?"

Jane arched an eyebrow. "Use it on my sister?"

I didn't have time to see Henri all weekend due to the demands of my other clients—the elderly matron and the professor—as well as citing my standing Saturday night Red Hat commitment. He hadn't taken it well, but then, he was French. He should be used to disappointment. Weren't they always losing every war they fought?

To tell the truth, I was still struggling with

the remnants of my feelings for Jim. And I didn't want to go any further with Henri until I resolved them. So I hadn't made the extra effort to see him that I might have even a week earlier.

By Monday night, though, I couldn't avoid Henri any longer. I was preparing dinner for him and a client at his apartment, and he had asked me to stay and play hostess. I'd have been more enthusiastic about the additional billable hours if even one of the invoices I'd sent to The Triumph Group so far had been paid. Maybe that was another reason I'd been avoiding him. I was going to have to confront Henri about the unpaid bills after dinner, and I was looking forward to that experience even less than to telling him I wasn't spending the night. Jane had advised me to address it directly, without emotion, but then Jane didn't know how many nights I'd been spending in Henri's bed.

Dinner was simmering on the stove when Henri arrived, half an hour earlier than I'd expected. He rarely made it home before six o'clock, and it was barely half past five.

"Henri? Is that you?"

"Yes, Ellie. It's me." He sounded tired.

Since the last time we'd made love, he was using fewer and fewer of the French endearments that had so captivated me when I'd first met him.

"What time is your client coming?"

He frowned. "Actually, there is no client."

My stomach sank to the cold Mexican tile beneath my feet. "No client?"

"I wanted to see you, and since you've been avoiding me . . ."

He'd lied to manipulate me. Of course, my passive-aggressive approach of telling him I was too busy to go out to dinner or a movie over the weekend wasn't much of an improvement on his plain, old-fashioned untruth.

"Well, then, we can have a lovely, quiet dinner," I said with an enthusiasm I was far from feeling.

"I'd like that." He looked so vulnerable at that moment that guilt yanked my stomach back up to its normal resting place and squeezed it tight.

"Can I get you a glass of wine?"

"Yes, please."

The habit of fussing over an exhausted man who had just come from the office was as inbred in me as not wearing white shoes after Labor Day or throwing my arm across the chest of the child in the passenger seat of my car when I had to slam on the brakes. I poured Henri a glass of an impeccable chardonnay, and then I poured an even bigger one for myself. Because although he might be exhausted, I still had to ask him when my invoices were going to get paid. I'd been living on credit in anticipation of that income, and the limit on my Visa was fast approaching. I hadn't even bought a dress for the Cannon Ball. I hadn't really allowed myself to think about how I was going to swing that.

Henri sank onto the leather sofa and I followed him, but I left a cushion between us whereas before I would have cuddled up right beside him. The way his eyes narrowed told me he noticed the difference. Funny, that had happened with me and Jim, too, although over a longer period of time and in that instance, I'm not sure either of us noticed when it started to happen.

"I want you to tell me the truth," Henri said, twisting the wineglass stem between his fingers. "What's his name?"

"Whose name?" I decided to take the coy

approach. Answer a question with a question.

"The other man. There must be someone, because suddenly I am like . . . ," he paused, ". . . a burden to you."

He sounded like a hurt little boy. His pride was obviously wounded. I wondered if it made me a bad person if his jealousy secretly thrilled me, even if I wasn't sure I wanted to be involved with him any longer.

"There's no other man."

"No? Impossible. There must be someone."

"There's no one." The lie fell so easily from my lips.

"Then what has happened?"

What had happened? I still thought he was incredibly sexy and charming, when he wanted to be. And then it hit me. My feelings for Henri had started to change the moment I'd started to feel like his wife instead of his lover. And the fact that he hadn't paid me for my work had only contributed to my sense of being taken for granted. I felt like I was still married to Jim, only with a French accent and without the foundation of a shared history.

I gulped my wine in three substantial

swallows, and then coughed when everything from my eyes to my throat burned like
fire.

"It's . . . well, it's . . . complicated." I man-
gled the words, but the sentiment was clear.
Henri's eyes widened.

"There is someone else."

"No, there's not. There used to be someone else—"

"Used to be?"

"My husband. I mean, my ex-husband."

"He wants you back?"

"No. Maybe. I'm not sure. He keeps calling."

"And you would go crawling back to him
like a dog?" He sniffed with Gallic disdain.

"No!" I snapped. "I'm not crawling back to
anyone. But maybe I'm not ready yet for
this." I waved my hand back and forth between us. "Maybe it's too soon." Although
even as I said the words, I was pretty sure
that wasn't the real reason at all.

"Then you will not need me to escort you
to your party at the end of the month?" In a
moment of post-coital bliss, I had asked
Henri to be my date for the Cannon Ball.

"No, I'd still like you to go with me."

He set his wineglass down on the coffee

table with a snap. "I am not here for your convenience."

Now that made me angry, because if anything, I had been the one to be there for his convenience over the last month. "I never said you were." I was going to have to placate him, because, frankly, the prospect of trying to find another date for the Cannon Ball was far more wearying than humoring Henri. "Please don't be angry."

And now I couldn't even ask him about the unpaid invoices, at least not right then. I'd thought the divorce had complicated my life, but that was nothing compared to what I'd done to it myself in the last six weeks.

"You can make it up to me," he said, and now he was smiling his charming smile once again.

"Oh?" If he tried to lead me toward the bedroom, I was going to develop a splitting headache.

"You can feed me some of that delicious dinner I smell."

Whew. I felt like I'd dodged a bullet. "Sure. Just give me a minute to finish it up."

I unfolded myself from the couch and escaped to the kitchen, feeling like I had perhaps won the battle, but the outcome of the war was definitely in doubt.

Henri's cell phone rang in the middle of dinner, and for once I didn't resent the interruption. In fact, the phone call gave me the excuse to clean up the kitchen, kiss his cheek good-bye since he was still talking on the phone, and escape to my house for the remainder of the evening.

Once I arrived home, though, I received a phone call of my own. I had just slid my nightgown over my head when the phone rang. Hoping it wasn't Henri, I sat down on the bed and gingerly picked up the receiver.

"Hello?"

"It's me." Well, of course it was. With a frustrated "omph," I punched the pillow next to me and plopped it against the headboard. Might as well get comfortable for the duration.

"Yes, I remember your voice." Mine dripped with sarcasm.

"I know, I know. But this is a real thing."

As opposed to all the unreal—or surreal— things Jim had been calling me about since

I'd moved into the house on Woodlawn Avenue?

"What do you need?" I swung my legs onto the bed and leaned back, exhausted.

"It's about Courtney's horse."

When she was six years old, my daughter had developed an undying love for anything with hooves, a mane, and a tail. Jim had indulged her by buying her a pony which we had paid a fortune to board at a local riding school. The pony had been followed by a succession of horses, each more expensive than the last. What we spent on feed could have been used to pay my utilities, phone, and Internet in one fell swoop. Now that Courtney had gone off to college, we'd dithered about what to do with Cupcake, the aging bay that apparently ate his weight in oats on a weekly basis.

"I can't keep paying for the horse, Ellie." This time Jim didn't sound angry or defiant. Instead, his voice held a note of despair I hadn't heard since those exhausting twenty-hour days of his residency.

"I know it's expensive, but it means a lot to Courtney." I studied my bare bedroom walls, wondering when I'd ever get around to hanging pictures.

"Let's face it, Ellie. Courtney will probably never come back to Nashville to live. We need to sell him. He'd make a good horse for a little girl just learning to ride."

"Have you asked Courtney about this?"

He was quiet for a moment.

I sighed. "I can't do that for you, Jim. If you want to sell the horse, then you need to talk to her about it."

"Well, there's one alternative."

"What's that?"

"I was telling Greta about your new company." Greta Price owned and operated Cumberland Farms & Stables, Cupcake's official residence.

The hairs on the back of my neck stood up against the pillow. "And?"

"She thought we could work out some sort of barter system."

"We? Would that be the royal 'we', Jim? Or do you mean that *I* could work out a trade with her?"

"Well, she's not currently in need of any thoracic surgery."

Okay, I did smile at his joke, but I was still peeved.

"If you want me to take on that responsibility, then just ask me to do it. Don't try to sneak it by me like I'm too stupid to notice what you're doing." I might be tired, but I wasn't that tired.

"I'm sorry, Ellie. I know you're not stupid. I guess I just feel guilty about the whole thing."

I wanted to tell him that he darn well should feel guilty, but what would that help? I knew that Jim loved Connor and Courtney and had always worked hard to give them the best of everything. I couldn't fault him on that score.

I heard a tinkling sound over the phone line, like ice cubes clinking in a glass. Drinking and dialing yet again. That wasn't something he'd ever done when we were married.

His voice softened. "Remember when we gave her that first pony?"

"We? That was all your doing." But I smiled in spite of myself as the image of a tiny Courtney sitting tall in the saddle sprang into my mind. It had been one of those few moments in life when I was privileged to see sheer, unadulterated joy on my child's face. That joy, and not her begging and pleading, were what had compelled us to continue to underwrite her equine addiction.

"We were toast from that moment on," I said, relaxing into the memory.

He laughed. "Yeah. Once your child's discovered her drug of choice, you're compelled to keep supplying her with her fix."

Jim and I had spent a lot of time sitting together in the bleachers at horse shows all over the Southeast, proud and anxious and hopeful and fearful just like all the other parents who watched their children compete in any sport.

"Remember when she fell?" My fingers tightened around the phone cord. That had been one of the most harrowing moments of my life. At eleven, she'd broken her collarbone when she'd been thrown by her horse when it balked at a water jump. Jim might be the physician in the family, but he'd turned a ripe shade of green when we saw the paramedics load her onto that stretcher.

"I wanted to shoot that horse," he said.

"She wouldn't let you."

He chuckled. "Always was a tough kid."

I sighed. "Jim, I'll work something out with Greta. Courtney's lost enough this year, with

the divorce and everything. I'm sure we can figure something out."

"No, Ellie. I won't let you do it. I was wrong to even call and ask. It's just that . . ."

"That what?" My knuckles had gone white. Slowly, I unwrapped the phone cord that bound them.

"I didn't think it would be like this."

"What wouldn't be like this?" But I knew what he meant, even if he couldn't quite articulate it.

"A new start. Tiffany."

I winced when he said her name.

"I thought I'd found the way to get out from under all the pressure," he said, "but instead it's twice as strong."

It was a rare but important moment of insight for a man who preferred action to reflection, so I kept my mouth shut, merely murmuring in agreement. I'd learned a little something about unwanted advice from Jane's kibitzing sister last Saturday night.

"I'll talk to Greta," I said, getting up from the bed to pull back the covers, "and see how much of the slack I can pick up. Maybe between the two of us we can manage." For the first time since the divorce, Jim and I

were cooperating and it felt much better than all those months of acrimony.

"That would be great."

"Okay. I'll let you know what she says." I got back in the bed, still tired but somehow less exhausted.

"Ellie?"

"Yeah?"

"Thanks. I appreciate it."

"You're welcome, Jim. Good night."

"Good night."

This time I didn't need to slam down the receiver. I slipped it gently into its cradle and slid down in the bed, pulling the covers up to my chin.

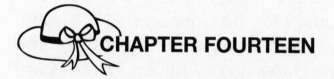

CHAPTER FOURTEEN

A Novice Opponent

Henri was out of town the rest of the week, traveling on business, and I could go about my routine of doing small jobs for my other clients and working on the flower beds in my backyard. I tried to avoid the section along the back fence where Marvin Etherington had been found, but some weeds had sprung up among the impatiens and I was forced to deal with them. By now, I knew the difference between a lot of things—not just plants and weeds. But other things still had me confused. Like Officer McFarland's continued pursuit of me. Frankly, I suspected that he wasn't even assigned to the Etherington case; he was simply using it as a pretense to keep in touch.

Sure enough, he called and asked me to have dinner on Friday night, and in the interest of security for the Cannon Ball, I agreed. I was ready to suggest a restaurant in some suburb like Bellevue or Antioch, somewhere I wasn't likely to see anyone I knew. But Officer McFarland was one step ahead of me.

"I thought we'd eat at Green Hills Grille."

Great. We were sure to run into at least a dozen people I knew, and most of them would be dialing Jim's number on their cell phones the moment they left the restaurant.

"Okay. I'll meet you there. What time?" At least I'd have my own car and could make a quick escape if necessary.

"Is seven okay?"

"That's great."

Security officers . . . security officers . . . security officers, I kept forcing myself to repeat in my head.

"I'll see you then, Miz Hall."

"You know, if we're having dinner, you might as well call me Ellie."

"And you can call me Will."

"Okay, Will. See you then."

Back in college, I'd perfected the fine art of dressing for a date with a boy you never wanted to go out with again. In those days, I'd favored high-collared blouses and baggy sweaters and they'd done the trick. But at fifty, a blouse like that was bound to make me look like Granny on the Sylvester and Tweety cartoons, and a baggy sweater only emphasized the matching set of luggage under my eyes.

So I settled for nice slacks and a sweater set with pearls. If Will McFarland had a thing for mothers, then a mother was what he was going to get.

I purposely arrived at Green Hills Grille just late enough so I knew he'd be there first but not late enough to be obnoxious. Will was waiting for me in a booth prominently positioned on a raised dais in the middle of the restaurant. No skulking in corners for Officer McFarland, and no way were we not going to be noticed. He had laid a long-stemmed red rose at my place.

"Hi." He stood up as I approached the booth.

"Hi." Okay, he really was very sweet. Once I sat down, he took his seat. Again, I was reminded of one of the little courtesies that had evaporated over the course of my marriage.

"Thanks for coming."

"You're welcome."

If our conversation was going to be this stilted throughout the whole meal, we were in big trouble. I unrolled my silverware from the cloth napkin and placed the square of fabric in my lap. It gave me something to do besides look at Will.

"How was your day?" His cheeks had a slight pink tinge, and he was trying so hard. But I felt like Florence Henderson out on a date with the kid who had played Greg Brady.

"Good. It was good." A neutral comment that didn't invite him any farther into my life than he already was.

"I talked with some of the guys, and you're all set for security."

I smiled, and it was genuine. "Thank you. I really, really appreciate it."

His hand reached across the table, and his fingers covered mine. "No problem. I was glad to help."

Thankfully, at that moment our waiter arrived with the menus. I retrieved my fingers from Will's and busied myself with looking over the specials.

"Order the lobster if you want," Will said. He was trying very hard to be mature and suave. It was quite sweet.

"Actually, I'm not that big on lobster. I think I'll have the tilapia." I chose an entrée on the modest end of the restaurant's price range, since I was going to feel guilty enough about letting him pay for dinner. I would try to pay for my share, of course, but a woman could always tell when a man was bent on picking up the tab.

The waiter took our orders, and we were left alone once more. Rats.

"So," I said, desperate for a topic of conversation, "how's the investigation going?"

"I can't really comment on that," Will replied. My face must have fallen, because he added, "I haven't found anyone else yet besides Mrs. Davenport who could have been Marvin's mystery woman."

"What about the preliminary autopsy? Any indication of what exactly killed him?"

"The M.E. thinks it was a gardening spade."

I practically choked on the water I was sipping.

"Is he sure?"

"Pretty sure. Said the shape of the weapon was consistent with your average gardening spade."

I thought of Grace appearing on my doorstep to teach me to garden and placing a spade in my hand. If anyone knew how to use one of those things, it was her. I fought the urge to gulp down my water. A moment later, the waiter appeared with the glass of chardonnay I'd ordered, and I fought the urge to gulp it down as well.

"I wouldn't think you could kill someone with one of those things."

Will nodded and looked very wise for someone half my age. "If you want to, you can turn anything into a murder weapon."

"So, what will you do next?"

"We can try to find the weapon, but after all this time, that's a long shot." He stopped and looked at me for a moment. "Didn't you say Mrs. Davenport was teaching you how to garden?"

"What? Oh, a little, I guess. Just how to pull weeds and things."

"Is she a big gardener, Mrs. Davenport?"

I couldn't lie to a policeman, even if I wanted to and even if I was out on a totally inappropriate date with him. "I guess you could say that." He'd probably arrest her if he knew the bridge club referred to her as the Queen of Spades.

The waiter arrived once more in the nick of time, this time bearing our dinner salads. "So," I said brightly, picking up my fork, "when did you graduate the police academy?"

If there was one thing I had learned in over two decades of marriage, it was the value of changing the subject when a man was on track to discovering something you didn't want him to know.

An hour later I was in the home stretch, finishing my coffee and crème brulée and thinking I was going to escape from dinner at Green Hills Grille with a man half my age without being noticed. Since Will, like any good police officer, had taken the seat that faced the door, my back had been to the entrance all evening. Perhaps that had contributed to the lack of recognition. The waiter slid the leather portfolio containing the bill onto the table, and Will and I reached for it at the same time.

"No way," he said, pulling it smoothly out from under my grasp and to his side of the table. "I asked you out for dinner. I'm paying."

I decided discretion was the better part of valor in this instance. "Okay, but I want my objection duly noted."

He blanched when he opened the portfolio and saw the total at the bottom of the bill. I bit my lip to hide my smile and turned my head to the side, just in time to see a couple walking right in front of my face as they passed the dais on their way to another part of the restaurant.

We were too close. There was no way he wasn't going to see me.

"Ellie!"

"Jim." I pasted a smile on my face and clutched the napkin in my lap for dear life. "Nice to see you." Although it wasn't very nice to see the woman who was with him. Heavily streaked blonde hair, too much eyeliner, and a pair of low-rise jeans that had apparently been spray-painted on. I'd never met her, of course, only conjured up her image in my mind based on descriptions I'd been given by Connor and Courtney. Those double-D cups, though, were a dead giveaway.

Why, why, why had I agreed to this dinner? And why hadn't I realized that if I went to one of Jim's favorite restaurants, I was very likely to run into him?

Jim stared at Will, and then he looked back at me, clearly puzzled.

"Jim, this is Will McFarland." I was going to act like a poised, confident adult if it killed me. "Will, this is my ex-husband, Jim Johnston."

"Pleased to meet you, sir." Will shook Jim's proffered hand over the little wall that separated our booth from the walkway through the restaurant. I tried very hard not to look at Tiffany, but I couldn't stop myself. She was like a cartoon character come to life, every curve and color exaggerated beyond life-sized proportions.

"Are you a friend of Connor's?" Jim asked

Will, looking as if he was trying to place Will's face among the slew of hairy-legged adolescent boys who had draped themselves across our furniture over the last few years. If only I could intervene before Will said—

"No, sir. I'm Ellie's date."

The look of astonishment on Jim's face was priceless. It made a warm glow not associated with the chardonnay I'd been drinking spread through my midsection. I would have given anything to have a camera. His head whipped back to look at me. "I thought you were dating some Frenchman?"

"I am." I looked him straight in the eye and kept my head up. "Will and I are just friends." Of course, that remark didn't sit too well with Will. He frowned.

Jim shook his head, skeptical at my description of my relationship with Will. But this time when he looked at me, there was a glint of respect in his eye that I hadn't seen in a very long time. Which only added to the heat rising up through me.

I stuck my hand over the booth toward my nemesis. "You must be Tiffany."

She looked at my hand like it was covered with rotting flesh. "Yeah, that's right."

"I'm Ellie." I'd envisioned this moment a million times, both the good and the bad versions. Well, she might not be willing to shake my hand, but that was because she knew I had the upper one. Ha!

"I know who you are." If looks could kill, I would be staked to an anthill, slathered with honey, and about to meet a very painful demise.

"Congratulations on your upcoming wedding." The words slipped out of my mouth before I could restrain them, but I was pretty sure that Tiffany wouldn't pick up on the insult. A cultured person never congratulated the bride; you always said "best wishes" to the woman and "congratulations" to the man for finding such a great girl who would agree to marry him. But congratulations were entirely in order for Tiffany, the husband-stealing tramp.

Not that I was still in any way bitter or jealous.

"Well, enjoy your meal," I said, hoping to get them moving along and away from Will and me.

"Huh?" Jim had clearly been lost in thought.

"It was nice to see you."

"Um, yeah. Nice to see you, too. Nice to meet you, Wayne."

My would-be-date bristled, and I hid my smile by dabbing at my lips with my napkin. "The name is Will," he said.

"Oh, of course."

"Come on, Jim, I'm hungry," Tiffany whined while she tugged at his shirt sleeve.

He looked at me for a long moment and then turned, reluctantly, and followed her across the restaurant. I had the satisfaction of watching her throw a little hissy fit in his ear as they wound their way through the other tables.

"That was weird," Will said. "What are the odds of running into him here?"

I sighed. "Never forget," I advised Will, "that Nashville isn't a big city. It's just a small town with suburbs."

As it turned out, though, I couldn't escape my encounter with Jim and Tiffany entirely unscathed. While Will waited, I slipped to the women's restroom. Over the last few years, my bladder had decided to shrink by a third of its capacity.

I opened the door and walked into the restroom, innocent as a lamb, and made use of the facilities. It wasn't until I was exiting the stall that disaster struck.

The door opened, and in walked Tiffany.

I smiled, nodded, and turned toward the sink to wash my hands. Even though I would have given a year of Jim's alimony checks to be magically transported out of that restroom, I could never walk out without having washed my hands. I wasn't a nurse, and the daughter of a nurse, for nothing.

"I want to talk to you," Tiffany announced. Her words stopped me in my tracks.

"I really don't think we have anything to talk about." I figured she wanted to berate me for not letting her wear my mother's wedding dress or some other piece of nonsense. She was younger than Will, although she had more of that beaten-down-by-life look around the eyes. Were those the beginnings of crow's feet that I saw? She also reeked of cigarette smoke, a fact which surprised me given that Jim was such a health nut and a thoracic surgeon to boot. He'd removed his fair share of cancerous tumors from people's lungs.

"Leave Jim alone," Tiffany snapped. She was clutching the shoulder strap of her sequined purse with a death grip. "I'm warning you."

My eyes must have bugged out of my head. "You're what?" When I was in junior high, all of the catfights and fistfights between girls had occurred in the restroom, away from the prying eyes of the teachers and administration. Tiffany had clearly cornered me here to have it out where Jim couldn't see.

"Stay away from Jim."

"That shouldn't be a problem, since I'm not married to him anymore."

"And quit calling him."

"I haven't been calling him."

That one threw her for a moment. She pursed her lips, and I could practically hear the wheels turning in her head as she tried to process that information. I felt a sharp little pain in the vicinity of my heart, and I was surprised to realize what it was. Pity. Pure, unadulterated pity.

"He keeps telling me stuff you've said."

"If you don't want him talking to me, then

tell him to quit calling. Heavens knows I've tried."

Her over-plucked eyebrows, or what was left of them, arched in surprise. And then I saw tears start to well up in her eyes. Again, I felt that sharp little pang. I didn't want to feel it, but I did.

"I'm not trying to come between you and Jim," I assured her, although even as I said the words, I wondered why on earth I was being nice to this woman. She had known Jim was married the first time she brought him a plate of buffalo wings. He hadn't even been smart enough to take off his wedding ring.

"Then why does he want to postpone the wedding?"

"What?"

"You heard me." She wiped away a tear that slid down her layers of mascara and onto her cheek in a dark blob. "He says we ought to push back the wedding."

"I didn't have anything to do with that."

"Then why doesn't he want to get married?" she wailed.

I looked at her then, really looked at her, and what I saw beneath the layers of makeup and behind the surgically enhanced anatomy was a confused, scared young woman. How sad, at not even twenty-five, to think you needed silicone, collagen, and bleached blond hair to attract a decent guy. Although, come to think of it, those three things seemed more likely to draw the attention of the exact opposite of a good man.

"I have no idea why he's gotten cold feet. Why don't you ask him?"

"He won't talk to me." She started to blubber, and I reached over to give the paper towel machine a few cranks. I yanked off a hunk of brown paper and handed it to her.

"Here."

She blew her nose into it with a less than ladylike honk. "Thanks."

I was silent, then, while she finished with her nose and wiped the tears from her eyes. Finally, she threw the wadded paper towel in the trash and looked at me again.

"Why are you being so nice to me? I'm being a bitch to you."

I wasn't sure I could explain it myself. For all those months, I'd built her up in my mind as this kind of überwoman, a sexual goddess with whom my aging face and body could never compete. But the truth, I real-

ized, standing in the middle of the ladies'
restroom at Green Hills Grille, was that
Tiffany was just a young, uneducated girl
with bad taste in makeup and plastic sur-
geons.

I couldn't believe it, but I actually felt sorry
for her.

"It takes two to tango," I said, surprising
myself. "Jim ruined our marriage, not you."
Only even as I said that, I was forced to admit to myself that while Jim's defection to
Tiffany had been the death blow, our marriage had been in decline for some time.

"I came in here to fight," she said.

"I know."

She looked as sad as I felt. "Any advice
on how to handle him?"

I guess she was young enough—and
naïve enough—to think that I might actually
answer that question. But I wasn't so mature as to take the high road and hand her
all the secret stuff I knew about Jim on a silver platter.

"Feed him lots of garlic," I said. "He really
likes it."

Her forehead wrinkled. "Really?"

"Absolutely. Key to his heart."

Well, not really. Actually, garlic gave him tremendous gas.

"I'd better go." I grabbed my purse from the bathroom counter where I'd left it when I washed my hands. "Good night." And I fled the bathroom feeling, for good and for ill, every one of my fifty years.

 **CHAPTER FIFTEEN**

Finessing a Queen

Thankfully, the next night was Saturday and the weekly bridge game. We were meeting at my house, and I spent the day cleaning and baking, in hopes that such mundane activities would take my mind off the disturbing events of the previous evening.

"Tonight," Linda said after we'd filled our plates and sat down at my dining room table, "we're going to focus on how to finesse." Linda sat across from me, Grace on my left and Jane on my right.

I knew what the word meant, but I wasn't sure what it had to do with bridge. "What's a *finesse*?"

"It's a way of slipping a lower honor card past a higher one to take the trick." Linda laid some cards out on the scarred surface of the table. "For example, let's say that you have the ace and three of clubs in your hand, and the dummy—me—has the queen and several low clubs in hers."

"Okay." I didn't see where this was going. Jane watched Linda's lesson with interest, but Grace seemed distracted and unusually quiet. Before I could ask her if anything was wrong, though, Linda plowed ahead with my lesson.

"You want to try and take a trick with the queen from the dummy for an extra winner, but you don't know which of your opponents has the king, right?"

"Uh huh."

"If Grace, the person to your left, has the king, then you can make the queen a winner by finessing."

"What if Jane has the king?" I said, nodding to her on my right.

"If the last person to play has the king, then your finesse won't work. But you have a fifty-fifty chance of taking the trick, and sometimes in bridge those are pretty good odds."

I looked at the cards in front of me. "So, how do I play it? Do I just go ahead and lead my ace?"

"No. You lead weakness to strength."

"What do you mean?"

Jane plucked a three of clubs and laid it in the middle of the table. "Lead with your low club. If Grace has the king and plays it, you play a low card and then your queen can take the trick the next time clubs are played."

"And if Grace doesn't play the king?"

"Then you play the queen from the dummy. If Grace was holding it back, you take the trick. If Jane, on your right, has the king, then you lose."

"Shouldn't you try for something that you know is going to work?"

"Finessing is about taking extra winners, not for tricks you need to make your contract."

"Just remember, lead from weakness to strength," Linda reminded me as she began to deal the cards for real. "And remember, too, that it's okay to take risks. Sometimes they pay off. You just have to know when they're worth it."

"How do you know that?" I'd never been very good at trying to slip something past anyone, queen or otherwise. And I rarely ever anticipated someone making an effort to slip something past me, although I had caught Connor red-handed that time he'd tried to sneak a sixpack of beer out of the refrigerator.

Jane nodded her agreement. "Calculated risks can pay off. You just have to know the odds and plan accordingly."

"Like with you and Roz," Linda said.

At the mention of that name, I started to feel queasy. I'd spent even more time in the past week in my futile effort to find shuttle buses and valet parking for the ball. Roz had taken to leaving daily messages on my answering machine and blitzing me with e-mails. I'd just been screening her calls and ignoring the e-mails, but I expected her to show up on my doorstep in the near future.

"Why do I need to finesse Roz?" I had enough drama in my life. The last thing I needed was to add to it.

Linda gave me a piercing look. "Ellie, you know she set you up for a fall. And you know she's going to keep doing it as long as you move in the same social circles."

"Well, after next week, the only social circle I'll be moving in is when I join the mall walkers at Green Hills." I couldn't seem to make myself admit my failure to Roz. I was like a person tramping down the railroad tracks, knowing a train was barreling toward me but somehow determined not to be the first to flinch.

"It would be better to confront her sooner than later," Jane advised.

Grace had been uncharacteristically silent all evening. I looked over at her. "What do you think, Grace? Should I have it out with Roz?"

I hadn't expected the solemn, almost grieving expression that covered her face. "Sometimes the truth has to come out," she said, her shoulders rounded as if she bore a great burden. Since her usual posture was bolt upright, I knew something was wrong.

"Grace? Are you feeling okay?"

"I'm fine, Ellie. Just feeling my age tonight." Her thin smile didn't reassure me any more than her feeble answer did. "I'm sure you should do as Linda says."

"I'd rather not confront Roz." Despite their

well-meant advice, these women had no idea of the history between Roz and me. Years of enmity, and my theft of Jim's affections, couldn't be solved so easily.

"We're not saying confront her, Ellie." Linda waved a hand at the cards on the table. "We're saying finesse her. Slip one past her. So that the next time she tries to set you up, she'll think twice."

"It sounds pretty complicated."

"It's time for a power play." Linda leaned forward. "I've been in Nashville society for a long time, and one thing I know is that women like Roz will always be a part of the equation. But, if you can learn to manage them, your life suddenly gets a whole lot easier."

The mere idea that I could ever "manage" Roz Crowley was ludicrous. No one in her life had ever been able to put a leash on her.

"I'm not the woman for that job," I protested.

"On the contrary, you're exactly the woman for the job," Linda said.

Because of Linda pushing so hard for me to finesse Roz, I was grumpy the rest of the evening and couldn't even enjoy it when I pulled off several successful finesses of the bridge variety. Didn't the other three understand that I was no match for my oldest enemy? Sure I'd won the battle over Jim, but she would fight to her last breath before she let me win the battle for the upper hand in Nashville society.

I found it both a little scary and a little Zen how many principles of bridge were turning out to be quite handy in my everyday life. Or at least in this strange new post-divorce existence. That lesson on finessing a queen, for example, proved quite helpful not forty-eight hours later when I was pushing a grocery cart down the aisle at Harris-Teeter.

Most important moments in life catch us unaware, just as this one did me. I had been stewing over the whole "finessing a queen" thing since Saturday. But today was Monday, the start of a new week, and I needed to forget about Roz and focus on how in the world to find shuttle buses for the ball. Not to mention figuring out what I was going to do about Henri and Will. And the myriad of other difficulties that seemed to swamp me every time I thought about them.

So there I was, pulling a stack of ninety-nine cent frozen pizzas out of the freezer case when I saw her out of the corner of my eye.

Roz Crowley.

She, of course, was not wearing faded jeans and a Target T-shirt like I was. No, she looked like a million dollars in her chic little separates from Sigfrid Olsen.

For a moment, I debated the pros and cons of climbing into the freezer case and trying to hide out behind the wall of frozen pizzas. I didn't have the chance to give it a try, though.

"Ellie!" She spit out my name somewhere between a bark and a screech.

I turned, slowly, careful to look surprised to see her. My eyebrows were arched so high that they hurt.

"Oh. Hello, Roz." I don't know if I could have sounded so cool if I weren't standing with the door to the freezer case open. "Nice to see you."

Her eyes narrowed above the forced smile she'd plastered on her face. "I've left you several messages but you haven't called me back."

"Sorry." I pitched the pizzas into the basket of my cart and prayed she wouldn't check out the other contents too closely. Everything in there had a generic or a store brand label. "My new business has really taken off and I've been swamped." I resisted the urge to cross my fingers behind my back.

"I need to know about the transportation arrangements. I assume you have made them?"

"Why wouldn't I have?" I was pretty good at feigning innocence from all those years of convincing my kids that I had no idea who had eaten all the Girl Scout Thin Mint cookies.

Her eyes narrowed further, if that was physically possible. "What company's doing the shuttles?"

She might as well have pinned me up against the frozen pizzas and shone a bright lamp in my eyes.

"You wouldn't believe me if I told you. It's going to be something very special."

I could tell she didn't believe me. "I'm the chair of the ball. I think you can tell me."

"Nope. It's going to be a surprise." And it was, even to me, so I wasn't lying. Still, guilt thickened my tongue and raised my heart rate.

"And the security?"

"Taken care of. All the off-duty Metro officers we need."

Her eyebrow arched, then, in pure skepticism. "How did you manage that?"

"Connections." And an excruciating dinner at Green Hills Grille.

"I always worry when I think someone's being less than truthful with me." She took a step closer, totally violating my personal space. And I couldn't retreat since the freezer case had my back.

"Don't screw this up, Ellie, like you do everything else."

"If I screw this up, Roz, it will be because you used Nashville's biggest charity event to get back at me for stealing your boyfriend!"

All the breath whooshed out of my lungs on the wings of those words. I couldn't believe I'd actually said that.

"You've got to be kidding." Roz rolled her eyes, but it was an affected gesture. I could tell from the tightening of her nostrils that I'd scored a direct hit. Only in an outright battle, I knew I couldn't beat her. She had money, power, connections. Lord, she was going to squash me like a bug. She'd been waiting years for the opportunity.

"Look, Roz," I said, swallowing the large knot in my throat that was my pride. "I'm sorry about Jim. But that was a long time ago, and clearly I'm getting my just desserts now."

But even that didn't seem to mollify her. Her perfectly made up cheeks took on a fiery tone.

"You think this is about Jim?" She was looking at me in patent disbelief.

I didn't know what to say.

"I could care less about Jim Johnston," she sneered. "Although I will say I admire him for finally coming to his senses."

"Wait a minute." The cold tile beneath my feet was starting to spin. "If you don't hate me because of Jim, then why?"

"You really don't know?"

"No."

I couldn't tell whether my denial made her mad or happy. She looked up at the ceiling, then down at her impeccable navy pumps, and then finally back at me. And when she did, she had tears in her eyes.

"Your mother never told you?"

"Never told me what?"

Her mouth opened and closed wordlessly, much as mine had done when Jim had asked me if Tiffany could wear my mom's wedding dress.

"My father . . ."

Just the start of that sentence was like a sucker punch to the stomach.

"He and your mother—"

"No!" I was not going to let her stand there and slander my mother. Roz was a jealous, bitter, vindictive—

"Oh, yes. Oh, yes. For *years.*" She drew out the last word like it was a knife coming out of its sheath.

"No way." I thought of my mom, collapsed on the couch at the end of a long day with her feet in a tub of hot water and Epsom salts. As far back as I could remember, her face had been lined and worn. She was the last person in the world who would have had an affair with her boss. Besides, I knew who my father was. Kevin Michael Hall had died in Korea three months before I was born. I had his eyes and his strong chin. One look at the portrait of my dad in his dress uniform confirmed my paternity.

"No, Roz, my mother wasn't involved with

your father." And then the light dawned. "Good Lord! You think we're sisters?"

I couldn't help it. I burst out laughing. Not a very politic thing to do at that exact moment, but it wasn't intentional.

"My mom always said—"

"Your mom was a bitter, jealous woman." I'd been young, but not too young to pick up on that fact. I'd always resented when my mom threw Roz's accomplishments in my face, and if I protested her doing that, she would tell me tales of Roz's horrible mother.

Evidently the apple didn't fall too far from the tree.

"It has to be true," Roz hissed. "He was always talking about you, going on about your grades, your hard work, your accomplishments. *Ellie* this and *Ellie* that. I hated the sound of your name."

Another shopper bumped against me trying to get to the frozen pizzas. I moved aside, and Roz moved with me.

"Look, Roz, I can show you a copy of my birth certificate if you want. Your dad was a doctor. If he had thought he was my father, his name would be on my birth certificate.

He would never have messed with something like that."

Right there, right in front of my eyes, she deflated like a balloon stuck with a hat pin. Her face crumpled as much as it could, given the amount of Botox it contained. I half expected her to go swirling and spinning off through the store.

For the first time in my life, I felt sorry for Roz Crowley. Suddenly, I didn't feel the need to finesse anything. I'd taken an extra winner without even trying.

"I'm sorry, Roz," I said and tried to sidle around the side of my cart. I was going to try and do something kind, like put a hand on her shoulder and pat her as Grace so often did to me. But before I could get anywhere near her, she threw back her shoulders and glared at me with those laser-beam eyes.

"If you ever, ever repeat this to anyone, I'll—"

"What, Roz? What else could you possibly do to me?" For a myriad of reasons, she and I had been destined for enmity. I didn't know if I could let go of all those years of bitterness and jealousy right there in the frozen food aisle at Harris-Teeter, but at least I could offer a truce.

"No, Roz. I'm not going to repeat this to anyone." I looked down into my cart. "My pizzas are starting to thaw. I'd better go."

I could tell she hated my generosity, but she seemed to accept it nonetheless.

"Fine." She smoothed her hair with one hand. "Just make sure you don't foul up the ball."

"Good-bye, Roz." I pushed the cart past her and gladly followed.

The last time I had been this stunned by a revelation was when I had curled up on my living room sofa while Jim went upstairs to pack his bags. I guess in life, people are finessing us, slipping things by us all the time, and most of the time we don't even notice. Sometimes, though, we slip things by ourselves, and maybe that's even worse.

 **CHAPTER SIXTEEN**

Becoming a Captain

By the end of the week, Henri was back in town, but I still hadn't found the right moment to push him about my unpaid invoices. I was too cowardly, though, to quit working for him until I got a check. So I spent that week just as I had the one before—organizing his meals, his laundry and dry cleaning, his maid service. I even took his luxury car to have the oil changed and the tires rotated.

By Friday, I decided enough was enough.

Time to beard the lion in his den. Far more professional to beard the lion in his downtown high-rise than in his, well, actual den. Every time I'd tried to introduce the subject while standing in his apartment, I had wound up either being seduced or running away from his attempts at seduction.

The bloom was definitely off the rose, I thought, as I found a parking garage near his office and managed to wedge my land yacht into a spot designated for compact cars. By now, I was far more concerned with the money Henri owed me than with his ability to make me feel special and sexy.

I took the elevator to the twenty-fifth floor and followed the signs for The Triumph Group. When I entered the suite of offices, I was surprised to find that Henri's business consisted of only a very young receptionist in the outer office and two closed doors beyond that, one marked with Henri's name.

"I'm Ellie John—I mean, Hall. Ellie Hall. I'd like to see Mr. Paradis."

The girl gave me the once over. "What is this regarding?"

"Business." I had worn my robin's egg blue suit for courage. The receptionist evidently knew her designer labels, because she nodded her approval.

"I'll see if he's available."

She picked up the phone and spoke in low tones while I wandered to the opposite side of the small reception area and pretended to inspect the artwork, really just framed copies of a generic landscape like you'd find in any office building anywhere.

"Mr. Paradis says it's not a convenient time. Perhaps you would like to come back after lunch?"

"You're kidding." I verbalized my thought before I could stop myself. "I mean, it's imperative that I speak with him right away."

From behind the door bearing Henri's nameplate, I heard muffled voices, one of them a woman's. Maybe I should have felt some shooting rush of jealousy, but I only felt annoyed. I was tired of the game-playing.

"I'll just show myself in." Without waiting for her response, I walked past her desk and threw open the door to Henri's office.

"Ellie!" He was halfway between the door and his desk, standing there with a confused look on his face. "This isn't a good time to talk."

How could I not know that something was going on? Henri looked guilty but also a bit smug, and then I noticed that there was another door in the wall to my right. Whoever he had been talking to, that door was apparently her escape route.

"I'm afraid it can't wait."

"What is it, then? What is so important that you must interrupt my work?"

I thrust the file I was holding into his hands. "Here are the unpaid invoices from Your Better Half. I took the liberty of making you additional copies. As you can see, some of them are more than thirty days past due."

He scowled. "Yes, yes. I know this already, and I promised you that I would see to them."

"Yes, you did promise. But nothing seems to have been done about it."

He shoved his fingers through his hair, unknowingly spiking the ends so that they stood straight out from his head. I'd never seen him do that before.

"You came all the way downtown for this?"

"Yes." I crossed my arms over my chest, prepared to stand there until doomsday if that's what it took to get the money I was owed.

"I'm afraid our accountant isn't in right now."

"I thought you said there was an accounting department. A bunch of Italians."

"Of course there is. But they are actually in Italy, *ma petite.*" In the blink of an eye, he dropped his defensive posture and came toward me. "When Jason, my partner, returns, I will have him call Italy immediately. Really, Eleanor, there is no need to be so dramatic."

"When do you expect him back?"

His smile faded. "Jason? Soon."

And then I heard a toilet flushing from behind the closed door. "Who's that?"

For the first time since I'd known him, I was given the opportunity to see Henri speechless. More sounds followed the flush—water running and the snap of paper towels being pulled from a dispenser—and then the door opened.

The woman who emerged from the bathroom was stunning, half my age, and obviously French. You could tell by her cheekbones and her shoes. Also, she looked at me with that Gallic disdain that I'd seen on Henri's face on several occasions.

"Henri? Who is this?" She dismissed me, robin's egg blue suit and all, with a flick of her hair over her shoulder.

"This is Eleanor. She's the woman who has been helping me with my domestic arrangements."

"Oh, but of course. Your little wife." Only she said it in French. *"Bien sur. Votre petite mariée."* Even my high school classes ensured I could translate that much.

"Ellie, this is Giselle. Giselle Paradis."

I smiled, trying very hard to be pleasant in the face of the other woman's hauteur. "Nice to meet you. I didn't know Henri's daughter was coming to visit."

Her eyes grew the slightest bit wider, and then she smiled like a cat about to devour a mouse that it had been toying with. "Daughter? Oh, no, madame. You misunderstand. I am Henri's wife."

"Sorry?"

"Giselle is my wife. She arrived unexpectedly last night."

I was at a complete loss for words. A shiver ran down my spine, and then it settled as a knot in my stomach.

"I flew in from Paris to make sure Henri was not being too naughty here among the Southern belles." She made it sound like the women of Nashville ran around in hoop skirts and pantaloons while hopping in and out of horse-drawn carriages.

Finally, I found my voice. "I'm sure he's as well-behaved here as he is at home." A statement that provided me with all the leeway of its double meaning.

She frowned. "Yes, well, now that I am here, I will look after his . . . how did he say it? . . . domestic arrangements."

At that moment, it dawned on me that she was looking at me the same way I had looked at Tiffany Trask the week before at Green Hills Grille. As if she couldn't believe her husband would involve himself with someone so lacking in sophistication, someone so clearly devoid of refinement and gentility.

Well, how did that saying go? One man's trash was another man's treasure?

"Of course. You'll want to resume your wifely duties." Wifely duties? My cheeks flamed. "I mean, you'll want to take over the household management." I gestured toward the folder of invoices Henri still held in his hand. "Those are up to date, so it would be simplest to terminate my services today." I kept myself from saying, "right this very moment before I take a club to your no-good husband." After all, about the only thing I had left was my pride. I was going to tie a knot in it and hang on.

"Yes. I think that would be for the best," Giselle snapped. Clearly she was losing patience with our conversation.

Henri had been uncharacteristically mute during this exchange, but at that point, he seemed to collect himself. "I'll just walk Ellie to the elevator, *ma chère*." His use of the endearment that had weakened my knees now had the opposite effect of straightening my spine.

"That's not necessary. I can find my way out."

"Oh, but I insist. I won't be a moment, darling."

Giselle arched an eyebrow but offered no protest.

"Nice to meet you," I said inanely before spinning on my heel and making a beeline for the door. I didn't particularly want Henri to walk me anywhere. Mostly I just wanted to flee the building—and the greater Nashville area—as quickly as possible.

But he wasn't going to allow me to make a quick escape. He didn't say anything until we passed the receptionist and were safely in the deserted hallway. I strode to the bank of elevators and punched the DOWN call button.

"Ellie! Wait." His hand covered mine on the button. I snatched my fingers back as if I'd placed them on a hot stove.

"No, Henri."

"But I can explain."

I snorted. "I'm sure you can. But the bottom line is you told me you were divorced. I would never have slept with you if I'd known you were married."

"But I am divorced." He actually had the gall to look wounded. "I did not lie about that."

"Well, Giselle doesn't seem to be aware that you two no longer share a legal bond."

"Oh, no, *ma chère.* I am not divorced from Giselle. Marie, I am divorced from Marie. She was my first wife."

It was the closest I'd ever come in my life to committing homicide. Any reasonable jury would have declared me not guilty. Still, if I wound up in jail, I wouldn't be available to enjoy my total humiliation when all the transportation arrangements for the Cannon Ball turned into a disaster.

"You knew what I assumed when you told me you were divorced."

"Yes, but I did not lie."

"You turned me into an adulteress!" I hadn't meant to shriek the words quite so loudly. Down the hall, an office door opened and a woman's head popped out.

"Everything okay down there?" She was a formidable-looking tank of a woman with gun-metal gray hair pulled back in a severe style.

"Everything's fine." I waved, trying to act nonchalant. "No problem here."

"Then keep it down. Some of us are trying to work." The door slammed.

"Ellie, please don't be mad." Henri put his hands on my upper arms and tried to draw me closer. "I cannot help it if I was be-witched by your beauty."

I was pretty sure the only reason he put his hands on my arms was to keep me from slapping him. Really, though, the person I wanted to slap was me. For being so stupid. For thinking a man like Henri would want

anything more from me than sex. For hem-
ming and hawing about those invoices
when he had played me like a fiddle. I felt
more ashamed of how I'd fallen for his spiel
hook, line, and sinker than of being duped
by Jim. My ex-husband, at least, could
boast two decades of dependability and
fidelity before middle-age had addled his
brain.

"The only thing that bewitched you was
the possibility of *getting some.*" And then
my mouth went round with shock, like a little "o." I'd never used an expression like
that in my life.

"Is that what you think?" Henri dropped
his hands and drew himself up to his full
height. "That I am just some alley cat on the
prowl?"

Evidently, I'd offended him. I let out a bark
of laughter. "No, Henri. I would never com-
pare you to an alley cat. That would be insulting to felines everywhere!"

Happily for me, the elevator bell dinged at
just that moment. The doors slid open, and
I stepped inside.

"If those invoices aren't paid within five
business days, I'll turn the matter over to
my attorney."

His face darkened like a thundercloud. "You ungrateful little—"

Fortunately, the doors closed, shutting out the rest of Henri's invective.

I fled to Jane's house out of instinct. I don't know why I sought her out rather than Linda or Grace. Mostly, I guess, it was because I hoped she could help me sort out this horrible social-life-and-work-life cocktail I'd mixed up for myself.

"Ellie? What's wrong?" She took one look at my face and waved me inside. I'd cried all the way to the parking garage, all the way up Broadway, and all the way down Twenty-First Avenue where I'd almost plowed through a group of Vanderbilt co-eds.

"He's married," I sobbed. "Henri's married."

That was all I needed to say. Jane led me to her sofa and handed me a box of tissues. "What happened?"

"I went to confront him about the invoices."

"What invoices?"

I burst into fresh sobs.

"The ones he hasn't been paying." I

flushed with embarrassment. I hadn't wanted any of them to know what a miserable businesswoman I'd turned out to be, despite Jane's tutelage.

"He still hasn't paid you a dime?"

"Not a cent."

"And you kept working for him?"

I let that one pass and took the opportunity to blow my nose into the wad of tissues in my hand.

"So how do you know he's married?"

"She was there."

"His wife was there?" She winced.

I nodded miserably.

"What did she look like?"

"Young. Elegant. French."

"Damn."

"You can say that again."

Jane shot me a weak smile. "I could, but I'll refrain." She was quiet for a moment, obviously thinking about something. "Well, now that he's revealed his hand, you can become the captain."

"What?" Either I was far more distressed than I thought or Jane had started speaking in tongues.

"In bridge, when you're bidding back and forth with your partner, the first one to reveal

the point range of her cards by bidding a certain thing limits their hand."

"Limits their hand?"

"It means that they've pretty much told everyone at the table what kind of cards they have."

"What does that have to do with the captain thing?" I said, sniffing.

"Once your partner limits his hand, then you take charge of the bidding. Your partner has revealed all her—or his—secrets. Since you haven't, you take charge of the bidding process."

"And this has what to do with Henri?" Honestly, sometimes I wondered about these women and their fanaticism for a recreational card game.

"Look, now that you know his secret, you have the power."

"To do what?"

"Well, for one thing, you can get him to pay those invoices."

"What am I supposed to do? Blackmail him?"

"Exactly."

I was speechless for a moment. "I can't threaten to rat him out to his wife."

"Why not?"

"Because I would never do that." I stopped and swallowed back the knot that lodged in my throat. "I know how it feels to be cheated on. The last thing I would want is to hear the truth from the other woman."

"You don't have to actually tell her. You just have to threaten to tell her."

That brought me up short. Because I hadn't stopped to consider that the threat alone would probably force Henri's hand.

"Do all captains resort to blackmail?"

Jane chuckled. "Only the really good ones."

I smiled back at her through my tears. Henri's betrayal still hurt, even if I'd begun to pull away from our romantic involvement. But the idea that I was in any way the same kind of woman as the despised Tiffany was even more painful. I'd been so sure she was pure, unadulterated—or adulterated as the case might be—evil. But did I even know for sure that she'd known Jim was married when they became involved? Jim hadn't said, and I certainly hadn't asked. She might be as innocent as I was. And even if she wasn't, Jim was the one who should have known better. He was the one with the wedding ring on his finger.

"So you think I can get Henri to write me a check?"

"If you play your cards right."

"Captain, huh?"

"The ball's in your court."

"So what do I do?"

Jane stood up. "I just took a pound cake out of the oven. Let's have a slice and draw up a plan."

By the time I left Jane's house and stumbled across the yard to my own front door, I was exhausted, even though it was barely noon. I really wasn't in the mood to deal with who I found sitting on my front steps. Jim. With a dozen red roses in hand and a look of contrition in his eyes.

"Hello, Ellie."

Honestly, I wished a hole like the police had dug in my backyard would open up and swallow me.

"Go away, Jim." I was too tired for any measure of diplomacy. "I'm really not up to this."

Honestly, I'd expected him to call or show up before now. I figured once Tiffany told him about our bathroom conversation at the

Green Hills Grille that he'd come by and chastise me. But as the week wore on and he didn't show, I began to think she hadn't told him what had happened. And then I'd spent way too much time wondering why she hadn't told him instead of writing copy for Your Better Half's Web site or calling the leads on potential clients Jane had e-mailed me.

He stood up and held out the flowers. "I brought you these."

It had been six years since he'd given me flowers of any kind and more than a decade since I'd been presented with roses.

"I don't want them."

"Please. Take them." If he'd had a hat, it would have been in his hands. The sharply sweet scent of the roses stung my nose.

"Jim, it's really not the time." I tried to keep my face slightly averted. I did not want him to know I'd been crying, and I definitely did not want any probing questions about why. The last thing I needed was Jim learning that Henri was married. He'd never let me live that one down.

I tried to brush past him to get to the front door, but he stepped in front of me. "Ellie, stop. I'm worried about you."

And he was. I could see it in his eyes, big and brown and full of concern. Eyes that had looked at me in just that way countless times over the years, and always, always that look had been both my comfort and the undoing of my composure.

If I thought I'd cried all my tears at Jane's, I was wrong.

"Shh. It's okay." Somehow, I wound up with my head against his chest, and I was sobbing into his shirt. He smelled like Jim— the slightest hint of Gray Flannel mixed with antibacterial soap. His arms came around me at waist height, holding me securely as they'd always done. We fit together perfectly, like two puzzle pieces, the result of years of practice.

I knew I shouldn't indulge myself, but I did it anyway. I let Jim hold me and murmur reassuring, mindless words in my ear. I sobbed against his shoulder, dampening his shirt, until the new well of tears ran dry. And then I just rested my head there for several long moments because I didn't have the courage to lift it up and look at him. I felt warm and safe, a different feeling from the excitement I'd found with Henri but one more likely to last over time.

"I have to tell you something."

"What?" I mumbled into his shirt.

"I'm a first class jerk."

I sighed, stepped back, wiped away the last traces of my tears, and looked at him. "This is not particularly new information."

Now his eyes were filled with sadness. "No, I guess it's not."

I looked down at my feet, unsure what to do next.

"Ellie, I've also been a fool. An idiot. And a bunch of other names that I shouldn't say in front of a lady."

"You'll get no argument from me."

The whole moment had a hugely surreal quality. I half expected clocks to start slithering down walls and over pieces of furniture.

"I've broken it off with Tiffany."

That caught me by surprise. I looked up. "Why?"

He grimaced. "Actually, that's been coming on for a while. Ever since we started planning the wedding."

I wanted to feel vindicated. I wanted to crow out in triumph and rub his nose in his admission of failure and wrongdoing. Before that morning, I might have. But now that I was myself the "other" woman, I was feeling slightly less righteous.

"And so you think if you dump Tiffany you can just show up here with a dozen roses and all is forgiven?"

At least he had the grace to blush. "I'm stupid, but I'm not that stupid."

"Then why are you here?" My chest was tight, but whether it was hope or grief constricting me, I couldn't say.

He shifted from one foot to the other. "Well, to apologize, I guess."

"And?"

"I know you don't want me back, but, Ellie, for old times sake, I was wondering . . ."

"Wondering what?"

"Would you at least let me buy you dinner sometime?"

If he'd shown up like this a month ago, I might have responded very differently. But in the last six weeks, I'd learned a lot— some of it good and some of it not. One important thing, though, I'd come to realize was that I wouldn't have been so utterly destroyed when Jim left if I'd had more things in my life that were just for me.

Another thing I'd come to realize was that Jim was not the only guilty party in the situation. Yes, his had been the greater offense. But I'd known for years that our marriage wasn't what it had once been. We'd been complacent enough to let comfort take the place of intimacy. Stress and children and the busyness of our lives had driven us apart long before Tiffany's impressive cleavage had burst onto the scene.

"There's no going back, Jim." Nothing said that more clearly than the fact that we were standing on the front porch of my home. Mine alone. Not the one we had once shared.

"I know. I guess I'm just realizing exactly how bad I've fouled up."

My smile was so sad it felt more like a frown. "It's not exactly news to me."

And yet, I could see that he was really suffering. Men's mid-life crises might be the butt of a lot of jokes, but when it was your man suffering through one, it really wasn't very funny.

"So can I call you sometime? Maybe take you out to dinner?"

I paused. In the last six weeks, I'd gone on dates with a married philanderer and a young man half my age. Dinner with my ex-husband would make the hat trick complete.

"Okay. I guess."

And then something occurred to me. Standing in front of me was the answer to several of my current problems, as well as a great way to tweak Roz's nose. The Cannon Ball was a week away, and I was pretty sure Henri was no longer my escort. Plus there was one thing I still needed to take care of.

"I tell you what, Jim."

"What?"

"Buy me a dress for the Cannon Ball, and you can be my date."

"A dress?" He blanched. "Ellie, you know I'm broke."

"Jim, I know exactly what you're worth and what you own. And it's a whole lot more than I have."

He stared at me like I'd grown another head. "You're serious, aren't you?"

"Absolutely."

He looked down at the roses, thought for a moment, and then lifted his eyes to me.

"Okay. I'll do it."

"Fine. I'll charge it at Elliott's." I couldn't resist that dig.

To my surprise, Jim smiled instead of

scowled. "You're really something, you know that?"

After a day of tears, it felt good to return his smile. "Oh, yes, honey. I'm well aware of that."

I also knew that as risky as it might be, I could develop a liking for becoming the captain.

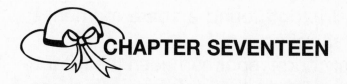 **CHAPTER SEVENTEEN**

Asking for Aces

The last thing I needed to be doing on the Saturday night one week before the Cannon Ball was playing bridge. I had too many other things on my mind. Will McFarland and his investigation. The approaching date of the Cannon Ball. My humiliation-slash-revelation at Henri's hands.

I had spent the rest of the day after Jim left canvassing limo services, taxi companies, and even the local school system for buses to serve as shuttles for the ball. My attempts to find someone to handle the valet parking had fared slightly better. I'd bribed, cajoled, and otherwise unduly influenced a handful of Connor's friends to help me out, although they were little more than a drop in the proverbial bucket. And though I'd blackmailed Jim into buying me a dress, I hadn't found a spare moment to actually shop for one.

The only bright spot had been the total silence from Roz. I thought maybe our confrontation at Harris-Teeter had subdued her until Linda told me she was simply out of town. Roz had gone to New York City for a final fitting for her gown for the ball. This news made me feel more than a little like a sooty Cinderella.

One other bright spot, too, had been the FedEx envelope that arrived at my doorstep early that afternoon. It contained a nice big check from The Triumph Group. Apparently when Henri was properly motivated, he could get the Italians in accounting to move quite swiftly.

Despite all these complications and a preference for climbing into bed and pulling the covers up over my head, by seven o'clock Saturday evening I found myself ringing

Linda's doorbell, a plate of still-warm-from-the-oven blondies in hand.

"Hi, Ellie." Linda let me in and relieved me of the blondies. "We've got big plans for tonight."

"Big plans?" It sounded like about the last thing I needed.

"Don't frown. We're just excited because we're going to talk about slam bidding."

"What's that?"

"When you bid at the highest levels. Very exciting stuff."

And it actually did turn out to be pretty exciting.

"There are two kinds of slams," Linda explained as the four of us sat down at the table to play. "Little and grand. With a little slam, you must take all the tricks but one."

"And a grand slam is all thirteen?"

"Exactly."

I was glad to have something else to concentrate on besides all my current life complications, even if the pressure at these stratospheric levels was enough to give me a nosebleed. The ladies walked me through bidding slams in a trump suit and in no-trump.

"If you're bidding a slam in no-trump, you

have to account for all the aces, so you have to ask your partner how many she has." Once again, Linda sat across from me with Grace on my left and Jane on my right.

"I thought you weren't allowed to talk to each other like that."

Linda smiled. "You ask by bidding. Let's say you have two of the four aces in your hand and enough high card points and support from your partner to know you might have a slam. Then you need to know if your partner has one or both of the two remaining aces."

"Why do you need to know about aces?"

"You need to know what kind of support you can count on from your partner. In no-trump, all the aces are winners. If your partner only has one of the two missing aces, you can only bid a little slam. But if your partner has them both, you can bid a grand slam."

"So how do I ask for aces?"

Like just about everything else in bridge, it turned out to be a matter of understanding the carefully coded language. If I bid four no-trump, then I was asking my partner how many aces she had. If she responded with a bid of five clubs, it meant she either had none or all four.

"How will I know whether it's one or four?"

Grace chuckled at this. "Well, if you don't have a couple of aces in your own hand, you wouldn't be bidding four no-trump to begin with."

I laughed and nodded. "Point taken."

"If your partner has one ace, she'll bid 5 ♦. If she has two, it's 5 ♥. Three would be 5 ♠."

"And then I'll know if we have all the aces and can bid a grand slam?"

"You've got it." Linda smiled. "And six weeks ago you were telling us you were hopeless at cards."

Well, six weeks ago I'd assumed I was hopeless at almost everything. These three ladies, though, had shown me just how wrong I'd been. True, my life was far from perfect. But at least it was mine. Although it would be nice if life could be like bridge and I could ask for aces so I'd have some idea if I held all the cards I needed to make my very own grand slam.

Sunday morning found me not out in the backyard pulling the last remaining weeds, but on my way to Cumberland Farms & Stables to negotiate for the exercise and feeding of Cupcake. Part of me knew I was sacrificing too much to hang on to the past the horse represented, but another part of me didn't know if I could live with the guilt of telling Courtney that Cupcake had to go. If nothing else, it was a beautiful morning for a drive, and so I headed south, grateful for a reprieve from my worries over the Cannon Ball and avoiding Will, the lovestruck cop.

I'd known Greta Price for years, since the day Jim bought Courtney her first pony without consulting me. He'd gotten the hugs and kisses and sparkling looks of adoration from a young Courtney. I'd gotten the task of chauffeuring her to and from the stables several times a week. As I pulled into the gravel driveway, Greta, fresh-scrubbed with hair stuffed into a ponytail, appeared from around the corner of one of the barns and gave me a jaunty wave.

"Morning, Ellie."

I returned her greeting and joined her in the sunshine. "How are you?"

"Can't complain." Greta was one of those women who was either drawn to horses because she resembled them, or she had

come to resemble them after spending so much time around them. She wasn't unattractive. On the contrary, she glowed from the combination of sun, wind, and work-induced sweat.

"Thanks for taking the time for me."

She smiled. "No problem. How's Courtney? College going okay?"

"Well enough that she only calls home when she needs money."

"Good." Greta turned and started walking toward the barns, and I fell into step beside her.

"I guess you know Jim and I are divorced."

"He mentioned it when he called."

"Neither of us really has the means right now for Cupcake's upkeep."

Greta nodded sagely. "Do you want me to let folks know he's for sale?"

"Well, actually, I was wondering if we could trade services, so to speak. I think Jim mentioned that to you."

"He did. What is it your new company does?"

"It's called Your Better Half. We do all the things you're too busy to do yourself."

"Like muck out stables?"

It took me a moment to realize she was kidding. "I'm afraid not," I said with a laugh. "More like errands, shopping, hostessing events, things like that."

She stopped and turned toward me. "I'd like to help you out, Ellie. You and Jim have been good customers all these years. But I just don't need that kind of help."

My stomach fell to the tops of my ancient running shoes. "You sure?"

"Yep." We'd reached the door of the nearest barn. Greta opened it and motioned me inside.

The interior of the barn was cool and dark. No horses whinnied here, though. Instead, it was more of a carriage house. "What's all this?"

Greta led me down the center of the barn toward a lighted room at the back of the building. "Carriages, wagons, pony carts. I started collecting all this stuff a few years back. Don't get much call to use a lot of it. Folks will hire out a wagon for a hay ride or a carriage for a wedding. Pony cart for a birthday party. That kind of thing."

"There must be twenty of them in here."

Greta ducked her head sheepishly. "Guess

I went a little bit overboard. But I'm just partial to horse-drawn travel."

"Oh my gosh. That's it!" The idea kicked me in the head like one of Greta's horses. I turned toward her, and my face was probably bright enough to light up Nashville. "Do you have enough horses to pull all of these?"

"At the same time?" Greta's brow furrowed.

"Yes. Do you have enough horses?"

She smiled. "Well, what I don't have I could probably borrow or rent from some of the other stables in the area."

"How much?"

"To do what?"

"To rent all of these for one night."

She looked at me like I'd lost my mind, and maybe I had. But I was giddy with excitement.

"I don't know. Including drivers? And would you use them here on the farm?"

"No. In town."

Greta thought for a moment and then named a figure that stole the color from my cheeks. The number was sky high. It was also almost the exact amount of the check

I'd received from Henri in the FedEx envelope yesterday.

"Could I book them for next Saturday
night?"

"Are you kidding me?" Greta's eyes darkened. "This isn't some kind of weird joke?"

"No. I want to book all of these for next
Saturday night. Could you find drivers in
time?"

"They might not all be professionals.
Maybe some of my experienced older students, too. Would that be okay?"

"That would be fine."

"Well, okay. Sure. It's a deal."

The knowledge that it would take all the
money I'd made in the last six weeks to underwrite my crazy scheme scared me, but I
also knew never to look a gift horse in the
mouth. So to speak.

"And about Cupcake—"

"Are you kidding?" Greta started walking
toward the office again. "If you're serious
about this, Cupcake can be my guest for a
couple of months. Think of it as a free gift
with purchase."

"Thanks, Greta."

I followed her to the office where she filled
out a contract. I signed my name in big,

bold script. And then I thought about how even if you know when to ask for aces, you don't always know where to ask for them. Sometimes you can find them in the most surprising places.

After all the times I'd told Jim to quit calling me, I was delighted when he phoned that evening.

"You sound happy," he said. I laughed and told him about my conversation that morning with Greta.

"Brilliant. Although the wagons may be a bit of a stretch for some of the high-end folks."

"I'm going to cover the benches in them with some old satin sheets and buy some fancy throw pillows. They'll think they're traveling in a sedan chair with a sultan's harem."

"You did it, Ellie. You saved Cupcake." He actually sounded proud of me.

"Just for the short term. You're responsible for the two months after that."

He was quiet for a moment, and then he said, "I guess I could sell my Harley. That ought to keep old Cupcake in oats for awhile."

If I hadn't been sitting on the couch, my knees might have buckled under me. Jim considering selling his Harley? Was the world coming to an end?

"You'd really do that?"

"I'm pretty sure Greta's not doing this for free, and I doubt the Cannon Ball budgeted the kind of money we're talking about for shuttle buses. You must be forking out a pretty penny."

"I am. Now if I can just round up some more valet parking attendants."

"How many do you need?"

My heartbeat accelerated. "About twenty. I've already hired most of Connor's friends who still live here. Why, do you know where I can find some?"

"I can probably swing some of the boys from my fraternity at Vandy. I'm on the alumni advisory council."

"They'd do it just because you're on the advisory council?"

Jim's sigh wasn't one of exasperation— more like one filled with resignation. "They will when I tell them how much I'm going to donate to their house renovation fund."

"I thought you were broke?"

"Well, if I don't need the Harley, I probably don't need the boat, either."

Okay, the world was definitely in danger of coming to an end. Jim loved his high-priced toys like Courtney loved her horses.

"You'd really do that?"

"I told you, Ellie. I've been a fool. If selling the Harley and the boat convinces you I'm sincere, it's not much of a price to pay."

I was so, so tempted to let down my guard at that moment. Even after all that had happened, I was still vulnerable to him. That thought both terrified and electrified me.

"Thank you." I didn't know what else to say.

"I actually called to see what color dress you're wearing to the ball. Thought I'd get a tie and cummerbund to match."

I swallowed against the sudden lump in my throat. Because this man on the phone, whoever he had become, was sounding more and more each moment like the man I had married. Not the man I'd been married to.

"I don't know yet."

"You don't have a dress? I gave you carte blanche at Elliott's."

"I know. Tomorrow. I'll swing by there tomorrow. And I'll let you know about the color as soon as I pick something out."

Jim chuckled. "You really must be busy if you can't take time to buy a ball gown."

In the months before Jim walked out, a chuckle like that would have provoked me into a defensive outburst. Now, I could hear the affectionate bemusement in his tone.

"I guess priorities have a way of shifting."

He was quiet for a moment. "Yes, they do. And sometimes they have a way of shifting back."

I wasn't ready to offer any olive branches quite yet, though. "Pick me up at five on Saturday. I need to be out there early."

"Five?"

"Is that a problem?"

"No. No, no problem." Although I could tell from his tone that clearly it was. Still, he didn't balk. "Just need to reschedule a few things."

"Okay. See you then. And Jim?"

"Yeah?"

"Thanks for your help with the parking attendants."

"My pleasure," he said. And for the first time in a long time, I could tell that he really meant it.

I finally got to the last of the weeds in the flower bed late that afternoon. Except for Red Hat meetings, I'd studiously avoided Grace. I kept waiting for her to show up on my doorstep, exhumation order in hand, furious that I'd implicated her to Will McFarland. Instead, she showed up in my backyard carrying a long garment bag.

"There you are. I rang the bell twice and you didn't answer."

"Sorry." I rocked back onto my heels and brushed the dirt off my gardening gloves. Then I leveraged myself to my feet. "Just trying to get the last bed finished."

Grace's gaze swept around the yard and the now-immaculate flower beds. "A good layer of mulch and you'll be done with this first go round."

First go round? My head swam. "There's more?"

Grace smiled. "A real garden takes years. But you've got the good bones for one now."

"So to speak." Oops. I really hadn't meant to bring up Marvin Etherington. "Sorry."

"Why are you sorry?"

I brushed away her question just as I'd brushed the dirt from my gloves. "What's that?" I asked, nodding toward the garment bag in her arms.

"You said Saturday night that you didn't have a dress for the ball."

Oh, dear. And now she'd come to offer me the loan of one. Probably a mother-of-the-bride dress from one of her children's weddings. I was going to have to handle this very delicately.

"That's very thoughtful, Grace. Why don't we have a glass of tea and you can show it to me?" I didn't mean to sound like a teacher patronizing a student who'd brought her first show-and-tell to school.

We went inside and I poured us both iced tea in my nicest glasses, plastic tumblers that said, world's best barbecue on the side. "Okay. What have you got?"

Grace looked like the cat that ate the canary. "Something you might not be expecting." She snagged the hanger on the kitchen door frame and then unzipped the bag. I could see a glimmer of very pale pink underneath black tulle. Grace slipped the bag from around the dress and then shook out the skirt, spilling yards and yards of the luxurious materials.

The glass of iced tea slipped from my suddenly nerveless fingers and hit the floor with a thud and a splash. "Oh my God." The dress was magnificent.

"I wore it years ago to the Cannon Ball myself."

"You attended the ball?" I didn't know whether to grab a mop or grill Grace immediately. She'd been a socialite? Why hadn't she ever mentioned it?

"Don't move," she ordered me, and I was still stunned enough to obey. She grabbed a dish towel from the counter and threw it over the spilled tea. Then she wiped it up and threw the towel into the sink.

Finally, though, my paralysis dissolved. I grabbed a roll of paper towels and attacked the liquid the towel had missed. "When did you go to the ball?"

"Fred Lewallen, my second husband, was a widower. His late wife had been involved in the Cannon Ball for years. We went once, after we married, but neither of us was much interested in that kind of thing."

"And you wore this?" I rinsed off my hands, dried them thoroughly, and went to inspect the dress more closely. It was as beautiful up close as it had been from across the room. The strapless pink satin sheath was covered with rows of black tulle that stood out like little ruffles. "Wait a minute. Is this—?"

"Chanel? Yes, it is."

I had thought the robin's egg blue suit deserved to be worshipped and adored, but clearly it was only a minor deity in the pantheon of fashion. Before me at this moment was the true goddess.

"You're going to let me wear your vintage Chanel?" And then the guilt returned. "I can't."

Grace frowned. "What do you mean you can't? It should fit." Then she smiled. "I used to be taller. And have a little more meat on my bones."

If only the mess I'd made for Grace was as easy to clean up as the spilled tea. I swallowed the lump in my throat and summoned my courage. "I don't think you'll want to loan me this dress when you hear what I have to say."

And so I confessed my sins to the Queen of Spades. How I'd unwittingly made Will McFarland suspect her. How he was going to be showing up with an exhumation order in his hand any day now. How I'd embroiled her in a murder investigation without meaning to. And to my surprise, she laughed.

"Grace? This isn't funny. It's very serious."

"Ellie, I've known for weeks where that policeman got his information. And he delivered the exhumation order several days ago."

I blanched. "And you're not mad at me?"

Grace walked toward me and patted my cheek. "I know you didn't mean any harm. And to tell you the truth, I wasn't at all surprised when you found Marvin's remains."

"You weren't? Why not?"

"Why not?" She smiled sadly. "Because I helped put him there."

**CHAPTER EIGHTEEN**

Making a Slam

"You what?" Surely Grace didn't mean what I thought she meant.

"I helped put Marvin Etherington in that hole."

"You mean you killed him?"

Grace waved an impatient hand. "No, of course not. Flossie did that. I just helped her bury him."

"Why didn't you call the police?" And why didn't she look more concerned? Or anxious? Or guilty?

"She didn't mean to kill him when she threw the spade at him. He'd just knocked her around pretty good, and she thought he was going after the girls next. I guess she didn't know her own strength. He told her he had no intention of giving her a divorce, and if she tried, he'd make sure the girls were taken away from her." Grace shivered. "She knew what would happen to those girls if they were left alone with Marvin."

"But—"

"I told you this before, when you first moved in. Things were different back then. Marvin had no family to mourn him, and no one was going to miss him except the string of floozies he carried on with." For the first time, emotion colored her cheeks. "I was not going to let those little girls grow up without their mother. She made a mistake— a terrible one—but there was no battered wife defense in those days. Flossie would have been thrown in jail and left there to rot."

I sagged against the counter, all the fight drained out of me. Grace had a point, but she'd also just confessed her role in helping to cover up a murder. "What are we going to do?" I asked.

"Do?" Grace took a sip of her tea. "Well, you're going to go try on this dress, and then I'm going to alter it so you can wear it Saturday night."

"Grace, we can't pretend like all of this never happened. You have to tell Officer McFarland the truth."

Grace reached up and unhooked the hanger from the door frame. She carefully draped the gown across her arms. "I don't have to do any such thing. It wouldn't make a bit of difference to anyone at this late date."

"But Marvin's daughters?"

"They both died young, God rest their souls. One to cancer, the other in a car crash. At least they didn't spend the years they had burdened with the knowledge of their mother's crime."

"And you still think that's best? Keeping it a secret?"

Grace nodded. "I've seen a lot of life, El-lie, and I know one thing for sure. Sometimes the cure is worse than the disease."

Was she right? And if I didn't think she was, what was I willing to do about it?

"Come on, now," Grace said. "Come try on this dress."

And since I didn't know what else to do, I followed her out of the room.

"Jim? It's me." I twirled the phone cord around my finger as I'd done when we were dating. If I'd been sitting on the bed in my dorm room instead of standing in my kitchen on Woodlawn Avenue, it could easily have been the Ellie of thirty years ago calling her new boyfriend.

"Ellie? Is everything okay?"

"Fine. Everything's fine. I just thought you might want to know . . ." Now that I had him on the line, I was beset by nerves. Ridiculous. What was wrong with me?

Jim waited for me to finish my sentence, and when I didn't, he said, "So, what do I need to know? The secret password for the Cannon Ball? Maybe a secret handshake?"

I smiled and then swallowed the unexpected anxiety. After all, didn't I have the upper hand with him? There was no reason to feel like an awkward adolescent.

"My dress. For the ball. Just thought you might want to know the color."

"Sure."

Then more silence. Why was I having

such a hard time communicating such a simple piece of information?

"Do you want me to guess?" He was clearly amused, but not in a mean way.

"No, no. It's pink and black. Vintage Chanel."

Jim let out a low whistle. "Nice."

The warmth, the interest in his tone poured over my heart like a thick balm. How ironic that the man who'd broken my heart was the one man whose interest and affection could begin to heal it.

"Me, too. I mean, I'm looking forward to Saturday night, too."

"Not as much as I am."

Jim might not be French, but what he lacked in the suave department he more than made up for in earnestness.

"Ellie?"

"Yes."

"Thank you for asking me to take you to the ball."

In his voice were all the qualities that had drained away over time. Attraction. Desire. Love.

"You're welcome," I said, still on shaky enough ground that my conversation was less than brilliant.

"Vintage Chanel, huh?"

"Yes."

"I'm looking forward to it. See you on Saturday."

We said our good-byes, and while I knew it wasn't possible for my body to ever feel twenty years old again, I now knew that it was entirely possible for my heart to feel the way it had then.

By the Saturday morning of the ball, I was still wrestling with my conscience, at least as much as the demands of the last few days would allow. I'd met with all the frat boys and made sure they had the appropriate uniform—white polo shirts and khaki pants. I'd also checked to make sure they all had a legal driver's license and were properly bonded. In addition, I'd made several trips out to Greta's stables to go over how many people she could transport in the given period of time before and after the ball. Finally, I'd had to break down and call Will McFarland to do a final check of the schedule and postings for the security guards. I'd managed to escape that conversation without agreeing to another dinner

date or implicating Grace in Marvin Etherington's murder. All in all, not a bad week's
work.

Jane, Grace, and Linda turned up at the
Gatewood Botanical Garden and Museum
that morning to serve as my committee for
the day. We checked and double-checked
schedules, counted out pillows and blan-
kets for the wagons and carriages, and
even managed to squeeze in a quick lunch
at the restaurant next to the gift shop.

"I couldn't have done it without you
ladies," I said, lifting my glass in a toast as
the waiter slid salads under our noses. It
was my first official outing with the Queens
of Woodlawn Avenue.

"That's what we're here for," Jane said
with a smile, sipping the champagne I'd ordered to celebrate.

"Roz will be pea green." Linda tipped her
glass toward me in a salute. "Nicely done."

"Thanks." Although after my confrontation
with Roz in the frozen food aisle, I was feeling a lot less triumphant.

"I hope you enjoy the ball, Cinderella,"
Grace said.

"Well, I'll certainly have the loveliest
dress." We exchanged smiles, although

they held a hint of sadness. By unspoken mutual agreement, we hadn't discussed Marvin Etherington any further. I was still debating what to do about the information Grace had revealed.

"What time is Henri picking you up?" Jane asked.

"Actually, I'm not going with Henri."

Jane's eyebrows shot up. "Really? Then who's the lucky man."

"Um, Jim, actually."

Down her eyebrows went beneath her blonde bouffant hairdo until they were almost knitted together. "Jim? Your ex-husband?"

"He wants to reconcile."

All three had identical looks of horror on their faces. "You're not thinking of taking him back, are you?" Linda demanded, green eyes blazing. "After what he's done?"

"The only thing I'm doing is allowing him to escort me to the ball."

"Be careful," Jane warned. "Especially of ex-husbands bearing gifts."

"I'll be careful," I reassured them, but I knew that keeping my guard up would take some effort on my part. I hadn't loved the man for more than a quarter of a century for nothing.

Jim arrived at the house promptly at five as I'd requested, a good sign for a man who had, in my experience, been regularly detained by patients in need of attention. Many an evening I'd scraped a burned dinner into the trash and turned on the television to watch our favorite shows alone.

"You look stunning." He leaned forward to kiss my cheek, and I let him. A frisson of something akin to the champagne I'd drunk at lunch washed down my spine.

"Thanks. You look pretty good yourself." And he did, in his black tuxedo, pink-and-black paisley bow tie, and cummerbund.

"I brought you this." From behind his back, he pulled out a large, square, black velvet box.

"What's this?" I'd been expecting flowers at most. A corsage, or maybe a bouquet of roses.

"I decided that if I didn't need the Harley or the boat, I probably didn't need the new golf clubs, either."

My fingers trembled as I opened the box. "Oh, Jim."

There, against the white satin, lay the most exquisite strand of black pearls I'd ever seen. The diamond clasp twinkled in the sunlight streaming through my living room curtains.

"You shouldn't have." My heart fluttered in my throat.

"I think they're more than deserved."

I looked up from the pearls and met his gaze, searching for any double meanings or hidden agendas in his eyes. All that I saw, though, was a mixture of sorrow, regret, and painful hope.

"Thank you." I could accept the pearls, but I wasn't sure I was ready to risk what went with them. Tonight, though, I wasn't going to tackle any of the life issues facing me. Tonight, I was simply going to enjoy the ball.

Jim helped me fasten the necklace. "Shall we?" He offered me his arm, and I took it. I felt like a girl going to her first prom as he led me down the sidewalk to the little roadster.

We were the first to arrive, of course, because I wanted to make sure the parking ran smoothly and that Greta had everything she needed.

"We're just fine," Greta assured me as she led a horse from a trailer and walked it toward one of the carriages. "Should go off without a hitch." She chuckled. "Or with a number of hitches. Just no problems."

I fervently hoped so. Roz and her husband arrived hot on my heels. She looked around, incredulous, when the handsome young valet attendant opened the passenger door of their Mercedes to help her out of the car. She looked him up and down, searching for any signs of disrepute, and frowned when she couldn't find fault with his snowy polo and crisply pleated khakis. She frowned even more deeply when she saw Jim standing by my side. At this rate, her Botox would need refreshing by ten o'clock.

"What's all this? Where are the shuttle buses?"

"No buses tonight. We're all going to play Cinderella."

At that exact moment, Greta pulled up in front of us with the first carriage. She was wearing a top hot with a flower pinned to the brim. "Your carriage, madam?" Greta winked at me.

"But— You couldn't have— The shuttle service—"

"It's all under control, Roz."

"Without a committee? How did you do this?" Clearly she'd come ready to crow over my defeat, so my triumph left her completely baffled.

"With a little help from my friends." I opened the carriage door and motioned Roz inside. "Please, I think you should be the first couple to arrive in grand style."

If Roz had actually had any nails in her mouth, she definitely would have been spitting them. "If you went over budget . . ."

I thought of the big, fat check from Henri I'd sacrificed so I could have this moment. "It's all taken care of. Came in under budget, as a matter of fact."

She looked like she wanted to say more, but her portly husband climbed in the carriage beside her and said something to Greta. She flicked the reins, and the carriage started the long drive toward the museum.

I couldn't help beaming from ear to ear.

"You look like the cat that ate the canary," Jim said with a smile.

I beamed back. "And it was mighty tasty, too."

That evening was a night meant for walking on air, and so I did. Once I was sure that the parking attendants and Greta's fleet were flowing smoothly, I availed myself of a carriage and headed for the ball itself. I wanted to check in with Will and the security guards. So far, what little paparazzi Nashville possessed had been content to snap photos of the guests being driven off to the ball in open carriages. The only person with a camera permitted inside the ball, other than the official one, was the society photographer from the *Tennessean.*

Jim gallantly handed me into the next empty carriage and then hoisted himself in beside me. The decorations committee had strung lights in the trees that lined the driveway, and though it wasn't yet dark, the effect was still magical. The lights would have been wasted on guests traveling via shuttle buses.

"Roz looked fit to be tied," Jim said with a

smile. "The carriages are a great touch." He reached over and slid his hand around mine, giving my fingers a squeeze. "Nice job."

Despite my attempts to keep things with Jim on a friendly basis, his praise warmed me. "Thanks."

We rode in silence after that. I was glad for a chance to take a few breaths and re-group. So far so good, but the night was young, and we still had to get everyone back from the ball to the parking lot at the end of the evening. I took a few moments, though, to enjoy the early summer breeze on my face and my ex-husband's occa-sional appreciative glances at my cleavage in the strapless Chanel gown.

The carriage let us off at the museum. As I tried to step gracefully down, my heel caught in my skirt and I pitched forward with a small squeal.

"I've got you." Jim caught me and swung me into his arms. It had been a number of years, and a number of pounds, since he'd done that.

"I'm too heavy. Put me down." Secretly, though, I was thrilled that he could still bear my weight.

"Light as a feather," he said with gentle-manly savoir faire, but I had to grin at the slight signs of strain that etched his mouth.

"You're sweet to say so." He lowered my feet to the ground, and before I stepped away, I gave him a kiss on the cheek. "Thank you."

As we stepped through the museum en-trance, we were greeted by banks and banks of flowers lining the entrance hall. The theme for the ball, "A Midsummer's Garden," must have been thrown together at the last minute, since the original one had called for "An Autumnal Affair." I assumed that Roz's change of date for the ball had caused the decorations committee the same nightmare it had caused me.

"This is an allergy sufferer's nightmare," Jim whispered under his breath, and I had to cover my mouth with my hand to smother a giggle.

"Behave," I swiped at his shoulder, "or I'll never make any rank beyond transportation chair."

"You shouldn't have done such a good job with it," he shot back. "They'll make you do it again next year."

I frowned. I hadn't thought of that.

At the end of the hall, we found ourselves in the receiving line where Roz and her husband were greeting the guests. It was her role as the chair to play the lady of the manor. I looked around for a way to slip by her unnoticed, but no such luck. The line carried us up to her and the silver-haired Ben Crowley before I could manage my escape.

"Ellie!" she called, and everyone in the vicinity cocked an ear toward what was being said. "What a nice job with the transportation, although I do think you may be here late into the night cleaning up the horse poop." She tittered and then looked around, expecting others to join her in her amusement. The other guests, though, looked away, uncomfortable.

Hah! Score one for me.

"And I do smell a bit like a horse," she went on, trying to needle me into a response. "Hardly what I planned on doing while wearing Halston." She smoothed one hand down the skirt of her gown.

I pasted on my sweetest smile. "Well, the carriage was no problem for my Chanel."

Roz scowled and then quickly wiped the expression off her face before anyone else could see. "Well, do enjoy yourself. I'm sure you deserve it."

The look on her face said that she was sure I deserved a slow, painful death, but I doubted anyone else saw it. As always, Roz and I fought our own private war. Except that after her confession at Harris-Teeter, I wasn't in the mood for conflict any more. Her dislike of me was based on a delusion, and I no longer had any reason to feel guilty about Jim.

"Deserve it? She certainly does," Jim replied. "C'mon, Ellie. I want the first dance."

We left Roz seething in the entrance hall and made our way past all the beautifully decorated dining tables toward the dance floor. The items for the silent auction were in a tent off to the side, and beyond the dance floor a number of people had flowed onto the loggia that overlooked the reflecting pool. Linda, looking stunning in vintage Valentino, gave me the thumbs-up when we passed her.

Jim led me out onto the floor just as the band struck up, "Isn't It Romantic?" He pulled me close and off we went.

I'd forgotten how much I loved to dance with Jim. A lot of men hated to set foot on the dance floor, but not my husband. He'd bought ballroom dance lessons for my twentieth anniversary present.

I knew I should be off checking on the security guards, but it felt too nice and far too comfortable to be floating around the floor in his arms. He pulled me close each time he spun us around, and when he did he would nuzzle my ear. He'd always done that, but tonight the intimate gesture brought sharp tears to my eyes. How many wedding receptions, bar mitzvahs, and silver anniversary parties had we danced this way?

"Thank you for letting me come," Jim murmured in my ear.

I didn't know what to say. "You're welcome," didn't sound right, because I wouldn't have brought him if I'd had another option. I finally settled on, "It was nice of you to escort me." Noncommittal. Ambivalent. What I might say to an acquaintance rather than my former life partner.

The evening continued on in just that vein, with Jim moving closer (both literally and figuratively) and me trying to strike just the right balance between the yearnings building up in my midsection and the clamorings of common sense swamping my brain.

Whenever I felt too close to panic, I would grab Linda and retreat to the ladies' room.

Dinner was a delicious trout almondine. During the salad course I finally managed to slip away to check with Will McFarland, whom I had seen circling the dance floor moments before, watching me. When I caught up to him, he was behind a screen of shrubbery, barking into a walkie-talkie.

"Everything okay?"

He jumped about a mile.

"Sorry. I didn't mean to scare you."

He took a deep breath and blew it out. "No problem." He paused, and his gaze slid from my face down to my feet, lingering longer than necessary in a couple of areas. "Wow. You look amazing."

It never hurts for a fifty-year-old woman to be paid a sincere compliment by a man half her age. "Thank you. How is everything going, really?"

"Fine. A couple of people trying to crash the gate, but we got rid of them pretty quickly."

"Crashers? Really?" I was surprised. Surely anyone with an ounce of common sense would realize that there were no anonymous faces at an event like this. Everyone in this social circle knew who belonged and who didn't.

"You'd be surprised." He stood up a little taller. "Of course, we're trained to handle that sort of thing."

"I know. Thanks." Suddenly, Will looked every bit as young as he was. "You've been a true friend."

A shadow passed over his face. "A friend?"

I recognized the look of longing in his face. I had seen it every time I'd looked in the mirror in the months after Jim walked out. "Yes. A friend. A very good one."

"You know I want more." He looked straight into my eyes. I wanted to drop my gaze, but I owed him more than that.

"I know, Will. But I'm too old for you."

"I think that's for me to decide."

I wished I could still claim that righteous certainty that came with being young. "No. It isn't. But I want you to know that I'm flattered. Really, really flattered."

"But not flattered enough." There it was, the bald truth, dropped right there on the perfectly manicured lawn between us.

"Will, a relationship is about more than just attraction. It's about goals, experi-

ences, timing. It's especially about the timing."

"And if the timing was right?" he asked,
pushing.

"But it's not, is it? And wishing that it
would be won't make it so." I'd learned that
much, at least, over the last few months.

"So there's no hope for me?"

Well, you had to give him credit for per-
sistence. "No, I don't think so."

He looked away, and I realized that he
was trying to hide the play of emotion on his
face. After a long moment, his head swung
back toward me. "Okay, but will you at least
do me one favor?"

"Sure," I agreed, although with some re-
luctance.

"Will you dance with me?"

I looked around. We were alone behind
the shrubbery, but we could clearly hear the
strains of the dance orchestra.

"Here?"

"Yeah."

And that's how I came to be dancing with
a rookie police officer in the bushes at the
Cannon Ball. It's also where Jim found me a
few minutes later when he came looking for
me.

CHAPTER NINETEEN

Don't Send a Boy To Do a Man's Job, Part 2

"Who's this?" Jim bristled like our dog, Major, used to do whenever the Orkin man showed up with his five-gallon can of insect repellent.

"Jim, you remember Will. You met at Green Hills Grille a couple of weeks ago. Will . . . ," I hesitated for a moment. "My ex-husband, Jim," I said lamely.

They nodded at each other, and Will's arm tightened around my waist. "Is he bothering you? I can take him in if he is."

Take him in? "You mean as in jail?" I was well aware of the gun holster strapped to Will's waist. The last thing I needed was a showdown between my ex-husband and would-be lover at the Cannon Ball. If that happened, transportation would be the least of my worries.

"Looks more like you're the one who's bothering her, pal," Jim said, taking a step toward us.

I slipped out of Will's arms and took a step back so I could see both of them. "Gentlemen, that's enough." I turned to Will. "Officer McFarland, thank you for the dance. I appreciate your help."

Will looked mutinous. "Really. I can throw him out if he's bothering you."

I heaved a sigh of exasperation. "He's not bothering me. I promise. He's my date."

Will's eyes narrowed, and I thought for a moment he might take issue with my revelation. Finally, he frowned and said, "I'll check back with you later. Make sure he's behaving himself."

I couldn't help but smile at that, just to tweak Jim's nose a little. "Thanks. That would be great."

To my relief, Will turned and walked away

around the edge of the shrubbery, leaving Jim and I standing on the empty lawn. Jim had crossed his arms and now stood with his feet spread apart, like Connor's football coach used to do when he was angry.

"What is wrong with you?" I hissed. "Are you nuts?"

"Pardon me. I didn't expect to find my date in the bushes with one of Nashville's finest."

"We were only dancing."

I really, really, really shouldn't have been so thrilled by the jealousy leaking from every pore of my ex-husband's lanky frame, but I was only human. And I had the same amount of pride as the next woman, and Jim's response was like a salve to it.

"I would have been happy to go with you if you needed to talk to him."

"Look, Jim, I'm a big girl. I can take care of myself. I've learned that much this year at least."

He opened his mouth as if to say something and then shut it just as quickly.

I stepped toward him and put my arm through his. "Let's not spoil the evening." I gave his arm a squeeze. "Please."

The Jim of the last few years would have

divested himself of my arm and my presence as quickly as he could. But the Jim who was with me tonight responded in a very different manner.

"Okay. You win."

We moved toward the edge of the shrubbery, but before we'd quite turned the corner, he stopped and looked down at me. "Just promise me I'm not going to find you off in the bushes with any other guys tonight."

I couldn't suppress the giggle that rose to my lips. "I promise that if I go off in the bushes with anybody else tonight, it will be you. Okay?" Heavens, we sounded like a feuding couple at junior high church camp.

"Much better." And then he did something I wasn't expecting. He leaned down and kissed me softly on the lips. True, he wasn't as practiced or nuanced as Henri in the romance department, but the man had always known how to kiss.

And I had always been a sucker for it.

The rest of the ball passed in a blur of music and conversation. The tables for the dinner boasted gorgeous two-foot-tall center-

pieces of lilies and tulips, and the trout almondine was divine. I danced with Jim and
chatted with Linda's husband Bob—or,
rather, I talked and he listened in his usual
introverted silence. And I also basked in the
gushing enthusiasm of the planning committee members and other guests for the
horse-drawn carriage rides.

"Magical. Just magical," one woman who
was married to the ambassador to some
Eastern European country said when we
were standing in line for the powder room.
"Like Prague or Vienna." By the time we
reached the front of the line, she'd hired me
to take care of her Belle Meade mansion
during the frequent times when she and her
husband were out of the country.

All too soon, the evening was winding to a
close. Greta and company gave everyone
another ride to remember, this time down
the darkened driveway, which made the
fairy lights in the trees truly magical. She
told me later that she handed out enough
business cards to sink a ship. Cupcake
could wallow in the lap of equine luxury for
another couple of bonus months as a sort of
referral fee. The brothers of Phi Delta Tau
did a superb job ferrying all the Mer-

cedeses, BMWs, Acuras, and Volvos back and forth from the parking lots to their waiting owners. And Will and his fellow officers managed to pour the handful of guests who overindulged into cabs and send them home. When the lights came on at two o'clock in the morning, about the only people left were members of the planning committee and their spouses.

I was feeling strangely let down after all the tension I'd endured in the weeks leading up to the ball. Roz had studiously avoided me all evening. I was sure my success was like pouring salt into her wound, however self-inflicted it might be.

Jim and I were among the last couples to leave, and Greta herself drove us from the museum down the long drive to the parking lot. As we passed underneath the twinkling trees, Jim put his arm around me and pulled me close. I didn't resist. Maybe I couldn't resist. This was what a grand slam felt like in real life, and I wanted to bask in my triumph.

Once we were in Jim's car, we both rode in silence on the way home. I had no idea what Jim was thinking. Or, rather, I didn't really want to worry about what he was thinking.

Jim pulled up in my driveway, shut off the car, and turned toward me.

"Ellie?"

"Yes?"

I could see the question in his eyes, but I hadn't decided yet whether to acknowledge what he wanted or play dumb and pretend I didn't notice the desire that was plainly evident in the way he was looking at me.

"Would you like to come in for a cup of coffee?" I wasn't sure why I was even asking him the question. The digital clock on the car's dash said 2:37, and I was far too old to be staying up so late.

"No, thanks."

"Oh." Against my better judgment, disappointment stung my lungs like an indrawn breath of cold air.

"No, I don't think you do understand." Jim's gaze bore into me. "Ellie, I'd like to come in, but I have zero interest in coffee right at this moment."

I wished that such a pivotal moment in my life wouldn't occur when I was exhausted, sleepy, and way too influenced by the longing to fling myself into my no-good ex-husband's arms. Only was he still a no-good liar? Or had he truly come to his senses?

"Jim . . ."

"What?"

"If you come inside, it means no more Tiffany. Or Amber. Or Heather. Or whatever they name all those Hooters waitresses these days."

Jim looked sober as a judge. "Ellie, I swear to you that in all the years we've been married, Tiffany was the only time I wasn't faithful."

I searched his eyes, wanting to believe him but not gullible enough to let myself be swept away on a false promise. "Then why?"

"Why what?"

"Why Tiffany?"

He had been turned toward me, but at my question, he swiveled back to face the windshield and sank back in the driver's seat. Then he was quiet for a long moment. Finally, he mumbled, "I was afraid."

Those were the last words I expected to hear. "Afraid?" He had to be kidding. I was not going to buy some *I-hit-middle-age-and-came-face-to-face-with-mortality* excuse.

"Connor and Courtney were both launching their own lives, and you were so busy with all of your volunteer activities and the house."

"So? I would have thought that took the pressure off of you after all those years of trying to juggle work and family."

Jim wiped his hand across his forehead and gave a short laugh. "You'd think so, wouldn't you?" He shook his head. "Instead, I freaked out."

"I noticed."

"No, before Tiffany. That was when it happened."

"When what happened?"

He took a deep breath and swiveled his head to look at me. "I came home one Monday night. Just an ordinary Monday. But the kids were away at college, and you had gone out to a movie."

The pain in his eyes surprised and devastated me. "I would have thought you would have enjoyed a little peace and quiet to watch football."

"I'd have thought so, too. Instead, I had a panic attack."

"You never told me this."

His smile was half regret, half self-depre-cation. "I was ashamed."

"Ashamed? Of what?"

"Of falling apart when I realized . . ."

"Realized what?"

"That none of you really needed me any-more."

I was dumbstruck. "You can't be serious."

He went rigid. "I've never been more seri-ous in my life."

"You thought we didn't need you? Why on earth would you think that?"

"Because it was true."

I thought back to those last few years be-fore he'd left. Our relationship had drifted apart like two continents, gradually, imper-ceptibly. Until the day we'd woken up and realized we were no longer touching. Not mentally. Not emotionally. And certainly not physically. Our divorce had not been Jim's fault alone. No, we were both responsible. I had to acknowledge that I had felt the same way, like an unnecessary cog in a machine that would run just fine without me. If Henri had come into my life at that time, would I have been just as susceptible to him as Jim had been to Tiffany?

I looked at Jim, and we stared into each

other's eyes for a very long time. And somewhere in that locking of gazes, I made a decision. Jim was no Marvin Etherington. He was no playboy. He was truly sorry for what he'd done, and I still loved and missed him.

I reached down and opened the car door. Since he still had his key in the ignition, a warning chime sounded. This time, though, I wasn't going to listen to it.

"Fine, then. We'll skip the coffee."

The light that leapt to his eyes was visible even in the darkness of that summer night. "Are you sure?"

I laughed. "No. Are you?"

He smiled. "Completely."

"Then that will have to be enough." I slid out of the car and started up the walk. A moment later, I heard the driver's door slam and the sound of Jim's footsteps as he followed me up the walk to my front door.

When I woke up the next morning, the other side of the bed was empty.

Despair swamped me, and I flinched at the banging in my head. Sunlight streamed through the curtains, which someone must have opened. I certainly hoped it had been Jim.

And then I smelled bacon frying. Burning, actually. And I heard the sound of tuneless humming, deep-throated and male, from the vicinity of the kitchen.

I didn't know whether to be mortified, ashamed, or ecstatically happy, so I stretched like a cat underneath the covers, rolling my limbs out one by one. Finally, I slipped out of the bed and grabbed the satin robe I'd left draped over the clothes hamper.

"You're not supposed to be getting up."

I whirled around and found Jim leaning with one arm against the doorframe, looking rumpled and sexy. And he had a definite gleam in his eye. "Good morning, gorgeous."

"Good morning." He might be feeling all self-satisfied, but I was deluged with a strong sense of wariness. I had quite possibly just made the biggest mistake of my life.

"You have to get back in bed," he said.

"Why?" I didn't want to return to bed. I wanted to flee the house in panic.

"Because I can't bring you breakfast there if you're not in it."

"Who are you and what have you done with my husband?" The words slipped out before I could stop them, particularly the "h" word.

Jim smiled indulgently. "Now, now. Time for a fresh start, don't you think?" He stopped and sniffed the air. "Damn. I think the toast is burning."

Before we divorced, I would have shot back some sarcastic comment like, "Ya think?" and then followed him back to the kitchen, pushed him out of the way, and taken over the breakfast preparations. Not a very flattering admission, I have to say. Now, though, I simply smiled and said, "I've always found that if you put extra jam on the toast, no one notices a few black spots." And then I shucked the robe I'd donned and slid back into the bed.

Frankly, I think we were both astonished by our behavior. "Right. Right," Jim repeated, and then he disappeared back into the kitchen. He returned a few minutes later bearing a large tray containing my slightly charred breakfast. I propped some pillows against the headboard, settled in comfortably, and allowed him to place the tray on my lap.

"Bon appetit."

If I'd learned anything in all the months of loneliness, it was when to shut up and eat. So that's what I did. Jim stretched out on the bed beside me and before long was reaching over to steal bites of food off my tray.

"Ouch!" he protested when I finally slapped his hand away. "Don't bite the hand that feeds you."

"I wasn't biting. I was hitting." We were both smiling like a couple of infatuated school kids. I couldn't believe it. After all we'd been through, was it really going to turn out to be this easy and comfortable to reconcile?

And then his expression grew suddenly serious. "Ellie?"

"Yeah?" My hand stopped with a strip of blackened bacon halfway to my mouth.

"Can you do it? Can you really forgive me?"

I'd thought about that for a long time after we'd made love the night before. I'd lain awake, despite my exhaustion, listening to him snore softly and trying to sort through my feelings.

"I think so. I think I want to try."

He nodded. "Fair enough." And then he looked around the room. "Where's the box?"

"What box?"

"You know, the 'Jim & Ellie' box. The one you made at that party."

I tried to be nonchalant. "My memory box? I guess it must be around here somewhere."

Evidently both my breezy tone and my guilty expression gave me away. His eyes narrowed. "What did you do, burn it?"

I blushed. "No. Actually, I buried it."

Jim actually looked a little hurt. "Where? In the backyard?"

"Yes. Back there where they found—"

"Where they found what?"

I'd forgotten I hadn't told Jim about unearthing Marvin's remains. "It's a long story."

Jim sat up in the bed and then swung his feet over the side. "Well, you can tell it to me while I'm digging it up."

"What?"

"You heard me. You can tell me while I'm digging it up. Where's your shovel?" He started toward the door.

I set the breakfast tray to the side and

swung my legs over the side of the bed. "Jim, don't be ridiculous. It's just a box."

He looked back over his shoulder. "Maybe. But it was important to you. And it's a symbol."

"Jim, it doesn't matter."

He stopped and turned around. "Yes it does. You've given up enough for me, Ellie. You shouldn't have to sacrifice your memories, too. We can't start over, but we can pick up where we dropped the ball."

I smiled at his mixed metaphors, but I still didn't want him digging in my yard. It had taken me forever to plant all those impatiens. "Really, Jim, it's okay. It's not going anywhere."

"Yeah, but you might want it after you come back home."

I froze in place. "What?"

Jim stepped toward me and put his arms around me. "It's time to come home, Ellie. I know it's my fault you're in this . . . ," he waved an arm, "sad little house, but that's over and done with. We'll sell it. Maybe take another cruise. Just the two of us this time."

"I don't want to go on a cruise." Not really the point, but it was the only thing I could think of to say.

"Then we'll go to Europe. Paris, maybe."

"Jim, I'm not selling my house."

That brought him up short. "But I thought you wanted to get back together."

"I do. I mean, I think I do. But it's going to take time, and not everything's going to be just like it was."

"Meaning?"

"Meaning that this is my home now. I'm not sure I want to give it up." I felt a sharp pang at the thought of relinquishing my place amongst the Queens of Woodlawn Avenue. They'd seen me through my darkest times. No way was I going to relinquish them so easily.

"Ellie, you have to come home if we're going to make a go of it."

"Jim, I'm not ready to resume our marriage."

His eyes filled with hurt, confusion, and a fair amount of angry frustration. "Then what was last night?"

I clenched my fists at my sides and took a deep breath, praying for the courage I needed. "Last night was wonderful. But we're not married anymore. Now, if you'd like to ask me out again, I would probably accept."

"Ask you out? Probably accept?" He looked like I'd just told him Martians had landed on the front lawn. "Are you kidding me?"

"Jim, if we pick up where we left off, pre-Tiffany, we'll just find ourselves right back in the same situation we were in before."

"Are you going to throw her name up to me every time we disagree?" Now he was actually scowling.

"I'm not throwing up anything. Except maybe that awful bacon." I tried to joke, to lighten the mood, but Jim was having none of it.

He opened his mouth to say something, but I was never to hear those fateful words. Instead, the doorbell rang.

 **CHAPTER TWENTY**

The Partnership Desk

As I made a beeline for the front door, I glanced at the clock on the mantelpiece in the living room. It was almost one o'clock in the afternoon. Jim and I had stayed up most of the night, and then slept the morning away. I cinched my robe more tightly around me as the bell continued to ring. Maybe, if I was lucky, it was an overzealous Jehovah's Witness or some kid selling popcorn for his Boy Scout troop. I didn't want to have to explain Jim's presence to anyone I knew right now. I wasn't sure I could explain it even to myself.

I opened the door, and there stood Jane and Linda on my front porch. *Drat.* I peered around them to make sure Grace wasn't there, too, to make my exposure complete.

"Ellie! Finally." Jane brushed past me into the living room when I opened the storm door, Linda hot on her heels.

I knew they would want to do a post-mortem on the ball, but did it have to be right now? "I'm not sure this is really a good time to chat about last night."

"Last night?" Jane looked at me like I'd lost my mind. "Why would we want to talk about last night?"

Linda looked like she'd been crying. "Grace is in jail," she said. "We just got a call."

"Oh, no." The burned bacon turned to acid in my stomach. "When did this happen?"

"Last night, evidently," Jane said.

"She wouldn't let anyone call us until this morning," Linda added.

The thought of the fragile, elderly Grace spending the night in a jail cell sent shivers down my spine. And it was my fault she was there. Entirely my fault. I'd been so caught up in all my Cannon Ball drama that I had procrastinated dealing with the Marvin Etherington problem. And now Grace was paying the price.

"We have to get her out of there." I looked around the living room, not really sure what I thought I'd find that would help the situation. Then I looked down at my robe. "I'll get dressed."

Only when I looked back up at Jane and Linda, their faces were a mixture of surprise and consternation, with a hint of mirth. They weren't looking at me. Their gazes were fixed on a point beyond my right shoulder. I whirled around, and there stood Jim in the doorway, wearing nothing but his tuxedo pants. To my delight—and to my consternation since he was fifty, too—he looked like one of those sexy morning-after ads for men's cologne.

"Ladies," he said. "Good afternoon."

I was the only one with the good grace to blush. "Um, Linda, you remember Jim." I'd introduced them at the ball. "Jane, this is my ex-husband, Jim Johnston."

Jane, of course, consummate professional that she was, carried off the introduction with aplomb. "Hello, Jim."

Jim stepped into the room and shook hands with both of them. I was rendered speechless by the entire sequence of events, until Jim finally said, "Sounds like a friend of yours is in trouble."

That brought me back to my senses. I had to get Grace out of jail and I had to do it immediately.

"Did they say where we go to get her out? Do we post a bond or what?" I took a step toward the hallway. "I'll throw on some clothes and we can go." Then I looked at Jim. "Can you see yourself out?"

He looked at me like I'd grown another head. And then he frowned. "If you're going down to the jail, I'm going with you."

"I'll be with you in two shakes," I said to Jane and Linda before grabbing Jim by the arm and towing him from the room. Once we reached the privacy of my bedroom, I dropped his arm and whirled to face him.

"Look, I don't need a knight in shining armor right now. The other queens and I can take care of this."

"Other queens? What are you talking about?"

I only had time for the abridged version. "When I bought this house, I automatically got a spot in this bridge club. The Queens of Woodlawn Avenue. I'm the Queen of Hearts."

"Is that what the dining room arch means?"

"Exactly. And now Grace, the Queen of Spades, is in trouble and I've got to go help her."

He reached over and grabbed last night's shirt from the pile of clothes on the floor. "I'm going with you."

By this time, I had slid into a pair of jeans and pulled a T-shirt over my head. "Look, Jim, I don't mean to be rude, but I really don't need your help."

He sank down on the bed and pulled on his dress shoes with no socks. "I don't mean to be rude, either, but have you ever bailed anyone out of jail before?"

"No." I hadn't thought of that. "Have you?"

A faint blush tinged his cheeks. "A couple of times."

"Who?" How could I have been married to this man for more than twenty-five years and not know he'd bailed someone out of jail? And why was he blushing?

"Let's just say you might not know everything about my adolescence. Or Connor's."

I was too stunned to say anything for a moment. Then when I started breathing again, I said, "Connor was in jail?" I didn't know whether to be horrified or angry or both.

Jim looked suddenly serious again. "Ellie, just because you're the kids' mother doesn't mean you know everything about them."

I opened my mouth to protest, but he stood up and laid his fingers against my lips. "I'm not saying that makes you a bad mother. You're a great mother. But I have been there for them, as their father. Maybe not in all the ways you think I should have been, but also maybe more than you think."

That shut me up for a moment. "I still don't need you to help me bail out Grace."

"What are you going to use for money?"

Okay, I hadn't thought of that. Still, his playing the money card, so to speak, rankled. "I'm sure between the three of us, we can make bail." Although I hated to ask Linda and Jane to pay for my mistake.

"What's she charged with?"

I'd forgotten to ask. "I'm not sure. Accessory to murder, maybe? Tampering with evidence?"

"Murder?" He stood up. "Are you telling me you play bridge with a woman who's a killer?"

At that moment, I almost felt sorry for him. "Grace didn't kill anyone. She helped someone dispose of a body, the first Queen of Hearts' abusive husband, and it was over forty years ago."

"How long have you known this?" He slid his keys and pocket change from the dresser, slipped them into his front pocket, and then shoved his wallet into the right rear one. It was a series of actions I'd seen him do a hundred times over the years, and the comforting familiarity of the ritual made my throat go tight.

"Not long. They found the body weeks ago. Then I inadvertently put the police on Grace's tail. They must have arrested her last night." Although since Will McFarland had been working security at the ball, I wasn't sure who had done it.

I shoved my feet into my running shoes and grabbed my purse from the bedside table. "Grace is elderly, Jim. She really doesn't need to be in jail. And I don't need a lecture."

"Fine. Then we'd better get going."

I stopped short and put my hands on my hips. "Jim, you're not going."

"Yes, Ellie, I am. If for nothing else than to be moral support."

Okay, I was annoyed at his high-handedness. But I also had to acknowledge how nice it felt to know that he wanted to stand beside me in this mess.

"Besides," he said, his lips curved slightly upward in a smile that hinted at triumph, "my car is behind yours. You can't leave until I do."

I could have worked around that obstacle. We could have easily gone in Jane's car. Or Linda's. I had learned enough in the last few weeks, though, to know that it was okay to accept help when you needed it. Even from an ex-husband whom you didn't know quite what to do with.

"Okay, fine. You can go with us." I wagged a finger at him. "But you're not to take over. This is our problem to solve."

"Yes, ma'am," he said meekly, but everything else about him—body language, facial expression—practically crowed like a rooster. I could have taken umbrage. Instead, I decided to take the gift that fate had dropped in my lap.

"C'mon," I snapped. "We haven't got all day."

Jim ended up driving my car, since the four of us couldn't fit in the roadster. I'd like to say I breezed into the Criminal Justice Center and whisked Grace away in a matter of minutes, but it didn't quite happen that way. I might have thought I'd had Jim cowed into just going along for the ride, but the moment we hit the lobby of the CJC, he took over. And I let him.

Jane, Linda, and I sat on a bench for a really long time after Jim disappeared down a corridor to retrieve Grace. I wanted to confess to them and receive absolution for landing Grace in this mess, but I couldn't, so we sat in silence as my stomach wound into tighter and tighter knots. Finally, a lifetime later, Jim returned with a pale, tired Grace by his side.

"Grace!" I almost tripped over my own

feet in my haste to reach her. "Are you okay?"

"You're here." She smiled at me, tiredness etching her wrinkled face. "Good. I'm ready to go home."

I looked at Jim. "What about bail? Is it taken care of?"

Grace patted my hand. "Calm down, Ellie. I'm free to go. The DA may file charges later, but for now, I've confessed everything I know. I'm glad I decided to do it."

"I don't understand," I said to Grace. "I thought you'd been arrested."

"No, no. I came down here on my own last night. Thought it was time to tell the truth. And I knew if you were around, you'd try to stop me. So I waited until you were at the ball."

We were all standing around in a semicircle. Beyond Grace and Linda's shoulders, I could hear arguing and a scuffle as someone was hauled through the lobby. Jane and Linda moved back a little, and between them I could see the man causing the ruckus behind them. He was resisting the officer who was trying to guide him toward a corridor at the opposite end of the lobby, and he was spitting out invectives with a strong French accent.

"This is not to be permitted," the man shouted, just as I realized who it was.

"Henri?" I hadn't meant to call out. His head whipped around, and then he spied me across the lobby.

"Eleanor! You must help me. These men think I'm some kind of criminal."

I stepped toward him, and then a hand caught my arm. Jim's hand. "Ellie, don't."

I looked up at him. His eyes were filled with concern. "It's okay." Then I walked across the unforgiving tile toward Henri and the police officer.

"Henri? What's going on?" And then I realized who the officer was. "Will?"

Poor boy. A light leapt into his eyes at the sight of me, and then he quickly masked it. "Ellie? What are you doing here?"

I nodded back toward the bench. "My friend. Grace Davenport. We thought she'd been arrested."

Will's gaze followed my nod. "No. One of the guys told me Mrs. Davenport came in last night, wanting to come clean about Marvin Etherington. Since it wasn't urgent, she ended up having to wait a while to give her statement."

"Will they arrest her later?"

"We don't take too kindly to murder, even ones committed forty years ago." Will shrugged. "They'll pass her case on to the DA. I doubt they'll charge her with anything after all this time. Maybe a misdemeanor. Unlawful disposition of a body, or something like that."

"Thank heavens."

Will looked a little shamefaced. "Well, I might have blown my investigation a little bit out of proportion. To get your attention." He blushed. "Actually, I wasn't even assigned to the case."

Henri snorted. "What about me? What about this miscarriage of justice?"

Will twisted Henri's arm a little harder so that he gave a little grunt of pain. "This guy, on the other hand, may not see daylight for awhile. He's bilked people out of enough money to qualify for some state-run hospitality."

I took that for police-speak to mean that Henri had been perpetrating fraud of some kind and would wind up in jail. Another shiver crawled down my spine, but this time it was one of revulsion. What had I ever seen in this man?

Then I felt Jim's presence at my back. "Everything okay here?"

"Fine. Just fine." I turned to Henri. *"Au revoir, ma chère.* And thanks for the check." Boy, was I glad I had already cashed it. Then I looked at Will. "Thank you. For everything."

"No hard feelings?" he said, looking young and eager once more.

I smiled. "No. No hard feelings." I turned around, took Jim's hand in mine, and started walking back toward Grace.

"Ellie! Wait! You cannot just leave me here," Henri called as we walked away.

"C'mon," Will said to Henri. "You're going to booking." I didn't turn around again as Will hauled him away. Instead, I hurried back to Grace.

"Officer McFarland says he'd be surprised if the DA charged you." I slipped my hand out of Jim's and held it out to Grace. "So let's get you home."

She put her hand in mine, and then our strange little posse moved toward the entrance. I said a little prayer of thanksgiving, because things could have turned out so much worse.

That evening, when the excitement had died down and Jane and Linda had gone home, I remained at Grace's house. Jim had left a couple of hours earlier when the hospital paged him. I was grateful for a few minutes alone with Grace.

I'd ordered her to bed with instructions to rest while I fixed us some soup and crackers. Then I carried the food on a tray to her room, just as Jim had done for me that morning. After the events of the day, it seemed like a lifetime ago.

"Why did you do it, Grace?" I asked when she was settled back against her pillows and eating. "Why did you go to the police after all these years?"

She set her spoon down on the tray. "Maybe I just thought it was time." She must have seen from the frown on my face that I didn't believe her, because she added, "Maybe you convinced me that the truth should be told."

I still didn't think she was telling the whole story. "Why did you do it? Really?"

"Because I didn't want you to get in trouble." Her vehement response wasn't at all what I'd expected.

"Me? Why would I get in trouble?"

"When I told you the truth, I made you a party to the crime. I made my choice long ago to keep the secret and take any consequences that came with that decision. But you didn't."

"You gave yourself up for me?" I wasn't sure anyone had ever shown me that much loyalty in my whole life except for my mother.

Grace shrugged, trying to downplay the gravity of her decision. "What were they going to do to an old woman like me? Put me in jail?"

"But they might have. You didn't have to do that."

"You still don't understand, do you?"

"Understand what?"

"What it means to be one of the Queens of Woodlawn Avenue."

I didn't know what to say. Most people spent their entire lives searching for that kind of loyalty, and I had inadvertently stumbled into it at my lowest point. Talk about your blessings in disguise. Underneath those red hats were the answers to my prayers.

I took Grace's hand in mine and lightly squeezed her fingers. "I think I'm beginning to," I said. "Now, eat your soup."

Later, after she'd finished her meal and I'd cleared away the dishes, I broached another difficult topic while perched on the edge of Grace's bed.

"I hope you're not disappointed in me for taking Jim back."

Grace leaned back against the pillow and sighed. "Did I ever tell you how I met my second husband, Fred? The one who took me to the Cannon Ball?"

"No. I don't think so."

"I met him at a bridge tournament. I'd gone alone, so I signed up at the partnership desk."

"Partnership desk?"

"Tournaments always have them. For folks who don't have someone to play with. They match you with someone at a similar skill level."

"And they matched you with Fred?"

Her dreamy smile was contagious, and I

felt my own lips curve as the power of memory lit Grace's face from within.

"We didn't do so well in the tournament, but we did just fine for the next fifteen years. Until . . ."

"Until what?"

Her smile faded. "He had an affair."

Again, Grace had managed to surprise me. Hadn't she told me that she'd buried all three of her husbands with a smile on their faces?

"What happened?"

"It didn't last. He came back home, tail between his legs, but I wouldn't have any of it."

"But—"

"Then I went to another bridge tournament. I was single once again, so I signed up at the partnership desk."

"Is that how you met your third husband?"

Grace laughed. "No. That's how I wound up reconciling with Fred. You see, they assigned us as partners again."

"And you played bridge with him?"

"By the end of the tournament, we were doing a lot more than playing bridge." Her smile reminded me of the one I'd been wearing when I'd awakened this morning.

I twisted the bedspread between my fingers, wanting to ask a question but not wanting to intrude on a personal matter. Finally, I screwed up my courage and said, "And did he ever cheat on you again?"

Grace looked me in the eye. "Not that I know of. But Ellie, there are no guarantees."

"I know."

"Sometimes, if the cosmic partnership desk keeps throwing the same guy in your path, someone may be trying to tell you something."

Grace was giving her blessing to my reunion with Jim, but she was also warning me. Nothing was for sure. I just had to take the hand I was dealt and play it the best I could.

"Thanks, Grace." I leaned forward and brushed a kiss across her cheek. "You've been a tremendous help."

Her eyes were starting to drift closed, so I tucked the sheet up around her and stood up. "I'll do the dishes and then lock up when I leave."

"Thank you, Ellie. You're a good girl."

"Good night, Grace." Down the short hallway to the kitchen from her bedroom, I fought back tears. Grace's words about being a good girl echoed in my head. It was exactly what my mother used to say, and to tell the truth, I hadn't always believed it. Now, though, after half a century, I had finally figured out one thing.

Being good and being perfect were mutually exclusive. And since I'd never be the latter, I could only be the former. In the end, being good was good enough. It would have to be.

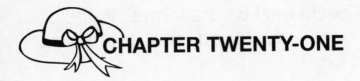

CHAPTER TWENTY-ONE

Drawing a New Line

Jim didn't come back to my house that evening, so I assumed he'd had to go back into surgery. I was grateful for the reprieve, because I had a lot of thinking to do. His blithe assumption that now that we'd reconciled in the bedroom I'd move right back into the rest of the house still bothered me.

I slept like a log and woke the next morning to find my refrigerator was as empty as my stomach. There was nothing for it but to throw on some clothes and make a quick run to Harris-Teeter. Of course, since I looked less than my best, I ran into lots of people I knew. One person stopped me in the bread aisle to rave about the carriage rides. Another expressed similar praise in front of the Saran Wrap and Ziploc bags. The one that really got to me, though, was when I ran into Cissy Crawford, a fixture in Nashville society, in front of the potato chips.

"I'm so glad Roz thought of the horse and carriage idea. Brilliant. Simply brilliant. I wish I'd done it when I was the chair."

My face froze, and I couldn't do anything but smile and nod. I was too stunned to set Cissy straight. At least, I was too stunned until I started pushing my cart forward again and looked up to see my nemesis heading straight toward me, her own cart piled high.

"Ellie." She greeted me with a curt nod. "You look terrible. Are you ill?"

After our last confrontation in this grocery store, I'd been ready to let bygones be bygones, live and let live, etc. Clearly Roz's antipathy for me had very little to do with reality and a lot more to do with her crazy mother. But her taking credit for my Cannon Ball success was too much.

"Roz." I returned her chilly nod. "I understand you're due some congratulations."

Her eyes narrowed, suddenly wary. "Am I?"

"I understand you had the brilliant idea to hire the carriages instead of using shuttle buses for the ball."

She blushed underneath her layers of LaPrairie makeup. "I'm sure I never—"

"I'm pretty sure you 'never,' too."

I was ready to blast her, to pin her to the wall with the force of my righteous indignation. After the last two months, I felt powerful enough to do it. A heady sense of command rose up in me. Finally, after all these years, I could take my enemy out at the knees, leaving her decimated and crippled right here in front of the Pringles.

And then I looked at Roz again. Really looked at her. I saw underneath the layers of expensive makeup, beyond the plastic surgery, deep into her normally brown eyes that were concealed behind blue contact lenses. At that moment, the need for revenge drained away. What good would it do? What point would it prove?

Instead, I said, "I'm going to send you something in the mail."

She blinked twice, confused. "What?"

"I'm going to send you something in the mail. My birth certificate."

She pursed her lips. "What would I do with your birth certificate?"

I smiled. Not in a Cruella De Vil kind of way. Just in a normal way. A relieved way. The old Ellie way.

"You can use it to put your fears to rest. We're not sisters. Your dad had nothing to do with me."

I knew better than to expect any kind of gratitude or similarly human response. Instead, I reached out, took a bag of pretzels from the shelf on my right, and tossed them into my cart.

She collected herself, and her spine went ramrod straight. "You can't do this."

"Do what?"

"You can't just say something like that and assume that it's over."

I could see in her eyes that the loss of our rivalry scared her. I had some sympathy for that. She'd been a part of how I defined myself for so long that it was like pulling up an anchor or letting go of a lifeline. And yet, how could either of us ever move forward if we didn't let go?

"Have a good day, Roz."

I grabbed my cart by the handle, and with my head held high, I pushed it past her, leaving her behind me, right where she belonged.

My trip to Harris-Teeter took longer than I had expected. Before I could get out of the store, I'd had to stop to hear three more rave reviews for the transportation at the Cannon Ball, talked to two women (divorcées, like myself) who had heard about Your Better Half and wanted to know if I was hiring, and been given the eye (and some free peaches) by the produce manager. All in all, not bad for a trip to the grocery store.

When I pulled into my driveway, though, another surprise lay in wait. Jim's sleek little car was there.

"Here goes nothing," I muttered as I grabbed the grocery bags from the back seat and made my way up the walk. He wasn't on the porch, though, as I'd expected. I turned the key and went in the house, but he wasn't there, either. Curious. And then I heard the strange sounds coming from the backyard. I walked to the kitchen, plopped the bags on the counter, and looked out the window.

With Grace's help, the view from my kitchen window had undergone a transformation. And while I hadn't yet achieved the lushness of her English garden backyard, I was doing pretty well. The best-looking thing between me and the fence, however, happened to be Jim, shirtless and sweating, as he dug up the flower bed at the rear of the yard.

Irritation flashed through me at first as I watched his well-muscled arms thrust the shovel into the ground, and then his spine curve and flex as he used one foot to push it into the ground. I even admired his backside, one of his best features, actually, as he bent to lift the dirt from the hole and then sent it flying off to the growing mound on his right. How unfair that a fifty-year-old man could look so good when I'd looked so awful after doing the same thing.

Quickly I put away the groceries that needed to be refrigerated, and then I was vain enough to make a quick stop in front of the bathroom mirror to fluff my hair and apply some lipstick. Not more than three minutes later, though, I was letting myself out the back door and crossing the yard.

"What are you doing?" I kept my voice carefully neutral.

Jim cast a quick look at me over his shoulder before thrusting the shovel into the ground yet again. He had to be getting pretty deep by this time.

"I'm digging."

"Yes. I can see that."

Okay, I'll admit a little thrill shot through me. He was very determined, very matter-of-fact, and the hair at the nape of his neck clung in sweaty little clumps that looked really manly.

I stopped when I was a few feet away from him. "Why are you digging up my impatiens?"

He threw a last shovelful of dirt onto the pile, struck the shovel into the ground, and leaned on the handle. "I'm retrieving something."

Another thrill followed the last one up my spine. "Buried treasure?" This time, I could keep my tone neutral but I couldn't keep the corners of my mouth from turning upward.

"Yep." He pulled a bandana from the back pocket of his jeans and wiped his forehead. I had to admit, the man still had a great pair of pecs. Cracking open people's chests was pretty physical work when you got right down to it.

"You gonna be long?"

He smiled, and I guess since things come in threes, the final shiver went up my spine. "Not too long."

And then, suddenly, I didn't want to dance around the subject anymore. "You don't have to do this."

His face grew sober as well. "Yes, I do."

"It's just a box."

"No, it's not."

"If I want it back, I'll dig it up."

For the first time, he looked away. "Maybe I don't want to wait that long."

I crossed my arms over my chest. "I can't just come back home like nothing happened, Jim."

I expected him to get a little angry and defensive, and I could tell from the way he took a deep breath and then slowly blew it out that those emotions were the first to surface. But whereas the Jim of old would have stomped off and found solace in his work or playing with one of his expensive toys or even turning to Tiffany, the man in front of me at that moment reacted quite differently than I expected.

"I don't know if I can make it right." He said the words to my shoes.

"What do you mean?"

He looked up then, and I could see the vulnerability in his eyes. It had been a long time since he'd let me see that.

"I did a lot of stupid things, Ellie. I don't know if I can ever make them up to you."

"So that's why you're digging up the box?" I'd thought it was to pressure me into coming back home, to lure me there with reminders of how safe and insulated my life had once been. Only as I'd learned, I'd never been truly safe at all.

He heaved a sigh. "Seemed like a good place to start."

Well, maybe he was right. But I still wasn't sure.

"We can't go back."

"No." He shook his head in agreement. "We can't."

"But maybe there's another option."

He went really still. "Another option?"

I smiled. My new smile. A real one that had found its own home on my face. "As I said before, you could ask me out. You were a pretty fun date the other night."

His smile was a bit wolfish. "Glad to be of service."

I went scarlet. Because my ex-husband

was flirting with me. Who would have ever thought it?

Jim turned back to the hole with his shovel and pulled out another scoop of dirt. With the next stab, though, I heard a dull thud instead of the crisp slicing of metal through dirt. Jim dropped to his knees and began digging with his hands. A few moments later, he pulled the memory box from its grave.

He laid it on the ground and brushed the dirt away from its top. The calligraphy lettering was smudged, but it was still there.

Jim & Ellie.

He stood up with the box and held it out to me like an offering. "Here you go."

I couldn't take it, though. Not yet.

"Tell you what. Why don't you hold onto it for me."

Jim frowned. "I don't want to play games, Ellie."

I almost bristled, but as I'd recently learned at Harris-Teeter, sometimes you had to let go of the past if you wanted to have empty hands to receive whatever the future might bring.

"I'm not playing games."

He looked confused for a moment, and

then a small flame of hope flickered in his eyes. "Hold onto it, huh?"

"Yes. I might want it back someday, though, so take good care of it."

"Okay." There was a world of emotions in that single word. Acceptance. Frustration. Regret. And, I believed, love. "Okay, if that's what you want."

By this time, the early summer sun was getting pretty strong, and my own forehead was starting to bead with sweat. "Would you like to come in and take a shower? I can fix us some lunch."

"What about the hole?"

I looked over at the poor, beleaguered section of my flower bed. "It can wait," I said with a smile. "Some things may be fleeting," my smile dimmed a little bit at these words, "but some things are here to stay."

"Which are we?" Jim asked tensely.

My smile returned. "I think I know," I said. "But I also plan to have a little fun finding out if I'm right."

I turned to lead him back to my house, but he caught me by the arm. "Ellie." His voice was deep and serious. "Don't get my hopes up just to pay me back."

I looked up into the eyes of the man I'd

loved for more than half my life. Suddenly, my throat was tight and I didn't feel so powerful anymore. "I want to forgive you," I whispered. "But it may take me some time to figure out how. I've got to draw a new line."

He dropped his hold on my arm, and the tears I saw in his eyes were almost my undoing. The old Ellie would have taken him in her arms to comfort and reassure him. The new Ellie, though, was a bit wiser. After all, she had to be—now that she was the Queen of Hearts.

"What are you talking about?"

"In bridge, when someone makes game, you draw a line under the score and start over."

Jim smiled and shook his head. "I'm not sure I want to understand."

I returned his smile. "That's okay. You don't need to understand it. Not as long as I finally do." I reached down and took his hand in mine. "Come on. I'll make you an omelet."

And so I held onto Jim's hand, he held onto the memory box, and we went into the house to have lunch, framed by my heart-shaped dining room arch.

EPILOGUE

A Fabulous Foursome

"A toast," Jane said, lifting her champagne flute and smiling, "to Ellie's first anniversary."

"Here, here," Linda and Grace echoed. All four of us clinked our glasses, and I took a sip of the ice cold champagne. It fizzed its way happily down my throat.

Had it really been a year since I'd moved into the house on Woodlawn Avenue? I beamed at the other three women as we guzzled our champagne.

"Don't let me forget," Jane said, setting her flute down on the table. "I've got a couple more business cards to pass on to you. Both of them sounded really interested in Your Better Half."

"Thanks. But if you keep sending me clients at this pace, I'm going to have to hire more people." I was learning every day how enjoyable—and how difficult—it was to run your own business. Besides myself, I now had three other divorced women on the payroll, all of whom I'd met through Red Hat functions. Most months it was nip and tuck, but Jane had assured me it would take a good five years to get myself firmly established. In the meantime, I was working very, very hard and loving every exhausting minute.

"I have good news, too," Linda said. "Well, not good news, exactly, but a good opportunity."

"For me?"

Linda nodded. "Adele Greenway's husband just got transferred to Raleigh."

My breath caught in my throat. Adele was Linda's co-chair for the Cannon Ball and heir apparent to chair the following year.

"I'm sorry to hear that."

"I am, too," Linda said. "Adele's great. So I'll need someone just as wonderful to fill her shoes." She paused. "What do you think, Ellie? Would you be willing to do it?"

Linda's offer was every social aspiration I'd ever dreamed of, wrapped up in ribbon and handed to me on a platter. But one thing I'd learned in the last year was that it was okay to say no.

"Would it be all right if I gave it some thought?" I didn't want to offend my friend, but I knew since she was truly my friend, she'd understand.

"Okay. But only a few days. If you don't think you can do it, I need to find someone else."

I leaned over to give her a hug. "Thank you, Linda. You know that just being asked means the world to me."

She returned my hug and then we both sat back with a laugh. "Champagne makes me maudlin," she said, wiping back a few stray tears.

Grace tapped her spoon against her water glass. "I have an announcement to make, too."

My breath caught in my throat. Grace's lawyer had been meeting with the DA off and on for several months, trying to convince the powers-that-be not to press charges.

"As of today, I'm a free woman," Grace said. "The District Attorney has decided to be merciful."

Relief flooded through me, and I leaned the other way, this time to hug Grace. "I'm so glad." I suddenly felt lighter than air.

"It was never your fault, Ellie." She patted my back reassuringly. "Oops."

The brims of our hats had bumped against one another. I reached up to straighten the enormous conflagration of ribbon and feathers on my head. I now had enough hats of my own to make a claim at being a true Red Hatter. Not as many as the others, of course, but given time, I'd give them a run for their money.

"Okay, ladies," Linda said. "Enough of the mushy-gushy stuff. Let's play cards."

"Now, Ellie," Grace said, leaning toward me. "Tonight, we're going to teach you how to respond to a takeout double if your opponent passes."

I laughed. "Wait a minute, Grace. I have something to say, too."

The other three leaned toward me in eager anticipation. "You're getting remarried?" Grace asked with excitement.

"No, no. Jim and I are doing fine, but we're not that far along yet." I smiled, though, thinking of the weekend before when Connor and Courtney had both been home from college. Connor had stayed with Jim at the house in Belle Meade, and Courtney had bunked with me on Woodlawn Avenue. The kids' happiness at seeing Jim and I together once again, even if we hadn't made any commitments for the future, had been an extra blessing.

"Then what is it?" Jane asked.

"Look, I don't want to seem ungrateful." I stopped, took a deep breath for courage, and then continued. "But I think it's time for the lessons to stop. I think it's time for me to take responsibility for my own hand."

The other three exchanged looks, and for a moment I was concerned. Then they all three burst into laughter.

Linda began to deal the cards. "Of course, Ellie. All you had to do was ask."

And it was true. Since the day Jane had arrived on my doorstep with that heavenly pound cake, these three women had responded to my every request. And that wasn't going to change anytime soon.

"You open the bidding," Grace said, nodding at me.

My fingers trembled a little as I scooped up my hand, fanned it out, and began to count my high card points. Three. Seven. Eleven. Fifteen. Nineteen. Twenty-three. It was all I could do not to hyperventilate. Balanced distribution. An obnoxiously large number of high card points. It was the hand of a lifetime, and one for which they'd been preparing me for a year.

"Two clubs," I said calmly without inflection, struggling to keep a straight face while my pulse raced through my veins. It was an opening bid that meant I'd hit the jackpot.

And I had, thanks to the Queens of Woodlawn Avenue.

The Red Hat Society®
isn't done yet!

Please turn this page
for a preview of
Regina Hale Sutherland's
next novel of fun, friendship,
and romance over fifty.

The Red Hat Society®'s
Domestic Goddess

*"I hate the word house-
wife; I don't like the word
home-maker either. I want
to be called Domestic
Goddess."*
—Roseanne

Feeling like the rabbit in *Alice in Wonderland*, Millie Truman pulled her gray Taurus
into the driveway of her condo and pushed
impatiently on her garage door opener.
Late. She was running late. But like the rabbit, at least she looked good. She spared a
quick glance into her rearview mirror, admir-
ing the new do. Cinnamon. Since she loved
the flavor so much, she'd taken a chance on
the color.

And it had paid off. Of course, now she
would have to hear her friends, Theresa and
Kim, say, "I told you so." They'd been bug-
ging her for a while to stop being so old-
fashioned and get a dye-job. She had to ad-

mit they were right; she looked much younger than fifty-five.

Except . . . had the beautician missed a gray hair? She reached up for the offensive strand, but it dissolved between her fingers like gossamer. A cobweb.

From cleaning Mitchell's apartment. It figured. Her youngest son was responsible for all the gray hair she'd just gotten rid of, too.

She'd stopped at his place after the beauty parlor, expecting to only have to do a quick dusting and vacuuming. But she found his loft apartment totally trashed, as her granddaughter would say, like the frat houses he and his brother had lived in during college. The big mess had probably not been the result of a party, though. It was just a consequence of his fast-paced lifestyle.

He'd done a drive-by while she was there, rushing in to pack a suitcase for a business trip for the automotive firm where he worked. Except *she* had wound up packing the suitcase, after finding it shoved under his bed.

She didn't want to think about what else she'd found under there. She brushed her hand through her cinnamon curls again, dislodging another cobweb and shuddering.

What had happened to his girlfriend Heather, who'd actually made an attempt to keep the apartment neat? Millie had asked, but Mitchell had just grinned and shrugged and made some smart remark about Suzy Homemaker types liking boring nine-to-five men like his brother, Steven, the insurance agent.

Suzy Homemaker, indeed, Millie sniffed. She preferred the term her fellow Red Hatters used, *Domestic Goddess.* Millie had reigned as one throughout thirty-one years of marriage, and she'd loved it. Like she'd told her dear husband, it was her *job.*

But Bruce died five years ago, and she should have been able to retire her tiara and spend less time cooking and cleaning and more time with her friends. But she'd still had Pop to take care of; he lived with her then . . . and Mitchell, the confirmed bachelor. At least she hadn't had to worry about Steven, who was happily married with a beautiful daughter. Then. She was a little worried about their marriage now.

But she didn't have time for that either. She had to clean up, bake her snack contribution for Movie Night at the community center, and meet Kim, a neighbor and fellow Red Hatter, for dinner.

Resisting the urge to check for more cobwebs, she tore her gaze from the mirror and noted that the door was up. But there was no room for her car in the one-stall garage of her end unit brick condo. Another car was already backed into it with its trunk lid lifted. She pressed the brake, stopping an inch shy of its front bumper.

"What in the world . . ."

A robber. That should have been her first thought. And she should have been fumbling in her purse for her cell phone to call 911 while backing away. But the black car looked vaguely familiar, or as familiar as the grill of a vehicle can look. And she'd feel pretty silly if she called the police on someone she knew, especially if it was, as she suspected, her oldest son.

Of the few who had a key to her place, Mitchell was probably on a plane by now. And Pop was in Arizona with his new wife. Or at least he had been when they'd talked a few nights ago. Process of elimination left Steven. But like Mitchell had just pointed out, he worked nine to five. And it was only three o'clock.

Hand trembling slightly, she shifted into park but left her car running as she stepped out. For a quick getaway? From her own house?

Maybe the cinnamon dye had leaked into her brain. Or she spent too much time with Kim. Kim was the daughter of a retired police chief; she suspected everyone of something. The scary part was that she was occasionally right.

Remembering that, Millie opened the back door of the Taurus and reached for something to use as a weapon. Her fingers closed over the handle of the vacuum, but the muscles in her shoulder protested as she started to lift it out.

She couldn't blame Mitchell for her cramped muscles though; those were courtesy of the aerobics class Kim had started at the condo community center. Millie couldn't very well not attend since it had been her idea for Kim to start the classes after school budget cuts cost her a Phys Ed teaching position. *But push-ups? Really?* Kim had a tendency to treat her new students like her old ones, teenagers.

Millie released the vacuum handle and reached for something else, pulling out a feather duster. Not very lethal. But with all the dust left on it from Mitchell's place, it might make a burglar sneeze hard enough for Millie to escape . . . if the need arose.

She drew in a quick, fortifying breath, then walked into the garage. The car parked in it was the same make and model Steven drove. While the trunk was open, the contents inside hadn't been taken from *her* house. She didn't own a laptop or a set of golf clubs. So unless her robber had a Robin Hood complex, she was safe.

And if he did . . . she preferred jewelry to golf clubs and computers. Rings and necklaces. Tiaras she could do without.

The door between the house and the garage creaked as it slowly opened. Millie ducked behind it and lifted the duster, hoping that her exercise-weary joints didn't creak as loudly as the door hinges. Her heart beat hard and fast against her ribs as a dark shadow emerged from the house.

Broad shoulders, thinning dark hair, expanding belly . . . he was not exactly her image of a cat burglar. He was her son. Steven caught sight of her and gasped, "Mom!"

Millie's heart rate subsided, and she breathed a sigh of relief.

Steven sneezed and gestured toward her weapon. "What the heck are you doing? Dusting the garage? You take this neatness thing a little too far."

"Steven?" It wasn't like she didn't recognize him; what she questioned was what he was doing at her house, at three o'clock.

"Did you have a golf outing?" she asked, waving the duster at his clubs in the trunk. "It's a great day for one."

Not that she had spent much time in the gorgeous, warm weather, which was unusual for such an early spring day in Michigan.

Steven didn't answer her, brushing a slightly shaking hand over his thinning hair instead. He had his father's hair, or premature lack thereof, as his younger brother relentlessly teased him. Maybe it was the hair loss, or his expanding waistline, but he always looked older than his almost thirty-six years. Today he looked even older, his face set in lines far too grim for a man his age.

"Bad game?" she teased, though he wasn't dressed for golf—he was wearing suit pants and a dress shirt. The jacket lay across the front seat of his car and his tie hung from the rearview mirror. He'd lost something all right, but it wasn't a golf game.

Her heart started beating fast again. Obviously she'd been right to worry about him.

"Mom—"

"Steven, what's going on? You're here in the afternoon, with the garage door down—"

"I shut the garage door because of your nosy neighbors. I already had a run-in with that crazy lady—"

"Crazy lady?"

"The neighbor who's packing."

He probably didn't mean luggage or a can of mace either. Besides being Hilltop Condominium's aerobic instructor, Kim was the unofficial neighborhood watch captain. Nothing and nobody got past her. "That's Kim."

"Dirty Harriet."

"Actually, Harry's the gun," she said, and if Kim had brought it out, she'd really been concerned. But since she'd left, she must have ruled Steven out as a burglar.

"She named her gun?"

Millie smiled. You really had to know Kim for a while before you realized she wasn't crazy. Just a little intense. "It's not real."

"Could have fooled me," he said, brushing that hand through his hair again. It was shaking even more.

But Millie didn't believe it was his run-in with Kim that had him so upset. "It's an air gun. Kind of like the BB guns you and Mitchell had growing up."

That they'd used to shoot each other before claiming the resulting welts on their skin were chicken pox. Millie might have fallen for it, too, had they not both had the chicken pox.

"Those can really hurt," Steven said. He would know.

"She didn't use Harry on you?" Millie asked, horrified. Because he looked like he was hurt. His brown eyes were dark and wounded, his mouth tight and devoid of his usual easy smile.

"No," he assured her, "but I could have done without meeting him today."

Somehow she knew he was talking about more than the uncomfortable sensation of looking down a gun barrel. As she looked again to his partially unpacked trunk, she had that uncomfortable sensation herself.

He shrugged, his broad shoulders bobbing slowly up and down as if they carried a burden too heavy for him to bear. His gaze kept sliding away from hers. He couldn't meet her eyes, like when he'd been a little boy and had, on the rare occasion, done something naughty. Unlike his younger brother, he'd never wanted her disapproval or disappointment.

"It's not a big deal," he said. "It's good to know someone's looking out for you."

"Hey, *I* look out for me!" She brandished the dark pink duster, leaving a trail of cobwebs across the garage floor that she'd just swept that morning. Now she *would* have to dust it . . . .

One half of Steven's mouth lifted in a half-hearted smile. "So now you're Dirty Harriet."

"I do feel pretty dirty," she admitted, letting him stall for time.

Unlike Mitchell, Steven had always confessed his misdeeds to her. She'd only had to wait a little while until his conscience got the better of him and he spilled all. He'd been the one to tell her what had really caused the welts on his and Mitchell's skin. BB's.

"I just finished cleaning your brother's apartment," she explained her dirtiness, hoping there were no more cobwebs in her hair.

Steven's face twisted into a disgusted grimace. "I don't know how he lives like that."

Millie knew that if it weren't for Steven's wife, Audrey, his house would look the same way. "I love it when you drop by, but I'm surprised—"

"It's so early," he finished for her, his voice thick with emotion, "and that I've brought luggage."

She hated to ask, afraid of what he might answer, so she just nodded.

"Audrey made me come home for lunch today. I thought—" He sighed, a ragged gust of air full of resignation. "It doesn't matter what I thought. I came home to my packed bags. She threw me out."

"Audrey threw you out?" Millie couldn't digest it; like the half-eaten pieces of pizza left in the boxes on Mitchell's coffee table, the thought made her queasy.

Steven and Audrey had met in college. While he'd finished, she'd dropped out to marry him. They'd been together seventeen years, married almost fifteen; they had Brigitte, who was just starting her teen years.

"No . . ."

He nodded, his hazel eyes filling with tears. "I don't understand it, Mom," he said, blinking furiously before lifting a box from his trunk and heading into the house with it. In the foyer, at the top of the stairs, which led to Pop's old apartment in the walk-out basement, he turned back and said, "And really I don't want to talk about it."

"But you and Audrey . . . you need to talk," she protested. "The *last* thing you should do is move out."

"It's what *she* wants, Mom. She doesn't want me around anymore."

Panic pressed heavily against Millie's heart, stealing her breath away more than any of Kim's outrageous exercises ever did. Steven, Audrey and Brigitte were the perfect family. Well, maybe not perfect. They had their arguments, but that was normal.

Except that things hadn't seemed normal for them lately. They'd been strained. But marriage was like a rubber band; it could get stretched to the limits but snap back tightly, not even showing any traces of how far it'd been stretched. Unless . . . it broke. The divorce rate proved how many times that happened.

"Steven," she said, reaching for his arm as he started down the stairs. "You're not giving up, not like this, not after so many years together."

He sighed and bowed his head, refusing to turn toward her. "Mom, it's not that simple anymore."

"Marriage isn't." Not that she could complain about hers. All her memories of Bruce were happy ones; at least the ones she'd kept alive were. Maybe there'd been others, but if so they were few and far between, and not worth remembering.

"But it shouldn't be this difficult, either," Steven said, running that slightly shaking hand over his hair.

"What's difficult?" Millie asked, desperately wanting to understand. Despite noticing the strain, she hadn't wanted to ask before. From the minute her sons had been born, she'd vowed not to become one of *those* mothers, the kind who interfered in their lives. She'd trusted them enough to let them live their own.

"Until . . ." he started, his voice thick with emotion, "she went back to school."

Audrey had recently gone back to college to finish up the nursing degree she'd started so many years ago. She wanted to be an RN. Millie had applauded her determination and been so inspired by it that she'd gotten serious about retiring her own tiara. Now a horrible thought occurred to Millie. "Oh, no! She met someone else."

He laughed, a short bitter sound. "No, but I almost wished she had."

"Steven!" She fought the temptation to whack him with the duster; her son was already hurting.

He jerked his hand through his thin hair again. His whole body was shaking now: with frustration and shock. While Millie had noticed the strain in their marriage, she wondered if *he* had. His next words confirmed that he hadn't. "If she'd found someone else, then I could actually understand why she threw me out."

"You need to talk," she maintained. "We'll go back to your house. Brigitte can come stay with me while you and Audrey work things out."

He shook his head and squeezed his dark eyes shut, probably trying to hold in the tears she saw glistening in them. "No, Mom, it's too late. Or it's too soon. I'm not sure what it is anymore."

It was not fair to him or Audrey but most especially not to Brigitte. *That poor girl . . .*

"Oh, Steven . . ." She squeezed his arm, trying to express her love, support and willingness to help any way she could. The phrase, *too little, too late,* taunted her. She refused to accept that. "You have to try."

He nodded. "I know. But not now. It—" One tear fell, sliding down the hard line of his taut jaw. "—hurts too much, Mom."

The shock, the pain . . . it was too fresh. She understood that. "But you will."

"After some time. But I have to ask you something, Mom."

"Of course you can stay here." But it was a little late to ask that since he'd apparently already brought some stuff down to Pop's old apartment. It consisted of a bedroom, bathroom and a family room with a little kitchenette in one corner.

Steven blinked, surprised again. "Well, that, too. I didn't think—"

"It's okay." That he hadn't asked her first. "Don't worry about it."

Obviously he didn't think she had a life. But she did and she actually needed more time for it. She'd thought she'd only had

Mitchell left to marry off before she could retire her tiara.

There was someone else she'd flirted with
the idea of making time for, though, but it
was definitely too soon for him. And Millie
was so old-fashioned, she'd never actually
learned to flirt. Was it as easy as getting a
dye-job?

"Mom? Are you okay?"

She nodded, pushing the crazy thought
from her mind. She didn't really need anyone or anything else in her life. Even with
Pop married and moved out, it was too full
now for her to fit in all the things she wanted
to do, like shopping and gambling excur-
sions with her Red Hat chapter, The Red
Hot Hatters of Hilltop. "Fine, fine, just
tired . . ."

He snorted. "From cleaning Mitchell's
place. I would have moved in with him, but
I couldn't stand his mess."

Which multiplied by Steven's would have
given Millie nightmares. She would have
had to beg Mitchell to hire a maid.

"I'm happy to have you here," she in-
sisted. But she hoped it wouldn't be for
long. While she wouldn't mind his company,
Steven belonged home with his family. The

connection between a mother and child was strong as ever, she could *feel* his heart breaking, and hers ached, too.

He let out another ragged sigh. "Thanks, Mom. I need to ask you for another favor, though."

"Anything."

"I need you to go . . ." He drew in a quick breath. "To my house."

He couldn't call it home. He'd only been gone a few hours, but he couldn't call it that anymore. Panic pressed on Millie's heart, too. She refused to believe it was too late, though. Maybe she could still help.

But how could she, who had never interfered before, interject herself into the middle of a battle between a husband and wife when she had no real idea what their problems were?

"Steven, I don't think it's my place."

"I just need you to pick up my briefcase. I've looked through the boxes I brought downstairs."

Boxes? He'd already moved boxes of his stuff from his home to the basement?

"And I checked the trunk again. I can't find it. I brought it home with me to do some work this afternoon. I had a couple of life insurance applications in it that I had to finish up."

He wasn't even going to take off the rest of the day to fight for or mourn the end of his marriage? Was it over that quickly and cleanly? Millie couldn't begin to understand. She hoped it was just as he'd said, that it was too fresh . . . and it hurt too much.

"I need my briefcase, Mom. Can you go get it for me? I can't go back there."

"Steven, you're going to have to. For Brigitte."

"I can't go back *because* of Brigitte. It's too soon. We all need time to adjust."

Millie worried that he was adjusting pretty quickly, then she saw his eyes and the tears he couldn't blink away. He was hurting, and he didn't want his daughter to see him in that kind of pain.

Millie hated seeing him in that kind of pain.

"Of course." She blinked fast, pushing back her own tears. "I'll go right now."

And give him a chance to pull himself together. *She* needed one, too.

She'd conveniently left the car running for a quick getaway. Hands shaking, she opened the door, then tossed the duster into the backseat. She rammed it into re-verse, then glanced into the rearview mirror *after* she'd already started back. Too late.

A man stood behind her, his outstretched arm clutching a leash. But she couldn't see the dog he usually walked at the end of it.

She slammed on the brakes, the seatbelt biting into her sore muscles and threw open her door. "I'm so sorry! Are you all right?"

She couldn't look down. She was too afraid to see whether or not a furry, gray body lay beneath the tire of her car.